MUSSELED OUT

The hull of the *El Ay* broke the surface. The crowd gasped. As we had all feared, there was a body entangled in the lines under the boat. Beside me, Livvie moaned. Lorrie Ann screamed and fell against her mother.

"What the . . . ? That's David Thwing," I whispered to Livvie.

"What? Where?"

"Hanging from the boat. That's not Peter Murray. It's David Thwing."

Livvie stood up straighter, looking over the heads of the crowd. "You're right. No way that's Peter. Much too tall."

"And the suit. I saw Thwing wearing a suit this morning."

"The Mussel King? Why would he be under Peter's boat?" Livvie asked.

I pushed through the crowd toward Jamie. As he tried to shoo me back, I grabbed his arm and pulled him close so he could hear me above the buzz of the spectators. He bent over, moving his ear close to my mouth.

"That's David Thwing," I told him. "I saw him this morning. He was dressed in a green suit." I stopped. I hadn't liked either the idea of him or the man himself, but the shear awfulness of what had happened to him overwhelmed me. To be caught, helpless, hauled into the cold, cold water and drowned . . .

Books by Barbara Ross

CLAMMED UP

BOILED OVER

MUSSELED OUT

FOGGED INN

ICED UNDER

STOWED AWAY

EGGNOG MURDER
(with Leslie Meier and Lee Hollis)

Published by Kensington Publishing Corporation

Musseled Out

Barbara Ross

KENSINGTON BOOKS

http://www.kensingtonbooks.com

KENSINGTON BOOKS are published by

Kensington Publishing Corp.
119 West 40th Street
New York, NY 10018

All Kensington titles, imprints and distributed lines are available at special quantity discounts for bulk purchases for sales promotion, premiums, fund-raising, educational or institutional use. Special book excerpts or customized printings can also be created to fit specific needs. For details, write or phone the office of the Kensington Special Sales Manager: Kensington Publishing Corp., 119 West 40th Street, New York, NY, 10018. Attn. Special Sales Department. Phone: 1-800-221-2647.

Kensington and the K logo Reg. U.S. Pat. & TM Off.

ISBN-13: 978-0-7582-8689-5
ISBN-10: 0-7582-8689-9
First Kensington Mass Market Edition: May 2015

eISBN-13: 978-0-7582-8690-1
eISBN-10: 0-7582-8690-2
First Kensington Electronic Edition: May 2015

10 9 8 7 6 5 4

Printed in the United States of America

*This book is dedicated to my bright, wise, funny, loving daughter, **Kate Carito**, the best writer in our family*

Chapter 1

My cell phone trilled as I pulled my boat up to the town pier in Busman's Harbor, Maine. I glanced at the display. OWEN QUIMBY. Owen was human resources director at the venture capital firm where I'd worked in New York. It was barely 8:00 AM, and I pictured him fidgeting at his desk, waiting for a "decent" hour to call.

I pressed ACCEPT. "Hold on a sec, Owen." I heard his impatient sigh as I tied up my family's Boston Whaler and then climbed onto the pier. "I'm here," I said into the phone.

"Julia." Owen's voice exuded a hearty faux-bonhomie. "So nice to talk to you. You've . . . missed my last few calls."

In his hesitation, I could almost hear him consider and eliminate words like "dodged" and "ignored," then settle on the less accusatory "missed." The truth was, I hadn't missed his calls. I'd dodged them.

Owen continued. "As you know, last March,

when the firm granted your request for a leave of absence to attend to family business, you said you'd be back in six months. Then you called after Labor Day to ask for more time, and we agreed. But it's almost the middle of October. We can't keep your position open much longer. It's not fair to your peers. If you're not coming back, I have to replace you."

Last March, I'd sublet my apartment in Manhattan and taken a leave from my job to race back to Busman's Harbor to save my family's clambake business from bankruptcy. Despite some heavy challenges, we'd succeeded. The Snowden Family Clambake Company—along with our tour boat, my mother's home in town, and Morrow Island, the private island where we held our clambakes— was safe, at least for the moment. I'd never intended to stay beyond this single season, but complications had ensued.

I was in love.

"I understand," I told Owen. And I did. I also knew he could replace me in a heartbeat. Business school graduates lusted after jobs like the one I'd occupied for six years. "I'm close to making a decision," I lied.

"You're actively considering returning to the firm?" He sounded skeptical.

I didn't blame him, but in the interest of preserving my options, I answered, "Absolutely."

"Make your decision quickly. You have until the end of the week, Julia. By Friday, I need to know your return date or that you're resigning. If you don't call by then, you'll be fired for cause—job abandonment. And I don't need to tell you how much harder it will be to find another position in this field if you're terminated."

"I understand," I reassured him.

We said our good-byes and I clicked off the phone, glancing at the time as I did. I was late.

"Let me get this." The rental agent, a kindly middle-aged woman dressed in neat wool slacks and a mustard-colored cardigan, jiggled a key in the lock. The door swung open and the dark hall-way flooded with light. "You'll find it looks quite different now that it's empty."

The last time I'd been in the apartment above Gleason's Hardware store, a friend of my sister's had lived there with her mother and young son. Back then, there'd been too much furniture and far too many toys crowded into the apartment's tiny rooms. The rental agent was right—it did look much bigger. I stepped inside.

The combination living room–kitchen area stretched from the front of the apartment to the back, big windows at each end making it bright and sunny. I passed through the main room and stepped into the bedroom, which was also bigger than I remembered. During my years in Manhattan, I'd known plenty of people who lived in less square footage than this. Heck, I had for most of my time there. The little apartment over Gleason's Hardware might do quite nicely.

It couldn't have been closer to my work. The window out the back looked down on the town pier and the Snowden Family Clambake's ticket kiosk. Just beyond the kiosk, the *Jacquie II*, the boat we used to bring two hundred customers—twice a day, every day, in the high season—to our private island for a real Maine clambake, stood quiet and empty at her mooring.

Summer had become fall. The Snowden Family Clambake was only open weekends, and after next Monday, Columbus Day, we'd shut down for the year.

I turned from the window and walked across the bare wood floor to the front of the apartment, where the windows looked out over Main Street. They felt tight, an important consideration with winter coming, though the October day was sunny and unseasonably warm. Leaning my forehead against the smooth glass and craning my neck, I could see my mother's house sitting at the top of the hill less than two blocks away. Maybe this wasn't such a great location. I loved my mother and I loved my job, but did I want to live where I could see both from my windows?

"Of course, you'll want a twelve-month lease," the agent said. "I'm sure they'll go for it. Especially because it's you."

"Twelve months?" I tried not to sound anxious.

"It's for your own protection. So they don't take money from you for nine months and then kick you out in the summer when they can get a much higher rent."

"I hadn't thought about a lease." I hadn't, in truth, thought about much of anything. During the clambake's busy season, there'd been no time. With the clambake winding down, I finally had time to think. Maybe too much time.

But a twelve-month lease sounded like forever. Maybe by next summer my relationship with my boyfriend, Chris Durand, would be in a place where we'd move in together. Chris and I had had our ups and downs, dizzying highs and appalling lows, but we'd been on an extended up since the end of August.

But having a boyfriend, and even a place to live, wouldn't solve the problem of having nothing to do. When I'd arrived in Busman's Harbor late last winter, there'd been so much work to do to save our business—negotiating with the bank to restructure our giant loan, building a business plan and budget from the ground up, beefing up our marketing. But that wouldn't keep me busy this winter. Or pay the rent.

So maybe I'd leave running the Snowden Family Clambake to my sister and her husband and return to my real life in Manhattan. I didn't know what I'd be doing next summer, or next week, for that matter. Stressed out as I was about the decision, it was wonderful to have options. Options were something I hadn't had for months.

"I'll let you know," I told the rental agent.

"Make a decision quickly," she said, echoing the words of Owen Quimby. "It won't stay empty long."

The agent locked up and we clattered down the noisy wooden stairs and pushed through the glass-paneled front door onto Main Street. We said good-bye at the corner and I headed around the block, back to the town pier.

A line of senior citizens milled about, waiting to board a large, gray bus, which idled noisily in the road. The driver stowed walkers and small suitcases in the luggage compartment underneath. In the way of small towns, most, though not all, of the faces in the line were familiar. Two stood out. Fiona and Viola Snugg, called Fee and Vee, ran their bed-and-breakfast, the Snuggles Inn, in the gingerbread-covered Victorian house across the street from my mother's. The sisters were family friends and honorary great aunts.

"Hello, dearie." Fee spotted me as I spotted her.

"Hullo." I gave each of them a peck on the cheek. "Where're you off to?"

"Campobello Island, overnight. So lovely to get away," Vee said. She had pink cheeks and masses of white hair piled on her head, and was dressed, as always, in a skirt, hose, and high heels. Her older sister, Fee, standing beside her, had on a practical pair of wool slacks and huge white sneakers. In her left hand, she clutched a walking stick, an ebony shaft with a silver head that had been their father's. Arthritis bent her back so badly, Fee was now shorter than my paltry five-foot-two.

I looked around at the crowd. Most of the people waiting to board the bus, except the most ancient of the ancient, had toiled endlessly through the high season, as Fee and Vee had. They spent their summers laundering sheets, cooking divine English breakfasts, and cheerfully advising their guests about every activity our peninsula had to offer. I was glad they were finally getting to enjoy themselves, and on such a beautiful autumn day. Traveling just over the Canadian border to the summer residence of Franklin Roosevelt would be a special treat.

"It'll be nice to be out of town," Fee commented, her eyes darting around, studying faces. The other people in line were engrossed in their own conversations. "You know, to get away from the tension."

"It's a bad business," Vee added.

"Indeed." I didn't want to say more. The lobstermen in town were feuding with the men from Coldport Island, our nearest lobstering neighbors, about the rights to set traps in nearby waters. It was a touchy subject that could generate aggressive arguments. I wasn't comfortable discussing it in public. Coldport Islanders didn't often come to town, particularly after the daily service that took tourists from Busman's Harbor to their island shut down after Labor Day. The weekly ferry they relied on through the off-season landed farther up the mid-coast at Rockland, which was where most Coldporters took care of their grocery shopping, doctor's appointments, and other mainland business. But a seniors tour to Campobello Island was

exactly the sort of thing that might attract someone from the island, so I kept my mouth shut, and
so did the Snugg sisters.

"Where's the other musketeer?" I asked. Usually,
the sisters went on these expeditions as a three-
some with Mrs. Gus, the wife of my favorite elderly
restaurateur, Gus Farnham.

The corners of Fee's mouth drooped. "She's too
poorly to come. Such a shame."

Like Fee, Mrs. Gus suffered with arthritis, though
I'd never before seen either woman give into it.
Mrs. Gus must have been feeling poorly, indeed.

Fee brightened. "We told her we'd bring her
something."

Vee smiled, too, and they were back in the spirit
of the adventure.

"Let's board!" the busman called.

I stood at the bottom of the bus's steps and the
driver stood at the top. Working together, we got
everyone aboard. I waved good-bye until they were
gone.

When the bus pulled out, I found myself standing across from the one thing that could bring me
down on such a beautiful day. Next to the Snowden
Family Clambake ticket booth on the town pier,
the two-by-four skeleton of a second kiosk rose.
The fancy carved sign next to it promised boat
rides and gourmet meals offered by LE SHACK,
DAVID THWING THE MUSSEL KING, PROPRIETOR. And

there, polishing sea gull dung off the sign with a white handkerchief, was the Mussel King himself.

The Snowden Family Clambake had never had a direct competitor. Sure, there were plenty of tour boats in Busman's Harbor, and plenty of places to get a tasty lobster dinner, but no one else combined them into a "dining experience," as we called it. Just when we'd gotten the clambake back on its feet, David Thwing had come along. I tried to see the situation rationally. To well-wishers and employees, I was upbeat about Thwing's planned venture. "Just proves someone else believes there's demand," I said, parroting words I'd used to soothe panicky entrepreneurs and nervous investors back in my venture capital days.

But my emotional self couldn't see it that way. *Why, oh why, oh why?* I'd fumed. *Why now?* The Snowden Family Clambake Company was saved, but barely. What if this new competition tipped us back into the red? We'd worked so hard. If the business went sideways again, we'd be right back where we started—owing tons of money, unable to support the family. It was all too much to think about.

David Thwing looked up and saw me. "Ms. Snowden," he called. "Ms. Snowden!"

I recognized him from his many appearances in *The Fog Horn*, Busman's Harbor's weekly newspaper, but I was surprised he recognized me. I ran the clambake company with my sister's husband, Sonny, and I'd happily let him lead the charge against Thwing. Sonny, our attack dog, had testified against Thwing at the public hearings as he'd sought space for his ticket kiosk on the town pier, docking rights for his tour boat, and so on. Thwing had prevailed in those early rounds. His successes irritated me, though I tried to be realistic about them. They infuriated Sonny.

I looked around the pier. It was Monday morning in the almost off-season and Thwing was the only person in sight. I sucked it up and crossed the road.

"Julia Snowden, we meet at last." Thwing extended a hand and gave me his best chamber-of-commerce smile. He was a rangy man in his mid-forties, his bald head surrounded by curly, light brown hair that stuck straight up at the edges like a clown's. His olive-green suit was a dead giveaway he was from out of town. In Busman's Harbor, the only men who wore suits were funeral directors, bankers, and lawyers, and then only at work.

"Nice to meet you," I responded through gritted teeth.

"I take it you're the saner member of the family. Your brother-in-law doesn't seem to want me in town. I hope you're not afraid of a little competition." He smiled an oily smile. He had a strange way of moving, like a marionette, all jerky elbows and knees.

"The Snowden Family Clambake has run a successful business in this harbor since my late father started it thirty-two years ago," I said, staring straight into his mud-brown eyes, "I'm sure we'll be fine."

I said it with more confidence than I felt. Thwing's restaurants offered superb seafood. I knew because I'd eaten several excellent meals at the flagship restaurant in Portland. Le Shack served upscale, gourmet food, including its signature mussels. Thwing had some sort of hotshot chef working for him and they'd been a runaway success. In the last few years, he'd expanded to become a mini-chain with five restaurants in Maine coast harbors stretching from Ogunquit to Bar Harbor.

"We'll see if your little family operation has what it takes to go head-to-head with professionals. I give you less than a season." He moved closer, towering over me. I was smaller and younger, but working in venture capital, I'd gone toe-to-toe with enough of these guys not to let him intimidate me. I moved around him and stepped over the threshold into his unfinished ticket kiosk.

"Mind if I take a look?" I asked, a little belatedly, since I was already inside.

"Be careful! That's a construction zone. Get away from there!" Thwing threw his weirdly articulated arms in the air, elbows bent at sharp angles. In his green suit, he reminded me of a lobster attempting to roust another from its den. He obviously wanted me out of his ticket booth. Which made me stubbornly determined to stay put. I planted myself in his doorway as I continued our conversation.

"How's the hunt for a venue going?" I asked, all innocence. "Find anything yet?" Thwing had received permission from the town to dock a tour boat and build a ticket booth, but I'd heard he lacked the one thing the Snowden Family Clambake had—a place to serve his food. Thwing needed a beautiful island or an isolated piece of beach on Eastclaw or Westclaw Point, the spits of land that surrounded Busman's vast outer harbor. He would find a site, I was sure of it. There was always someone looking to sell out. But once he'd done that, he'd have to get permission to build on it, even to have a dock where his passengers could disembark. He'd need a victualer's license and a liquor license and Sonny would be there, fighting him every step of the way.

Maybe we'd catch a break. I hoped so. If we didn't, if Thwing got all his permits and built his restaurant, my options might melt away. I'd feel duty bound to run the clambake next summer as we competed with him.

"As a matter of fact, I'm looking at some promising properties today." He pulled his phone from his suit pocket and glanced at the display. "Will you look at the time? If I don't get going, I'll be late."

Then he charged off in his weird, stalking pace in the direction of the back harbor.

Chapter 2

My business in town concluded, I steered our Boston Whaler back into the navy-blue water of Busman's inner harbor. Most of the pleasure boat moorings were empty. The sailboats and cabin cruisers had been hauled out and stored in one of the harbor boatyards, or loaded onto trailers for the long drive to warmer winter waters. Only a few stalwarts remained, hoping to grab one last day.

I tried to shake off my strange encounter with the unpleasant David Thwing. I'd put Sonny's personal animosity toward him down to the natural human impulse to vilify someone who posed a threat. But now that I'd met Thwing in person, I wasn't so sure. With his not-so-veiled insults and oily smile, there was a lot not to like about him.

As I reached the outer harbor, the chop increased and I held tightly to the wheel of the Whaler. There were six islands in the outer harbor, three of them inhabited. The largest was Chipmunk, home to a summer colony with a hundred homes. Ferry service had ended on the first of October, so only the hardiest of summer residents remained. Next week, the town of Busman's Harbor would turn off the great conduits that took fresh drinking water and electricity to the island and it would be abandoned for the winter.

Though the day was unseasonably warm, it was cold on the water, and got colder still when I passed Dinkum's Light and exited through the narrow mouth of the harbor into the North Atlantic. I shivered in the heavy flannel shirt I wore over a Snowden Family Clambake T-shirt, wishing I'd shrugged into a sweatshirt before I'd started the boat. Fortunately, the trip to Morrow Island, two miles down the coast, was a short one and I was soon tying up at our dock.

I'd been living in the little house by the dock on Morrow Island for five weeks. My sister Livvie, her husband Sonny, and their nine-year-old daughter, Page, had lived there all summer, but moved back to their home on the mainland after Labor Day so Page could more easily attend school and swim team practice. I'd happily moved from my mother's house in town where I'd been living since March out to the island. Fall was my favorite time of year to be there.

Le Roi, the island's Maine coon cat, ran down the dock to greet me. Like many of his breed, he often behaved like a dog—loving a good swim, playing fetch, and welcoming the human inhabitants home. Though he behaved like a dog, Le Roi thought like a cat, which is to say he believed he owned me and not the other way around. I bent down, gave him a good scratch around his magnificent ruff, and wondered what the owners of the apartment over Gleason's Hardware thought about pets. Until this year, Le Roi had spent his winters with the island's former caretakers, but that was no longer an option. My niece, Page, had loved living with Le Roi for the summer, but my sister, Livvie, exhausted by the early months of pregnancy, had announced the cat wasn't coming home with them.

"What am I going to do with you?" I asked Le Roi. What was I going to do with me?

I looked up at Morrow Island, a thirteen-and-a-half-acre hunk of rock in the North Atlantic. The old great lawn led up from the dock to its first plateau, which had been home to the formal gardens in my great-grandparents' time. Now it held the croquet, badminton, and bocce courts the clambake guests played on while they waited for their meals. It also held the pavilion where we served chowder, twin lobsters, steamed clams, and the rest of the food at long picnic tables. The attached bar, souvenir shop, and small commercial kitchen waited for the last surge of guests before their long winter's rest.

Farther up the lawn, at the top of the island, stood Windsholme, the stone "cottage" built by my mother's ancestors. Half-burned in a fire in the spring, it too awaited a decision. Fix it up, or tear it down? Either would be breathtakingly expensive. I softened the focus of my gaze to blur the orange hazard fence surrounding it. A slight breeze rippled through the colorful leaves and the island seemed to sigh with contentment. I sighed, too. I was home.

The hardwood for the clambake fire was piled beside the fire pit. The lengths were twice what I could fit into the wood stove in the house. The day was gorgeous, but by late afternoon I'd need the stove's heat to be able to concentrate on anything beyond the cold in my toes and at the end of my nose. "No time like the present," I said to Le Roi and went for the axe. Le Roi, sensing work, scattered.

"Ahoy!" I straightened up from loading split logs into a wheelbarrow, grateful for the break. The *Flittermouse*, Quentin Tupper's sleek racing sailboat, glided into our dock. "Give me a hand here?" he shouted.

I ran over to take the lines. "To what do I owe the honor?"

"I was out sailing, thought I'd drop in."

In June, Quentin had saved the Snowden Family Clambake by paying off our bank loan and becoming an investor in our business. He owned a house on Westclaw Point, directly across the narrows from Morrow Island, and he knew if our business went under, our island would be sold and developed.

As a classics major in college, Quentin had developed a tiny piece of computer code that was licensed and embedded in a ubiquitous operating system and every application it ran. The resulting royalties had made him rich beyond most people's dreams. He spent his life studiously avoiding all connections and obligations. Unlike the other rich people I knew, he served on no boards of companies, schools, or charities. He didn't collect art or stamps or celebrities. He answered to no one.

True to his word, he'd been a completely silent partner in the clambake company during the long, busy days of the summer, but now that things had slowed down, he'd taken to "dropping by."

"Want lunch?" I asked.

"Don't mind if I do."

I wheeled the firewood to the deck of the house, where Quentin helped me unload it. Inside the pine kitchen, I put bacon on to fry and took a juicy tomato off the windowsill. The last spoils of summer. My sister Livvie was the gardener, not me, and I was aware I was reaping the final rewards of her hard work.

Quentin sat at the table. Through the big kitchen windows behind him, the Atlantic Ocean stretched to the horizon. Despite his carefully constructed life, I sensed he sometimes craved company. He'd accepted me as a peer from the beginning, and an odd friendship had developed. I'd been away from Busman's Harbor since junior high myself and had no group of town friends to fall back on. If you'd didn't count my boyfriend, Chris, and my extended family, Quentin was my closest friend in Busman's Harbor.

"I looked at the apartment over Gleason's Hardware this morning," I told him.

He shook his head. "That's not right for you."

Quentin had opinions about everything, and no

inhibitions about expressing them. I wondered if he'd always been that way, or if he'd started losing his social skills when his ever-increasing fortune had allowed him to withdraw from other people.

I assembled our BLTs and put one on a plate in front of him along with a glass of iced tea, another symbol of the now-gone summer. "Why 'not right'?" I asked as I sat down.

He waved me off. He'd taken a bite of sandwich and his mouth was full. Summer had been kind to Quentin. It had lightened his dark blond hair, and he was tanned as only the leisure class, or the most determined tanning booth bunny, could be. Today, as usual, he wore a cotton sweater, tailored denim shirt, khakis, and boat shoes, no socks. His tan made his bright blue eyes look even brighter. Sonny had told me Quentin was gay, but most of the rest of what Sonny had told me about Quentin had turned out not to be true. When I'd tried asking him once about his romantic history, former attachments, and so on, in the way that friends do, a steel door had slammed shut, keeping me on the outside. My life was there for his dissection, but his was off limits to me. Whomever he might have longed or lusted for, Quentin was steadfastly alone.

"The apartment over Gleason's Hardware is not where you're going to end up," he said, with confidence, once he'd stopped chewing.

"The HR director from my old job called this morning. They'll hold my position open only until Friday. Maybe I'll go back to New York."

Quentin shook his head. "Nope. That's not right for you, either."

This was getting aggravating. Which reminded me. "I saw David Thwing on the pier today." *Speaking of aggravating.*

"That jerk," Quentin said. "Did he give you a hard time?"

"He said he didn't think the clambake company could handle the competition—that we'd last less than a season."

"Jerk," Quentin repeated. He sat back in his chair, his tanned forehead furrowed. "If he does get his business up and running, I'd feel better if you ran the clambake next season."

"Is that your intuition about what's 'right' for me?"

"No. That's my intuition about what's right for my investment."

When Quentin put his money into the clambake to save us from the bank, I'd agreed to stay on for only one summer, the one just past. Technically, he had no way to hold me, though he knew me well enough to know that if the clambake was threatened, I'd feel I had to stay to protect my family and the employees along with his investment.

"If he continues to be a jerk, let me know," Quentin said, twirling a nonexistent mustache. "We haf vays of dealing with pepple like hem."

He drank the last of his iced tea and stood up. I walked him back toward the *Flittermouse*. On the lawn, he stopped and looked up at the ruin of Windsholme. "What are you going to do about that?" he asked.

Another decision. "I don't know."

"You should at least get it fully secured to protect what's left from the winter weather, so you have the option of restoring it, if that's what you decide to do."

My family hadn't lived in the old mansion for three generations. I couldn't imagine a scenario where restoring it made sense.

"It's an architectural gem," Quentin said, as if he felt my pessimism. "And it's in better shape than you think it is."

"Let me get through the last clambake this weekend."

When we reached the *Flittermouse*, Quentin climbed aboard.

"What are those?" I pointed to three lobster buoys sitting on the deck. They had a thick neongreen stripe with thin navy-blue rings above and below it.

"I found them floating free out by Coldport Island when I was on my sail," Quentin said. "I figured I'd try to return them to their owner."

Quentin had built his granite mansion on land where his ancestors had kept a shack in order to preserve their rights to lobster in the narrows between Westclaw Point and Morrow Island. He was rich, but he still understood what lost gear meant to a working lobsterman.

"Any idea who?" Every lobsterman had a distinct set of colors and design for the buoys that marked his lobster traps.

"No idea," Quentin said. All buoys were marked

with the owner's lobstering license number, so Quentin
would have to track the owner down that way.

"Do you think they were cut loose?"

If the buoys were cut, it marked an escalation in
the dispute between Busman's Harbor's lobstermen and Coldport Island's. When lobstermen from
one harbor put their traps in an area traditionally
belonging to another, the first response was usually to turn the encroaching buoys upside down as
a warning. If that didn't work, the next step was to
pull up the offending traps and take the lobsters.
This could be done subtly by removing only part of
the catch or as an outright provocation, taking it all.
If the traps weren't moved as a result, the next step
was dropping your own traps over top of the out-
sider's traps, creating a tangled mess.

The next stage of this "gear war" was cutting the
line from the traps to the buoy, leaving "ghost
traps" on the ocean floor. The owner lost the expensive traps and the lobsters in them. Then, like
as not, he would retaliate. In some rare cases, if
it kept going, the gear war became a full-fledged
lobster war, with vandalized boats and shots fired.
Even murder wasn't unheard of.

"It's a bad business," Quentin said, using the
same words Vee Snugg had.

Chapter 3

I waved good-bye to Quentin as he sailed off on the *Flittermouse* and contemplated what to do with the rest of my day. There was clambake-related office work to be done, but how many warm afternoons did we have left?

I went upstairs, put on a sweatshirt, pulled my blond hair back in a ponytail and grabbed a book. Normally, I would have sat out on our dock, enjoying the endless view on the Atlantic side of Morrow Island, but despite the unseasonably warm day, it was fall and slightly breezy. I wanted a more protected spot.

I followed the path alongside the great lawn to the top of the island. Beyond Windsholme, the path wound downhill to our little beach. Rock outcroppings on either side of the cove would protect me from the breeze, and in fall, the view from the beach was arguably even more spectacular than the Atlantic side. Less than a mile across the deep channel that separated it from Morrow

Island, Westclaw Point rose in front of me. The leaves of the deciduous trees had turned a riot of reds, yellows, and golds. I positioned an Adirondack chair in the sun, plopped down, and pushed aside my worries—the tension in the town, David Thwing's threat of competition, and all the urgent decisions about my own life. I opened my book and was promptly pulled into its story.

By the time I looked up, it was after three o'clock. I shivered a bit, realizing a chill had brought me out of my reading trance.

A lobster boat floated lazily in the narrows between my beach and Westclaw Point. I didn't recognize it. I hadn't been back in town long enough to know the players.

Across from me, Quentin Tupper's towering, modern edifice of polished granite and glass rose from the boulders on which it stood. Most people referred to the house as a monstrosity, but I thought it fit perfectly—like it was thrust out of the rough landscape. The *Flittermouse* rested at its dock out front.

The lobster boat continued to float, apparently aimlessly. It turned its stern toward me and I read its name, *El Ay*. I said it aloud. L.A. Who in Busman's Harbor, or on Coldport Island for that matter, had close enough ties to Los Angeles to name their boat for that city?

I walked to the edge of the water to get a closer look. For the most part, lobstermen weren't aimless. They went about the business of hauling, emptying, baiting, and releasing their traps with machine-like efficiency. Even more worrying, I couldn't see anyone on the boat. Not the lobsterman, or his frequent assistant, the sternman.

"Ahoy!" I called, trying to get someone to wave back to me. "Ahoy!"

The sound of my voice carried across the water, but no one responded. Seconds ticked by. I pondered. Was this a real emergency, or was it a lobsterman grabbing some time away from his family to take a nap, or sleep it off?

"Ahoy!"

The water echoed the sound back at me. The boat turned again and began to drift sideways with the current. It wasn't anchored. Something was wrong.

I jogged up the path away from the beach and walked carefully out onto one of the big outcroppings that surrounded it, hoping the extra height would allow me to see into the boat. "Ahoy!"

No sound. No motion. No one. I ran to my house to call the Coast Guard on the radio.

When I got back to the beach with my binoculars, a small Coast Guard boat was already approaching the *El Ay*. A voice boomed through a loudspeaker. "Vessel *El Ay*, United States Coast Guard. Are you in distress? Repeat. Are you okay?"

The Maine Marine Patrol, no doubt alerted by the Coast Guard, approached from the opposite direction. On a signal from the Coast Guard, the Marine Patrol boat pulled alongside the lobster boat. Through the binoculars, I saw the officer shake his head. My stomach dropped. No one was aboard.

Across the water, I saw Quentin, out at the end of his dock, drawn by the commotion.

The Coast Guard boat approached and the three boats floated in tandem. Two Coast Guards-men, a tall man and a trim woman, boarded the *El Ay*. I held my breath.

They, too, emerged, shaking their heads. My stomach, already in a knot, clenched tighter.

As the Coast Guard prepared to tow the lobster boat to town, I sprinted up the path toward our Boston Whaler.

Chapter 4

By the time I got to town, word had spread and a crowd had gathered at the marina. The Coast Guard and Marine Patrol boats were tied up, as was the *El Ay*. More Coast Guardsmen had materialized and so had Busman's four on-duty town cops, who seemed most interested in keeping the crowd away from the boats. I joined the group at the back and caught snippets of conversation.

"—Coldport Island—"

"This has gone too far."

"—knew it would end in tragedy."

The crowd, at least, had decided the empty lobster boat was a result of the war with Coldport Island. I wasn't so sure. It could have been an accident. Lobstering was a dangerous job, especially if you were doing it alone.

The greatest danger was being caught in the line that held the traps together, and then hauled into the water as they were released over the stern. This far north you wouldn't last long in any season.

Even if you could break free of the line before you were pulled to the bottom, it would be five minutes to hypothermia, as little as fifteen until death. If the line became tangled in the propeller, and you were hauled under the boat, you were a goner for sure.

I could tell by the pinched looks on the faces of the officials, and the way they paced around the boat, that's what they were worried about.

"Oh my God, it's the *El Ay*." My sister, Livvie, appeared at my side. Four months pregnant with her second child, the curve of her belly was beginning to show on her tall athlete's frame. Her auburn hair was, if possible, more lustrous than ever. My sister was beautiful, and never more so than when she was pregnant.

"You know the owner?"

"You do, too. It's Peter Murray's boat."

"Oh no." Peter had been her husband Sonny's best friend since elementary school. His wife was named Lorrie Ann. Initials, L. A. *El Ay*. They had three children under six.

Livvie pointed to the front of the crowd, where Lorrie Ann Murray stood. She was a petite woman in her mid-twenties, with light brown hair cut in bangs in the front and cascading in waves to her shoulders in the back. Her mother, whom I'd never met but knew by sight, comforted her daughter while leaning on a walker. I couldn't imagine what Lorrie Ann was going through.

"I need to get to her," Livvie said, but as she

started moving forward, the cops motioned us back.

The Coast Guard and Marine Patrol moved the *El Ay* into a cradle and fixed the long lines around it, preparing to winch it up. The local cops, including my childhood guy friend Jamie Dawes, tried to move the crowd away. We grudgingly took a step or two, but we weren't leaving.

"You going to go arrest those Coldporters, now?" someone shouted in response to the request to move.

The *El Ay* rose slowly out of the water. The crowd hushed. The only thing we could hear was the whir of the winch and Lorrie Ann's panicked sobs.

"Get back," Jamie shouted in his most forceful cop voice.

The hull of the *El Ay* broke the surface. The crowd gasped. As we had all feared, there was a body entangled in the lines under the boat. Beside me, Livvie moaned. Lorrie Ann screamed and fell against her mother.

"What the . . . ? That's David Thwing," I whispered to Livvie.

"What? Where?"

"Hanging from the boat. That's not Peter Murray. It's David Thwing."

Livvie stood up straighter, looking over the heads of the crowd. "You're right. No way that's Peter. Much too tall."

"And the suit. I saw Thwing wearing a suit this morning."

"The Mussel King? Why would he be under Peter's boat?" Livvie asked.

I pushed through the crowd toward Jamie. As he tried to shoo me back, I grabbed his arm and pulled him close so he could hear me above the buzz of the spectators. He bent over, moving his ear to my mouth.

"That's David Thwing," I told him.

"The Mussel King, that guy Sonny's been yelling about?" Jamie stared at the figure dangling below the *El Ay*. "That isn't Peter," he agreed.

"I know. It's Thwing. I saw him this morning. He was dressed in a green suit." I stopped. I hadn't liked either the idea of David Thwing or the man himself, but the sheer awfulness of what had happened to him overwhelmed me. To be caught, helpless, hauled into the cold, cold water and drowned . . .

"Whoa, you okay?" Jamie put an arm out to steady me.

"Fine," I said. "Sorry."

"Any idea why Thwing would be on Peter Murray's lobster boat?"

"When I saw him this morning, he said he was scouting sites for his business. Maybe he went out with Peter to look at properties."

"What time was this?"

"Around nine, on the town pier. We talked for a few minutes and then he went off in the direction of the marina."

Jamie looked up at the *El Ay* again. "Thanks. You may have sped up the identification."

"Of course. Anything to help."

The crowd hadn't dispersed. Around us, people

seemed to have realized the corpse hanging below the *El Ay* wasn't its owner. There was mad speculating about Coldport, the identity of the body, and the whereabouts of Peter Murray.

Jamie turned away from me and demanded again that the crowd "move along." Nobody did. He gave up and walked off toward his chief, I assumed to pass along my information.

Out of the corner of my eye, I saw the outline of a familiar lobster boat docking not far from where the crowd stood. My brother-in-law, Sonny, secured his dad's boat, disembarked, and started toward the group. He wore his lobsterman's orange oilskin overalls, which matched the bright orange of his short hair.

Lorrie Ann whirled toward him. "You!" she shouted, dramatically pointing at Sonny. "You were supposed to be there. If you'd been there, this never would have happened!" Then she collapsed into her mother's arms.

Chapter 5

"What the heck is going on?" Sonny demanded. Livvie gave him a quick hug and we stood in a tight circle, the dockside crowd milling and talking around us.

"Peter's missing and David Thwing was found under the *El Ay*, caught in the trapline." I gave him the summary of what had happened.

"Let's get out of here." Sonny inclined his head toward his dad's lobster boat, the *Abby*, the nearest private place to talk. The three of us climbed aboard.

"Thwing is dead?" Sonny asked. "Couldn't have happened to a nicer guy."

"Sonny!" Livvie rebuked him. "Don't speak ill of the dead."

"I'm not going to pretend to like the guy because he's a goner," Sonny said. "If that jerk had anything to do with Peter being missing—"

"Maybe you shouldn't speak ill of the dead when everyone in town knows you hated him," I offered.

"And when the boat owner's wife just publicly blamed you for whatever happened."

Sonny exhaled noisily. "I don't know a thing about it. Honest."

"Were you supposed to go out with Peter today?" I asked.

"His sternman took off for parts unknown last week. He called a couple of days ago and told me he needed help hauling his traps."

The lobsterman (never called a lobsterperson or lobsterwoman, though there were an increasing number of those) was the captain and usually owned the boat. He piloted and made all the decisions, like where the traps would go and how frequently they were emptied. The sternman (never the sternperson or sternwoman, though there were more and more of them, too) did everything disgusting, including putting the rotting herring in the bait bags, for a small share of the value of the catch.

Sternmen, unless they were family, were known for their drifting ways. Peter and Sonny had been friends since their days at Busman's Elementary, and Sonny was a highly skilled lobsterman. It would be natural for Peter to ask Sonny for help.

"But you didn't go out with Peter," I said.

Sonny shook his head. "I got to the dock too late. I missed him."

Livvie's left eyebrow arched upward. "You left the house at six-forty-five."

Sonny stared at his boots. "I went to Gus's."

"Sonny!" Livvie was clearly surprised. "We've talked about this. There's nothing there but trouble."

The local lobstermen often met at Gus's restaurant for breakfast, especially at times in the season when going out early didn't offer an advantage. Lobstering usually started in the pre-dawn hours, when the seas were calmest. In a good season, which this had been, the peak of the catch came in August and September when the lobsterman and sternman put in twelve-hour-plus days doing exhausting physical work. In October, the lobsters were moving to deeper water to escape the winter cold. All that moving around meant the catch was down and time could be spared for jawboning at Gus's.

The territorial war with Coldport would be the main subject of conversation and that was what Livvie had warned Sonny against. No doubt, she feared the conversation at Gus's would work everyone up into a lather, and her impulsive husband would do something he'd regret.

"So you went to Gus's and then what?" Livvie prompted. I could tell she was already unhappy with the direction of the conversation.

"And nothing," Sonny answered. "I stayed too long at Gus's and missed Peter."

Livvie's hazel eyes widened slightly. It was the lamest of lies. If Sonny had set off in the morning to help his friend, he wouldn't "forget." Besides, I'd seen David Thwing on the dock at nine o'clock, which meant if Peter had taken Thwing out, he'd left after that. There was no way Sonny had spent two hours at Gus's, no matter how engaging the conversation.

I held my breath, waiting to see if Livvie would confront Sonny about his untruth. But she didn't. This was a discussion they'd have outside my presence.

"Did Peter say anything about taking David Thwing out on the *El Ay*?" I asked.

"No, and he was aware that if he'd told me Thwing was coming, I never would've been involved," Sonny said. "He knew I hated that guy."

"Everyone in town knew you hated that guy," Livvie said.

Sonny sighed. "None of this makes any sense."

"If Thwing's under the *El Ay*, where's Peter?" I asked.

Neither Sonny nor Livvie responded, which I took to mean they thought Peter was in the water, probably dead. Lobstermen and their spouses were usually fatalistic about the dangers of their profession, rarely acknowledging the risks they took.

"When you figured out you'd missed Peter, what did you do?" I asked.

"I went to my dad's and offered to haul his traps." Sonny's dad had had rotator cuff surgery, and Sonny, along with his brother, Kyle, had been helping out. "My dad said sure, so I took the *Abby* out. Been lobstering all day."

"By yourself?"

Sonny gestured around the boat. "You see anyone else? Kyle was under the weather." He nodded toward the place where several lobsterman had gathered around the Coast Guard officers. "I need to find out about the search."

The Coast Guard didn't involve civilians in searches

if they could avoid it. Regular people, even skilled fishermen, were difficult to direct and communicate with. But in a situation like this, where speed was essential, an exception would likely be made. No one knew the point in the ocean where Peter had left the *El Ay*, which meant the search area was huge. If there was any chance Peter was alive, either in a rubber dingy, stranded on one of dozens of islands or along the miles of empty coastline, he had to be found quickly, before exposure killed him.

Sonny gave Livvie a kiss on the cheek. She pulled him to her and hugged him fiercely. Neither of them acknowledged that Peter was likely dead, but their emotions couldn't be completely hidden. Sonny nuzzled her neck, then pulled away and walked purposefully, head bent, shoulders forward, toward a circle of lobstermen.

"Have dinner with us?" Livvie asked.

I smiled. "Previous engagement."

"Oh really?" The hint of a smile back.

I treasured that. My entire family had been opposed to, or at least unsupportive of, my relationship with Chris Durand. Chris had the kind of reputation an exceptionally good-looking man in a small town could too easily come by. In his case, it was well-earned. If one more pretty girl introduced herself to me and said, "Oh, *you're* the one," I was going to——well, I was going to be not the least bit surprised.

Plus, there was the issue of Chris's multi-day, unexplained disappearances, which had caused so much trouble between us. And, though he and Sonny had at one time been friends, there was friction in their current relationship I didn't understand and neither would explain.

But lately my family had softened. At least the females had. They saw I was serious about Chris, and, at least for Livvie and Mom, I think they hoped that meant I'd stay in Maine. For me, there were a lot more factors to consider besides being near Chris and my family. But Mom, Livvie, and Page were definitely Team Maine, even if that meant a grudging toleration of Chris as my boyfriend.

Livvie made no move to get off the *Abby*, and I felt a momentary pang. Was her invitation a way of putting off the pending "discussion" with Sonny about where he'd really been that morning? Or maybe avoiding the emotions surrounding Peter's disappearance?

"Do you need company?" I asked.

"No, no, no. I'm picking up Page from swim team practice in a little while. And I should call on Lorrie Ann." Livvie said it without enthusiasm. I didn't blame her. Lorrie Ann's dramatic, public accusation of Sonny still hung in the air.

I checked my phone. "I'm late as it is," I said. "Gotta run."

Livvie put on a brave smile as I left the dock. "See you tomorrow?"

"Sure." Maybe by tomorrow we'd have some answers.

Chapter 6

By the time I left the marina, boats streamed out to search for Peter Murray in the little daylight that remained.

As I walked the few blocks from the back harbor to my Mom's house to pick up my car, I turned my encounter with Thwing that morning over in my mind. Had he been as awful as I'd thought at the time? He'd made fun of our "little family operation" and predicted our doom. But he hadn't deserved what had happened to him. In my wildest imaginings, I'd never wished him dead.

When I arrived in Mom's yard, both doors to her garage were open. Not an unusual sight. The garage was old, barely big enough for modern cars. You had to pull in perfectly or you couldn't swing the old doors closed, and mostly we didn't bother.

In the eight months I'd been home, I'd been responsible for not one, but two accidents with my mother's car. The first had resulted in an expensive, but mostly insurance-covered, repair. The second had totaled the old Buick.

After that, Mom insisted that instead of buying a decent used car, we follow the time-honored Maine custom of acquiring a "winter beater." A winter beater was an impossibly cheap car meant to be coaxed through the snowdrifts and road salt of a Maine winter, which was inevitably followed by the big-enough-for-a-four-year-old-to-stand-up-in potholes of a Maine spring. The beater was discarded the moment a repair of more than a few dollars was required, which one hoped was after the threat of frost had passed.

I didn't like the idea, but also didn't have the kind of money needed to thwart it. I still held out hope that when all the Snowden Family Clambake money was accounted for at the end of the season, we'd be able to find the funds to buy Mom a new or at least newish car. But Mom had insisted and, as a coup de grace, had pointed out, that if we bought beaters we could get two and I'd have my own car. Mom was done sharing. I couldn't say I blamed her. So buying a disposable car became yet another way, in the weeks after Labor Day, I had kicked the can of life decision-making down the road.

I was the owner of a maroon Chevy Caprice while my mother had a thirty-year-old black Mercedes S Class that wasn't, at that moment, in our garage.

I wondered vaguely where Mom was. Probably the supermarket or hair salon. Across the street, the Snuggles Inn was closed up tight, the Snugg sisters off on their Campobello adventure.

I entered our house through the back door, the

one my mother never locked. Upstairs I undressed and slipped into the shower. I found clean jeans, underwear, and socks in my old room. It said something about my life that my stuff was spread out among Morrow Island, my mother's, and Chris's house, not one of them my own home.

On my way out, I pulled my car keys out of the catchall kitchen drawer. In a matter of minutes, I was on the main road up the peninsula, headed toward Chris Durand's house.

I pulled into the dooryard of Chris's cabin, which sat on a flat piece of land bordering Foundling Lake. He'd bought the old house from his parents when they could no longer take the winters and fled to Florida. To me, Chris's home ownership was a symbol of his absolute commitment to Busman's Harbor. He'd never lived anywhere else and he wasn't planning to. The white pickup he used for his landscaping business and the taxicab he owned were both parked at the edge of the drive.

Before my car stopped, the door to the cabin opened and Chris jogged toward me. He was a blur of green eyes, dimpled chin and broad shoulders. My heart fluttered as it always did when he came into view. It had been three and a half rocky months and I couldn't believe I still reacted the same way every time I saw the man.

I climbed out of my car.

"Hello, beautiful." He kissed me like he meant it.

"Hey, yourself." He opened the cabin door and we went inside.

Chris rented out the cabin in the summer, so for most of our time together, he'd lived on his vintage wooden sailboat, the *Dark Lady*. In the fall, when he'd moved back into his house, I'd had two happy surprises. The first had been the cabin itself. During the long winters, Chris had remodeled the first floor extensively. It was open and bright with a soaring great room that held a two-story hearth, a screened porch with gorgeous views of the lake, and a sleek, modern kitchen. Which is where I'd found the second surprise. Chris was a near-gourmet cook. I never would've guessed it. Nothing about him suggested it. In the frantic summer months, he'd occasionally scrambled me an egg in the cramped galley of the *Dark Lady*, but that was it.

Less delightful was the second floor of the cabin. As soon as his summer tenants had left, Chris had gutted it. He'd demolished every plaster and lathe wall back to the studs, and that's how it had remained. From the two-story living room, I could look up into each of the bedrooms as if it were a dollhouse.

"When are you going to put the walls back?" I'd asked once, careful to peel any judgment from my voice.

"When I've saved up the next slug of money for the heating system and the wiring," Chris had answered, matter-of-fact.

Though there was a half bath on the main floor, I'd made him put the door back on the upstairs bath and tack some wallboard to the studs. "What would your previous girlfriends have thought of this arrangement?"

"Not hardly any of 'em made it upstairs," he'd said. That had shut me up. And guaranteed I'd never ask another question like that, or look at the faux-fur rug in front of the fireplace the same way.

Chris busied himself in the kitchen, which was producing wonderful smells. "What can I do to help?"

"Build a fire?"

"Sounds wonderful." I was going to tell him about David Thwing and Peter Murray, but not yet. I needed to soak up the comfort of Chris's home before I could face that topic again.

The fire made, I poured myself a glass of wine and settled into a big, comfy chair. I was as happy as I had ever been in any relationship. Even though I was thirty, my "official" three and a half months with Chris was the longest I'd ever been with anyone. I suspected for Chris, who was thirty-four, that was true as well. At least the longest romantic, monogamous relationship.

As a couple, we'd had challenges. I was born in Busman's Harbor, but I'd gone away for prep school, college, business school, and work. In all, more than half my life had been lived outside of town. Chris had never left and never would. He was dug deep, as his purchase of his parents' home proved.

We'd broken up over the summer, when his occasional unexplained multi-day disappearances

aboard the *Dark Lady* had threatened my trust.
He'd returned from the last one in August, beg-
ging forgiveness and suggesting a compromise. He
wouldn't tell me where he'd been or what he'd
been doing, but he promised he wouldn't disappear again. We'd both put it in the past.

I loved him, and eventually I'd decided I also
trusted him. Though any woman with a boyfriend
who disappeared for days at a time might think
"secret family," I knew in my bones he hadn't been
with another woman. In fact, when I looked deep
inside myself, I was astonished at how sure of that I
was, especially given his romantic history. I was one
hundred percent confident in Chris's love.

I wasn't nearly as sure that he hadn't been doing
something criminal. I wasn't naive about what
someone with a boat might be doing so near the
Canadian border. But drugs? I couldn't see him
doing anything so hurtful to people.

So I'd made my peace with it, whatever it was.
Like an old lover, it was tucked in the past, acknowledged but not to be dissected.

"Supper's on." Chris shook my shoulder gently.
With the wine and the fire, somehow I'd fallen
asleep. Aside from chopping firewood, I'd probably worked less today than any day in the last eight
months, but I was exhausted. It must have been the
emotion as I'd watched the *El Ay* being winched
out of the water, dreading what we would see.
Then the shock of seeing David Thwing, then

comprehending the inevitable meaning of Peter Murray's absence from the boat.

Chris had made a meal of tiny Maine rock shrimp in a fresh tomato sauce over polenta, the very definition of comfort food. The sauce had a clean, bright citrusy taste that contrasted with the brininess of the shrimp and the sweet of the tomato. The creaminess of the polenta balanced the chewiness of the seafood.

At the kitchen island where we ate our meals, I felt myself reviving. "This is fantastic."

"Took me twenty minutes."

"I couldn't have done this in twenty hours." I was impressed. "How did you learn to make polenta?"

"My mother's Italian," he answered.

How did I not know this? "I thought she was French-Canadian."

"Nope. My dad is."

"How come you never talk about your family?" I realized there were no photos of Chris's parents or sister in the redone home.

"Not everyone is quite so . . ." Chris struggled for the right word. ". . . enmeshed in their family as you are, Julia."

I supposed not.

"What did you do today?" I asked.

"Closed cottages." In a job-scarce resort town, Chris supported himself by landscaping, driving a taxi, and working as a bouncer. October was the busy season for securing cottages left by the summer folk and the retirees who'd started their great migration south. After the fall cleanup was complete, the water turned off, and the last load of trash hauled to the dump, Chris would check on their homes over the long winter, making sure there were no signs of break-ins or damage from storms. Crowley's, the tourist-trap bar where Chris worked as a bouncer, was already open only on weekends, and at the New Year would close completely. His taxi would still be called on for short hops—older folks headed to the grocery store or the doctor's office were his stock in trade—but the long, lucrative trips to the train station in Brunswick and the jetport in Portland would be over until spring came around again.

"You?" Chris asked.

"I was out on the island and I saw this lobster boat floating in the channel." Because he'd been outdoors raking leaves all day, Chris hadn't heard the news. He listened intently as I told the story.

"David Thwing? Isn't he that guy you and Sonny hate?"

"*Hate* is a strong word," I said.

"I think it's a word I've heard each of you use. And this guy was on Peter Murray's boat?"

"He was under it, to be precise."

"And there's no sign of Peter?" Chris scowled.

"Nope. The Coast Guard is conducting a search and rescue." I wondered how long it would be before "search and rescue" became "search and recovery."

"Upsetting as all this is, there's something more that's bothering you," Chris said.

My face must have given me away. "I'm sure Sonny lied about where he was today."

"Why would he lie?"

"He was supposed to go out on the *El Ay*. Peter is missing and David Thwing is dead. Sonny says he missed the boat."

Chris made a sound like "*pbbbft*" to convey that my concerns meant nothing. "Do you honestly believe Sonny had something to do with the death of David Thwing? And, what, left Pete Murray, his best friend since grade school, in the water without telling anybody?"

"You're right," I admitted. "I don't believe Sonny would do anything of the kind." I tried to push my worries away. "I looked at the apartment over Gleason's Hardware today," I said to change the subject.

"Did you like it?"

"Yeah." Arguably, it was perfect.

"Did you take it?"

"Not yet." *Why am I hesitating?*

He seemed pleased at this tangible indication I might stay through the winter. "You know you can stay here," he said.

I took our dishes to the sink. Was he inviting me to live with him? This was the nature of our relationship. Chris was open to whatever happened. He spoke without filter, from the heart. I was the cautious, analytical one. The one who had to look at things from every angle, to weigh and consider. The first time Chris said, "I love you," I'd pretended I hadn't heard him. As a result, I'd almost lost my chance to say it back.

I pointed through the living room to the non-existent interior walls of the second story. "No, I can't live here," I said lightly.

We both understood it was my excuse for not moving too fast.

We cleaned the kitchen and adjourned to the living room. The evening had turned cool and I was grateful for the fire. Chris had neither TV nor Internet in his house. He didn't want the expense or the distraction. If there was an important football game on TV, he drove down the peninsula to watch it at Crowley's.

Our evenings together had evolved to a comfortable routine. The Red Sox on the radio, their success prolonging the season, me reading a book, and Chris tinkering with something house-related. I loved all of it—the crack of the bat, the excitement of the ballpark crowd rumbling into the room. I could have gone on like this, happily, for the rest of my life. But I wasn't naive enough to believe that life in Busman's Harbor would be a series of gentle fall evenings.

I was at a fork in the road. If I stepped out of my life in New York, the decision was permanent, whether I walked away or was fired, as Owen Quimby had threatened. I was still technically an employee of the firm. There was no gap in my resume. If I spent the winter in Busman's Harbor, there would be a gap, and in the boys'-club world of Manhattan venture capital, where personal lives of any type were discouraged, it would be impossible to explain away.

When I'd left New York, I had felt burned out from the relentless pace of my job. But after eight months away, I missed it. I loved advising my firm to invest in young entrepreneurs and then helping them grow their businesses. Midwifing a new product or technology was exhilarating. Sure, there were plenty of failures, but the companies that caught on provided lots of good jobs. I felt as if I was productive and contributing. Yes, my firm made lots of money, but for me, the money was just a way to keep score.

I also missed the vibrancy of New York City, where I could order any kind of food at any hour of the day or night and have it delivered to my apartment door. Once Crowley's closed for the winter, Hole in the Wall Pizza, a take-out joint in the supermarket plaza, would be the only place on the peninsula to get prepared food for dinner.

If I stayed in the harbor, what would I do? The Snowden Family Clambake was a seasonal business. In Busman's Harbor, jobs for MBAs weren't falling out of trees. I'd thought about looking for a job in Portland and spending the weekends with Chris, but at that point, I might as well stay in New York. And presumably, any meaningful job anywhere, would preclude coming back to run the clambake in the spring.

I'd turned it all over in my mind so many times, and hadn't found a solution. And now I had five days to give Owen Quimby my decision.

I heard the rumble of car tires coming up the drive at the same moment Chris did. He was out of his seat before the car door slammed.

When he opened the cabin door, Livvie stood there, fist poised to knock. Her eyes were swollen from crying. "It's for you," he called over his shoulder.

Livvie gestured that I should come outside. I grabbed a coat off the peg by the door and followed her. There was no privacy in Chris's home-without-walls.

"Livvie, what's the matter?" This was my assured little sister, who always rolled with whatever life handed her.

"Sonny's lying." Her voice cracked with emotion.

"About why he missed Peter's boat?"

She nodded. "He won't tell me where he was today."

She and Sonny had been a couple since high school. They'd essentially grown up together, and more than a decade into their relationship, they were a tight, loyal team. I couldn't recall an instance of him lying to her. And her tear-streaked face showed they'd had a doozy of an argument.

But my sister wouldn't have left her warm home after ten o'clock on a chilly Maine night because she and her husband had a fight. Something else was scaring her.

"Livvie, are you afraid Sonny had something to do with whatever happened aboard the *El Ay*?"

Her eyes grew wide, as if my putting the question in words was the first time she'd confronted the amorphous fear at the corners of her consciousness. She shook her head, clearing away the emotion. "No." She said it definitively, as if trying to push away her doubts and my own. "He would never. But he's covering up something. Will you talk to him?"

"Why in the world would he tell me if he wouldn't tell you?"

She patted the slight curve of her belly. "Because he's protecting me. I just don't know from what. And it's freaking me out and making me more scared that he won't tell. You can force him."

"I don't know." I didn't want to get between a married couple, particularly this one.

"You help everyone who asks you. You've helped solve two murders since you've been home. Why won't you help me?"

In the light shining from over Chris's front door, I could see tears running freely down her face. Against my better judgment, I agreed to talk to Sonny.

"Assuming they don't find Peter tonight, Sonny will go out searching early in the morning," Livvie said. "He'll call me when he gets back to the marina. Then I'll call you so you can go over and speak to him."

"Okay." I wasn't going to pretend to be enthusiastic.

"I want to know where he was *all day*," Livvie emphasized.

"We both saw him get off his dad's lobster boat this afternoon," I said. "We know where he was the rest of the day, out pulling traps."

"But that's the thing. We saw him come into the back harbor and head straight for the *Abby's* slip in the marina. No stop at the lobster pound. We were on the boat with the lobster tank right next to us. Did you look in it? If he was out lobstering all afternoon, *where are the lobsters?*"

Chapter 7

In the morning, I drove the Caprice back into the harbor to Gus's restaurant for breakfast. Chris followed in his truck. The place was mobbed with people who'd been out searching for Peter, hankering for warm food and hot coffee. Gus didn't depend on the summer trade. He actively discouraged outsiders. If he didn't know you, or if you didn't arrive with someone he knew, you didn't get served. When I'd first come back to Busman's Harbor, this policy had seemed snotty and odd, not to mention illegal, but now I treasured both the restaurant and its cantankerous proprietor. In the summer, Gus's was the place for the local people to shed their masks as colorful old salts and get away from the tourists. In the winter, Gus's, along with the post office, was ground zero for gossip. For Chris and me, it was "our place," the place where we'd re-met, and where my middle-school crush on

Chris had grown to friendship, which had led to love.

Gus had obviously relaxed his "no strangers" rule in response to the crisis. Coast Guardsmen and Maine Marine Patrol officers ate next to lobstermen, who ate next to some of the few pleasure boat owners left in the harbor.

As always, Gus cooked on the hulking stove behind the counter. I gave him a wave as we waited for a table to open up. I looked around for Sonny, though I had mixed feelings about finding him. I'd promised Livvie I'd talk to him about where he'd been the previous day, but it wasn't a conversation I looked forward to having. I was relieved he wasn't there.

As we waited, the buzz around us, as expected, was entirely about the *El Ay*, the body of David Thwing and the missing Peter Murray. Even inside the noisy restaurant, you could hear the beat of the Coast Guard helicopters' blades as they passed overhead.

When a booth opened up, Chris and I settled in. Gus arrived a few minutes later, carrying two cups of coffee. He pulled an old-fashioned order pad from his apron pocket.

"Clam hash, one poached egg, orange juice," I rattled off. Gus's menu hadn't changed since I was a child, and I had no need to consult it.

Gus, staring off into middle space, didn't write anything down.

"Blueberry pan—" Chris stopped when it was obvious Gus wasn't listening. "Gus?"

"What? Oh, sorry. Preoccupied." The old man's blue eyes stared down his beak nose at us.

"Everything okay?" I asked.

"No," Gus said and walked away.

Chris and I followed Gus back to the other room.

There were no pies in the case at the end of the counter. For as long as I could remember, Mrs. Gus had arisen at 5:00 AM to bake the world's most delicious pies for the restaurant. There were always several fruit offerings, which this time of year would trend heavily to apple,—apple and raisin, apple and cranberry, and so on—and several other pies as well—chocolate peanut butter, pecan, lemon meringue. The list was endless. The day before, Fee and Vee Snugg had said that Mrs. Gus was feeling poorly, but I had never, ever seen Gus's without pies.

"What's wrong, Gus?" Chris asked in a tone that demanded an answer, even from the irascible old bird.

Gus removed a cloth from the sink and studiously wiped off a clean bit of counter. "Mrs. Gus is in the hospital."

"I'm so sorry," I said. "Is she going to be okay?"

"I don't know. She's unconscious."

I was shocked. "Gus! What are you doing here? Go to your wife."

"Who's going to feed these people?" Gus gestured toward the crowd. "We've got this search going on."

"We will," I answered for both of us.

Chris had already moved behind the counter and was fastening a white apron around his waist. "What are you working on?"

Gus pushed the slips on the counter toward him. "Hash, pancakes, omelets. You sure?"

"Get out of here," Chris said firmly. "We'll be fine."

I took over the front-of-house duties—taking orders, clearing tables, and refilling coffees; work that was similar to what I did at the clambake—while Chris cooked the food. It didn't escape me that it took two of us to do the work of one elderly man, but we got it done.

Things slowed down by a little after nine. Chris made us each an egg and I poured coffee. I tried the hospital on my cell. Gus didn't carry a phone, and I couldn't make it through the maze of the automated answering system that handled the hospital's non-emergency calls.

"Should we stay open for lunch, or close up?"

Chris grinned. "I'm having fun. You got any place you need to be?"

A tiny nervous clench in my stomach reminded me that Livvie could call me at any time to tell me Sonny was back in the harbor from his search duties. I'd promised to talk to him and I had to honor that commitment. But it was important to the searchers and everyone else that Gus's stay open. Besides, I loved the easy rhythm Chris and I had developed working together. In the kitchen at his cabin, he was a solo act. At Gus's, we were a team.

"I'm in," I said.

* * *

Lunch was more challenging and I was grateful for Gus's limited, unchanging menu. The atmosphere in the packed restaurant was more somber than at breakfast, the discussions at the tables and counter subdued. It didn't take long to overhear that the words "search and recovery" had replaced "search and rescue." Coast Guard no longer had any hope of finding Peter Murray alive. It wasn't surprising. No one could survive half an hour in that water, much less twenty-four. The hope for a speedy rescue over, the Coast Guard had dismissed the volunteers from the search. Still, the community needed to come together in the face of a tragedy, and Gus's was the best place available.

In a back corner of the dining room, a group of lobstermen gathered around several tables they'd pushed together. They were young and old, but mainly middle-aged. In an era when most fishing was done from giant boats owned by giant corporations, lobstermen were the small businessmen of the sea. I recognized all of them by sight. They looked like they might have been members of the Busman's Harbor Chamber of Commerce. In fact, several of them were.

Sonny's dad, Bard Ramsey, was there, his arm in a blue sling held against his chest by Velcro. Bard sat at the head of the table, appropriate to his status as a highliner, the most highly skilled and successful lobsterman in our harbor. When he spotted me, he raised his good hand in a salute. "Howdy, darlin'. Coffees all round."

Farther down, along one of the crowded sides of the table, sat Sonny's younger brother, Kyle. All three Ramsey men shared the same big, barrel-chested build and bright orange hair, though Bard's had turned white and fell in long tight waves to below his ears, unlike his sons' buzz cuts. Kyle had been in town all summer working as his father's sternman, but in the busy tourist season, we hadn't crossed paths. I was shocked by how thin he was and how scruffy he looked. A torn pocket hung from his ill-fitting blue-and-black-checked shirt. He didn't acknowledge me and I didn't call attention to myself. His expression was serious and sad, but then, it wasn't a happy group. The men looked worn and worried. I didn't want to intrude as I filled their coffee cups.

Sonny wasn't at the long table, which didn't surprise me. Just because the Coast Guard had called off the civilian part of the search didn't mean Sonny would stop looking.

"It's those Coldporters, for sure," a young man with a powerful build and long brown hair said. "I say we go over there—"

"Go over there and what? Those cops are already asking questions. If we retaliate, best to do it on the water," another man interjected.

"The water's crawling with Coast Guard and Marine Patrol," said a man with a long beard flecked with gray. "The harbormaster's working double shifts. It's like the parking lot at Target on Black Friday out there. I'll be lucky if their propellers don't cut my buoy lines, much less those Coldporters."

"So what? We ignore this? Face facts. Poor Pete Murray is dead. He's one of our own. It can't go unanswered," the first lobsterman responded.

Bard lifted his good hand off the table, and one by one, the others stopped talking. "We do nothing," he said, "until we have a better idea of what's happened. Then we'll assess."

The others muttered their assent, though the young man who'd spoken first looked distinctly unhappy.

I'd hovered as long as I dared. I backed away from the table, coffee carafe in hand. The finality of Bard's pronouncement had caused them to fall into silence. None of them had mentioned the death of David Thwing. He wasn't one of theirs.

But it seemed to me the presence of Thwing on the boat was the strangest part of the story.

Even on a day when there was so much to talk about, the restaurant was empty by 1:30. The working people of Busman's Harbor didn't have time to dally. As I wiped the last table clean, Lieutenant Jerry Binder and Sergeant Tom Flynn of the Maine State Police Major Crimes Unit came down the stairs that led into the restaurant.

"Ms. Snowden, you're not the person I expected

to see here. Do you work for Gus now?" Binder said when he spotted me.

My relationship with Binder had been up and down. On the one hand, in the spring and summer, I'd helped him solve two murders. On the other, during the first investigation, he'd ignored me, and during the second, he'd used and misled me. Nonetheless, in August, we'd parted in a grudging truce. I thought he was a good cop. I wasn't sure what he thought of me.

"We're filling in for Gus," I explained. "His wife is sick."

"We?"

I looked behind me at the kitchen, which was spotless and empty. The click of the back door told me Chris had let himself out. He was not a fan of Binder and Flynn. I couldn't really blame him. They'd once arrested him for a murder he hadn't committed.

"Do you gentleman want something to eat?"

"It looks like you've closed up shop."

"If we keep it simple, I can probably rustle something up."

I stepped into Gus's walk-in refrigerator to sort out what we might have. I didn't want to reheat the grill. "Cheese sandwiches?" I called. It wasn't much, but it would get them through to the next meal.

Binder had a ski-slope nose, large brown eyes, and a bald head surrounded by a sandy brown fringe. He was average height and slender, and wore a tweed sports coat and a simple gold wedding ring. I knew from our previous time together he was a devoted husband and doting father to two young boys.

His partner, Flynn, was compact and broad-shouldered. He removed his jacket as he sat down, and his biceps and chest muscles were visible under his dark blue tailored shirt. I didn't know him as well as I knew Binder. He had an aversion to chitchat. His haircut said ex-military, and his accent was New England, but not Maine. Rhode Island, maybe.

"Sure," Binder answered for both of them. As I expected, Binder wanted lots of cheese, mayo, and mustard, and no lettuce or tomato. Sergeant Flynn of the toned, gym-rat body wanted all the veggies I could find, little cheese, no mayo.

"What brings you to town?" I asked. Binder and Flynn worked out of the state police office in Maine's capital, Augusta, an hour away. The Major Crimes Unit investigated homicides, child abuse and suspicious deaths for every city and town in Maine, except Portland and Bangor, which were large enough to have their own detectives.

While Flynn bit into his sandwich, Binder answered, "David Thwing."

"Isn't he a problem for the Coast Guard?"

"Peter Murray's a problem for the Coast Guard. At least for the moment. Thwing was murdered." He let that sink in. *Murdered.* I couldn't claim to be surprised. It was obvious something had gone terribly wrong on the *El Ay.* Was it murder-suicide?

Peter killed Thwing and jumped overboard? I couldn't imagine it. Peter was a passive, cheery man who never had a bad word for anyone. Besides, what relationship could he possibly have had with Thwing, and what could his motive have been?

"I understand you're the one who called the Coast Guard," Binder said.

"I saw the *El Ay* floating in the channel between Morrow Island and Westclaw Point. It was drifting, didn't look right."

"You were where at the time?"

"The beach on the island." They were all too familiar with the island due to the murder that had occurred there in the spring.

"Did you see anything at all? Any other boats?"

I didn't have to think about it. "There was no one else visible on the water when I got to the beach."

"I understand David Thwing was planning a business to compete with yours," Binder said.

So they knew that already. How long had they been in town?

"That's correct," I answered.

"I also understand your brother-in-law, Sonny Ramsey, was rather vocal in his opposition."

Where was this going? I didn't like the sound of it. "You'd best ask Sonny about that."

Flynn grunted. Sonny hadn't been exactly forthcoming with the police in their previous investigations. "We tried. Your sister says he's out on his father's boat, looking for Murray."

"Then he is."

"Civilian boats have been called off from the search."

"That wouldn't stop Sonny."

Binder couldn't argue with that. He knew from personal experience Sonny didn't respond well to authority figures. "Officer Dawes tells us you saw Mr. Thwing on the town pier yesterday morning," he said.

"I did. He was inspecting his new sign and ticket booth."

"Anyone else around?"

"Not a soul." Earlier that morning, the pier had been crowded with senior citizens waiting for their bus trip, but they'd left by the time I talked to Thwing.

Binder wiped his mouth with his napkin and stood. "Thank you. This has been helpful. What do we owe Gus?"

"A five will cover it," I answered.

Flynn stood up, too. "We'll need a formal statement. You spotted the empty boat and you may have been the last person aside from his killer to see Thwing alive. Come by the station when you're finished here."

I nodded. I'd be happy to have that over with. "One thing I don't get though. If Thwing was pulled under the boat by the trapline, how do you know he was murdered?"

Binder dropped his voice almost to a whisper, though we were alone in the restaurant. "We're awaiting more from the medical examiner, but

Thwing was bashed in the head before he went overboard. We think whoever did it tossed the body in the water to get rid of it and didn't know he got tangled in the lines."

I wasn't shocked. If Peter Murray had been under that boat, I would have believed it was an accident, but David Thwing? Clearly there was more to the story. I finished cleaning the tables. *David Thwing was murdered,* I thought with every swipe of the cloth. *Murdered, murdered, murdered.* And my brother-in-law was lying to his wife about something, but what?

Chapter 8

As soon as Binder and Flynn left, I dialed my cell phone. "Prawk, prawk, prawk, prawk." I made chicken noises into the phone.

"Very funny," Chris responded, without a trace of laughter in his voice. "I'm not afraid of those guys. I'm afraid of what I might do or say if I'm around them too long."

"Prawk, prawk. My point, exactly."

"Besides, I got a call for a taxi pickup at the train station in Brunswick. I have just enough time to get back to the cabin, switch my truck for my cab, and get there." The drive to Brunswick was forty-five minutes each way.

"Okay. Drive safely. I love you." It had taken me too long to say those words. Now I used them whenever I could.

"Love you, too."

I drove my car the few blocks from Gus's to Mom's house. Once again, my mother's car wasn't in her garage.

"Mom?" In the kitchen, the sink was empty. A single teacup and a luncheon plate sat in the drain board. "Mom!" The parlor was picked up. Upstairs, her bed was neatly made.

I would have been a lot more concerned if the place had been messy. My mother always left the house as if she might have to entertain visiting dignitaries on a moment's notice. I tried to remember the last time I'd seen her. The day before yesterday, I was certain.

Her car was gone, so she wasn't across the street at the Snuggles Inn. I remembered belatedly that Vee and Fee were out of town on their seniors' trip until later that afternoon in any case. Mom's cell went straight to voice mail. "Mom, call me when you get this, will you?"

I went out on the front porch and stood wondering what to do. I wasn't worried about my mom, but I had a strange feeling of dislocation. Peter Murray was missing. Gus hadn't been in his accustomed place behind the counter at his restaurant all day. There were no pies. And now this.

My cell phone rang. Livvie. She didn't even say hello. "Sonny's back in the harbor. The cops asked him to go straight to the station to give his statement. Not to even come home and shower first."

"On my way there."

I left a note on the kitchen table for Mom—*Please call me as soon as you get in!*—and ran out the door. I didn't think there was really any issue with my mother. She was a grown woman. I hadn't seen her for a couple of days, which normally wouldn't be cause for alarm.

As I hurried the two short blocks to the police station, I realized that my mother had never really been on her own. She'd married my dad right out of college, and during my dad's illness and for a long time afterward, Livvie, Sonny, and Page had practically lived at her house. Since the spring, I had *actually* lived there. The last five weeks when I'd been living on Morrow Island were the first time Mom had been alone twenty-four hours a day in almost thirty-five years.

As usual, Binder and Flynn had commandeered the multipurpose room at Busman's Harbor's ugly brick fire department-town offices-police complex for their investigation. When I entered the station, the door to their room was closed, but I could hear Sonny's booming voice coming from inside. I couldn't pick out the words, but I could tell he was protesting. I smiled at the civilian receptionist and sat on the bench across from her.

I didn't have to wait long. The door to the conference room flew open and Sonny stomped out. He rushed through the outside door into the parking lot. I followed.

"Sonny, wait!"

He wheeled around, his hands on his hips. He smelled of bait and salt water. "What?" he demanded.

"What do you mean, *what*? What happened? What did they want? Are you okay?"

His posture softened a bit, and some of the

bright red color drained from his freckled face. "I'm fine, just on edge. I hate that building and I hate being questioned by those guys." Sonny and the state police detectives were a mutual antagonizaton society. "They were following up on what Lorrie Ann said on the dock yesterday. That I was supposed to help Peter on his boat."

This was the crux of the matter. I gestured to Sonny that we should move away from the station house into the parking lot. He shuffled to the end of the sidewalk and planted himself. "Say what you've got to say," he said. "I have to go back to the marina to get my truck, and I'm not following you all over creation."

"Sonny, why were you too late to meet Peter yesterday? I want the truth."

Sonny squinted at me. "Did your sister put you up to this?"

"Yes, my poor, pregnant baby sister, your wife, whom you've upset terribly by lying, put me up to this."

The remark hit home. Sonny deflated like a pricked balloon. Hurting Livvie was more than he could bear. "I'd finished breakfast at Gus's and was on my way to meet Peter at the marina when I got a call on my cell from Busman's Harbor Hospital." He stopped, visibly upset. "They said Livvie was in the hospital, having a miscarriage. They said her life was in danger. I needed to get to the hospital right away."

"What!"

"I know." He paused for a moment to let me

absorb what he'd said. "I turned around and drove like a bat out of hell. But when I got to the emergency room, Livvie wasn't there. I was frantic. The nice girl at the desk tried to find Livvie. She called everywhere in the hospital—OB/GYN, Surgery, Recovery. Nothing. She called Livvie's doctor's office in the hospital annex, but her doctor was performing a caesarian on someone else and her receptionist wasn't in yet. Finally, I got a hold of myself and tried Livvie's cell. She picked up right away. She was at home, safe and sound."

Sonny was breathing heavily by the time he finished the story. The phony phone call had terrified him. My brother-in-law was deeply in love with his wife, adored his only child, and was as excited about the baby to come as I'd ever seen him.

"What did you do then?"

"I went home, just to make sure." After a scare like that, Sonny would have needed to see Livvie in the flesh to believe she was okay.

"I didn't go inside. I was still upset and I knew Livvie would be able to tell something was wrong. So I parked on the street and waited until I caught a glimpse of her working in the kitchen." He exhaled loudly, blowing away the tension. "You see why I can't tell her, don't you?"

I did. Sonny had lied to Livvie to shield her from the upsetting nature of the phone call. "Did you tell Binder and Flynn about the call?"

"Told them. Showed them my phone. Gave them permission to look at my phone records." Sonny pulled his cell phone from the pocket of his lobsterman's overalls and showed me the recent calls list. The three digits after the area code on the most recent incoming call were indeed, the Busman's Harbor Hospital exchange.

"Do you recognize the last four numbers?"

"Nope. I tried calling the number several times while I was frantic in the ER, but there was no answer. The girl at the desk in the emergency room tried it, too."

"Who do you think would play such a terrible trick on you? Was it a man or a woman?"

"I was so panicked and I could barely hear the voice, but it I think it was a man. I forget who he said he was. Something official."

"And you didn't recognize the voice?"

"C'mon, Julia. Of course not."

"Then what did you do, after you checked on Livvie at home?"

"I went back to the marina, but I'd missed Peter. I tried to raise him on the radio, to apologize for being so late, but got no answer. I didn't think anything of it. I figured he was pissed at me and he'd come around. So I went by my dad's to see if he wanted me to haul his traps."

"What time was it when you got to the marina?"

"Not sure." Sonny looked up at the sun. "It was before ten, because I got to my dad's house around ten."

"Then what happened?"

"Julia, I just went through this with the cops."

"Humor me."

I figured he still hoped to persuade me not to

tell Livvie about the phone call, so he did. "Nothing. I took Dad's boat out."

"Did you talk to anyone on the radio while you were at sea?"

"I never turned it on."

Really? Most lobstermen kept up a constant, jokey conversation with the other boats from their harbor within radio range. It was a way to stave off loneliness, and maybe gain a little intelligence about where they placed their traps and how well they were doing. It seemed especially odd that Sonny had kept his radio off on a day when he'd hoped to communicate with Peter Murray. And during a time when hostilities with Coldport Island were so high, it seemed dangerous to be disconnected from the other men from our harbor.

"Did you see anyone? At the marina when you left or out on the water?"

"No one."

"If you were hauling traps all day, why were there no lobsters in the tank on the *Abby* yesterday?" Livvie's question—*where are the lobsters?*—echoed in my ears.

"I didn't catch any lobsters."

"You didn't catch any lobsters!"

"Julia, will you quit repeating everything I say? It was just one of those days."

It was certainly possible to haul traps for a full day and not get any lobsters, particularly at this time of year when lobstermen were moving their traps to deeper water, trying to get ahead of the migrating lobsters. The traps would come up empty, or the lobsters inside would be too big or too small, or egg-bearing females that had to go right back into the water. So it *was* possible Sonny had worked all day and had no lobsters to drop off at the lobster pound, but unlikely. Bard Ramsey was a highly skilled lobsterman. I was sure the Ramsey family traps were well placed.

"What about your GPS? Won't that show where your boat went?"

"Stop talking like I need some kind of alibi. I told you. I wasn't with Peter. I didn't have anything to do with Thwing's death or whatever happened on that boat."

"What do you think happened?"

He rolled his big shoulders, which were spanned by the suspenders that held up his orange overalls, still called oilskins even though they were now made from PVC or rubber. "It's obvious isn't it? Thwing is out with Peter, looking at properties for his restaurant, like you said. The stupid landlubber gets his leg caught in the trapline and goes overboard with the traps. Peter jumps in to save him and detaches the traps before hypothermia sets in. Thwing is then hanging on the rest of the line, which gets caught in the propeller and hauled under the *El Ay.* Peter's unconscious from the cold by then. He drowns. End of story."

Though Sonny narrated his version of events as if he were telling a story about a trip to the grocery store, his voice was husky with emotion.

"Lieutenant Binder says Thwing was bashed on the head before he went into the water."

"Those traps fly off the back of the boat at tremendous speed. If you got caught in the line, you'd hit your head about a dozen times on the deck and the rails before you went over."

I had to admit, it was the most plausible version of events I'd heard. We stood in silence for a moment. I put my hand on his forearm. "I'm sorry about your friend, Sonny."

"Thanks. Now will you please tell your sister I had a good reason for missing Peter's boat yesterday and get her to back off?"

"You want Livvie to accept my say-so without hearing what the 'good' reason was? How long have you known my sister? You must know that won't work."

"Julia, please."

"I don't want to be in the middle of this," I said, reflecting once again that I never should have said yes to Livvie's request that I talk to her husband. I looked up and faced Sonny squarely. "You need to tell your wife what happened yesterday morning."

"But you can see that—"

"Talk to your wife, Sonny."

Chapter 9

"Ms. Snowden! Are you here to give your statement?"

Sergeant Flynn stood in the open doorway of the police station, eyeing Sonny and me where we stood at the end of the sidewalk, obviously engaged in an intense conversation. No one was fooled. Flynn didn't believe I'd happened to arrive to give my statement just as Sonny was leaving, and neither Sonny nor I believed Flynn believed it. I squinted at Sonny, throwing my best "tell it to your wife, buddy" look, and answered Flynn. "Yes, that's what I'm here for." Why not? Better to get it over with.

When Flynn ushered me into the multipurpose room, I was surprised. During their previous investigations, Binder and Flynn had taken the whole space over and filled it with whiteboards, computers, and boxes of documents. This time, they sat together at a small table in the corner. Maybe it was too early in the investigation for all that other stuff. My hopes rose. Was it possible the medical examiner might still conclude, as Sonny had, that Thwing's death was an accident?

Lieutenant Binder stood up from his seat at the long conference table. "Julia." Binder's voice was warm when he greeted me.

In the spring, when there'd been a murder on Morrow Island, I'd been desperate to save the clambake business and determined to reopen as quickly as possible. Binder had been determined to preserve his crime scene and methodically investigate the crime. Our relationship had been tested again over the summer when an employee of the clambake had become a murder suspect. My view during that investigation was Binder had used me to gain information while lying to me, or at least withholding critical information about the case. He'd apologized and we'd made peace. The truth was, we both knew I'd been instrumental in solving each of those cases.

It didn't take long for us to go over my sighting of Peter Murray's lobster boat. Binder nodded encouragingly as Flynn took notes. They also recorded my statement.

"Did you see any other boats in the narrows?" Binder asked. "Maybe before you began to wonder about the *El Ay*?"

"None." I knew the question was critical. The crew of another boat could be suspects or witnesses. "Quentin Tupper lives across from Morrow Island on Westclaw Point. He visited me for lunch, then left from our dock on the Atlantic side around one-thirty p.m. He would have sailed around the island

and crossed the narrows on the way to his dock. Maybe he can tell you if the *El Ay* was in the channel then."

I spelled Tupper's name for Flynn and looked up his cell number on my phone. I felt terrible as I did it. Quentin Tupper answered to no one and accepted no obligations. His whole life was constructed so he didn't have to be in any particular place at any particular time. The last thing he'd want would be to be questioned by the police.

Then Binder asked me about my interaction with Thwing the previous morning.

I told them what had transpired when I'd met Thwing on the pier.

"So not a nice guy?" Binder said.

"No, not nice," I confirmed. But people rarely got killed just for being jerks. "The rumors are flying around town. Some people think Thwing's murder, and especially Peter's disappearance, have to do with Coldport Island."

"The lobster war," Binder confirmed. "We're investigating all possibilities."

I stood to go.

"One more thing. Your brother-in-law was just here," Binder said. Flynn looked up from his note taking, but didn't announce he'd found me talking to Sonny in the parking lot. I didn't mention it, either. "You might let him know he'd be better off telling us the truth about where he was yesterday." Binder's tone wasn't accusatory. It was kind.

Sonny had told them the truth about the crazy

phone call, so they must believe he was lying about what he'd done the rest of the day. Again, Livvie's question about the missing lobsters echoed in my brain. "I'll tell him. You can't believe Sonny had anything to do with David Thwing's murder."

"I'm not willing to give you that reassurance," Binder answered. "Besides, the direction this investigation follows may not be entirely up to me. By this time tomorrow, it may be out of my hands."

He stood, and Flynn did, too. They'd told me all they were going to.

May be out of my hands. What did Binder mean by that? Was there some prosecutor in the background pushing him toward Sonny? Or was it because there were other agencies involved, like the Coast Guard and the Marine Patrol?

I jogged the short route from police headquarters to my mother's house. Still no car, still no Mom. My note sat unmoved on the kitchen table. I called Livvie.

"Sonny's home," she whispered. "In the shower. Did you talk to him?"

How had I gotten myself into this? "Yes, I did. He had a good reason for missing Peter's boat."

"Did he tell you what this good reason was?"

Livvie had been sad and scared when she'd first talked to me about Sonny's lie, but now she was angry. I had to get out of this. "You need to talk to your husband."

"He won't talk to me. I've never seen him like this. Tell me, do you believe what he told you, whatever it was?"

I did. I believed he'd received the awful phone call. It was too bizarre to be made up. But I didn't believe he'd floated around all afternoon without catching any lobsters.

I hesitated too long. Livvie said, "I see."

"No, I didn't mean—"

"It's okay, Julia."

Clearly, it wasn't. Before she could hang up, I asked, "When's the last time you talked to Mom?"

"I dunno. Sunday?"

Livvie and Mom normally talked every day. "Do you know where she is? Because she's not at the house."

"Oh, for goodness sake. Our mother is a grown woman," Livvie said. Exactly what I had thought. "I have more important things to worry about."

I had to admit she did.

After I hung up, I sat for a moment in the still kitchen. How could I help my sister? My brother-in-law had offered me a portion of the truth, but it raised more questions than it answered. Who would have called him with such a terrible story and why? He'd accounted for his morning up until he'd gone to his dad's house at ten o'clock, but nothing after that. He'd lied about where he'd been, even though the state police were in town conducting a murder investigation. And they didn't believe him, either.

The faster the murder got solved, the faster suspicion moved away from Sonny and perhaps he would tell my sister what he'd been doing yesterday afternoon. And the faster things could return to normal.

At least that was the theory.

Lorrie Ann had said to Sonny, "If you'd been there, this never would have happened." What did she mean by that? How would Sonny's presence have changed the outcome? And what did Lorrie Ann believe had happened aboard the *El Ay*?

I decided to find out.

Chapter 10

The Murrays lived in town, a short walk from Mom's. I didn't have much of a strategy beyond asking Lorrie Ann what she meant when she said if Sonny had been on the *El Ay* things would have turned out differently.

I assumed the Murray house would be filled with people. Lobstering was a dangerous profession, so the spouses tended to stick close together, supporting one another, especially in tragic circumstances. Normally, I would've expected Livvie to be there, but after the scene at the marina, I understood why she wasn't.

On the way, I stopped at the bakery and bought a dozen cranberry muffins. Since it was quarter to four, the owner threw in two more for free, emptying the case. I hoped when I got to Lorrie Ann's house, I'd blend into the crowd.

When I reached the Murrays' block, I was surprised how empty it was. No parked cars lined the street, no children played in the yard.

The Murray house was on the downslope of the harbor hill, attached to its neighbor on one side, without a view or much land or charm—in short, anything that would make it too expensive for a young working family to afford. The dark gray paint on the house was peeling; the roof shingles were frayed and missing.

There was a toddler's red tricycle on the front porch, which was crowded with cardboard boxes, outdoor furniture in various states of usability, and rubber boots and waders. Before I reached the steps, I heard a child whoop inside, then another protested and started to cry. A female voice I didn't recognize calmed the crying child as I knocked on the door.

I stood on the porch in the afternoon sunshine, suddenly feeling ridiculous with my white baker's box tied with string. This was a house of mourning. I had no business here, but it was too late to turn and run.

I heard a rumble across the floor. The door opened and Lorrie Ann's mother stood there. "Oh, hello, dear."

I thrust the baker's box forward a little too aggressively. "I've brought some muffins."

She blinked at the box zooming toward her, then turned into the house, pushing a walker in front of her. She had a rocking motion to her walk, one leg obviously stronger than the other. "C'min, c'min. I'm Belle, Lorrie Ann's mother."

I took one step forward and was in the little living room, which was strewn with toys and dark because the curtains were drawn. A giggle erupted from behind the sagging couch and a little girl, maybe three, poked a head full of blond curls out. A toddler poked his head out too, his eyes trained on his sister for clues. Was I friend or foe?

"This is Mavis and Toddy." Belle rolled on past them toward the threshold to the kitchen. "PeeWee's around here somewhere."

PeeWee?

She answered my unspoken question. "Peter Junior."

A moment later, a whip-skinny boy darted out of the hallway and ran around the living room as the other children screamed and chased him.

"Hush!" Belle hissed. She waved me toward the kitchen table. "Tea?"

"I don't want to impose."

"No, no. Nice to have company. Stop running!" she shouted toward the sounds of chaos rising in the living room.

"Is Lorrie Ann here?"

"Down cellar." Belle rolled over to a door nearby, opened it, and bellowed, "Lorrie Ann, company!"

"I told you, no visitors," Lorrie Ann shouted back.

"Well, ya got one anyway. Get up here."

"Inna minute!"

If I'd been uncomfortable before, this conversation caused ten times more awkwardness. "I'll go," I said to Belle. "I only came to bring the muffins."

"Don't be silly," Belle responded. She was petite, shorter than my five foot two, and had steel-gray hair pulled back in a bun and a throaty, smoker's voice.

The kettle whistled and Belle poured the water into three mugs, quickly dunking a single tea bag in and out of each of them. She rolled toward me and set the mug down, without the offer of milk or sugar, or one of the muffins I had brought. She made a second trip with her mug and then eased herself into the battered kitchen chair opposite me, wincing as she did.

"Had my hip replaced a month ago," she explained. "Too many years standing on the line at the cannery."

The cannery had closed when I was ten, done in by frozen food and better packaging and shipping that brought fresh fish to American supermarkets. Nonetheless, if Belle had worked at the cannery from the time she was a teenager, it would have meant twenty years on the line, a long time to be standing all day.

The basement door flew open, and Lorrie Ann stood, panting slightly and holding a huge basket of folded clothes. With three children under six, apparently household chores didn't stop because the man of the house was lost at sea.

"Oh, it's you. Come to try to patch things up between me and your unreliable brother-in-law?"

I jumped to my feet. "Lorrie Ann, I am so sorry about what's happened. I'm sure Sonny never thought any harm would come to Peter. He was"—*how to say this?*—"unavoidably detained."

She made a noise like *humpf.*

"Do you want to sit? Would you like some tea? I've brought muffins." I was babbling, offering her food in her own house. She stared out at me from under her long brown bangs and said nothing. She was small like me, though curvier.

She didn't respond, but she didn't move, either, so I kept trying. "I am so sorry about what's happened. I understand you're . . ." I hesitated to use the word *grieving*, because I saw no signs of grief. If Lorrie Ann still held on to hope, I didn't want to be the person to take it away. "I do wonder," I continued, "why you thought Sonny being aboard the *El Ay* would have made a difference. What do you think happened?"

She still didn't respond, so I tried again, more calmly. "If you know what happened, or what might have happened on board your husband's boat, you need to tell the police."

"I've spoken to the police twice," she said wearily. "Endless questions."

I was dying to know what the questions had been, and how Lorrie Ann had answered, but she remained standing, laundry basket still in her arms.

Throughout our conversation, Belle sat at the kitchen table, eyes ping-ponging between her daughter and me. There was a crash, a yelp, and a cry from the living room. Lorrie Ann said, "Mother."

Belle got up and wheeled away to investigate.

"Please go," Lorrie Ann said to me. "I asked my mother not to let anyone in, but she's . . ." Her shoulders moved up and down, an invitation to fill in the blank about her mother. *Independent? Contrary? Thinks she knows what's best?*

"Of course," I said. I was in her home, after all, and it was obvious she wasn't going to answer my prying questions.

She didn't walk me to the door. I made my way back across the living room, dodging the running children and the toys.

Belle looked up, a teary Mavis in her lap. "Come see us again," she said in her smoker's rumble.

I let myself out.

I stood on the sidewalk in the sharp-focused, deeply slanted shadows of the late afternoon. The Murray household seemed to be in a state of suspended animation. Peter might have been away on an overnight fishing trip. I hoped if he had drowned, as everyone but Lorrie Ann seemed to believe, the Coast Guard would find his body, and find it soon, for his family's sake. How long could Lorrie Ann go on as she was, refusing the support of her friends, acting as if nothing had happened?

What to do next? Sonny claimed that, after he'd missed meeting Peter, he'd gone to his dad's house, arriving around ten. There he'd seen both his father and brother, Kyle, who'd been "under the weather," unable to accompany Sonny to haul traps.

If Sonny was lying about what he'd been doing

the afternoon of the murder, he could only lie about it easily because he'd ended up on the *Abby* alone. I went along to the Ramsey house to confirm what Sonny had told me. The more parts of Sonny's story I could nail down as true, the more I could zero in on the lie and the reasons behind it.

The Ramsey cottage was just a few blocks from the Murrays. I hoped Bard would be home. I walked the short distance and rapped on the Ramseys' sea-green front door.

"Julia Snowden, as I live and breathe. Come in." Bard Ramsey loomed in the doorway, his arm in the blue sling. He stepped aside so I could enter.

Sonny's dad and his much younger brother, Kyle, had been a part of my life almost as long as Sonny had been a part of Livvie's. Sonny's mom had died when he was in middle school. I was fuzzy on the details of her death. I hadn't known Sonny back then, but I'd seen the fallout. Bard, always a hard drinker, had gone fully down the road to alcoholism. An aunt had stepped in and done the heavy work with Kyle, who had been a toddler at the time, but she'd left town ten years later, eager to reclaim something of a life of her own.

Once the aunt was gone, Livvie had insisted on inviting Bard and Kyle to every one of our family holidays. I couldn't blame her. They were her family, and why shouldn't Page spend her holidays and birthdays surrounded by all her living grandparents?

Bard Ramsey wasn't a nasty drunk. He wasn't loud or argumentative or insulting. In fact, the more he drank, the more expansive and flattering he became. "You're like the perfect American family," he said to us one Christmas. "A successful businessman, his beautiful wife, two wonderful girls. Every time I come to your home, I want to stand up and salute the flag."

I never detected sarcasm in his tone, or envy. But his little speeches put me on edge. We weren't a perfect family, for one thing. His son had been the center of family battles for years. When Livvie had kept flunking out of prep schools to get back to Busman's High and to Sonny, when she'd announced she wasn't going to college so she could stay in town and marry him, and finally when she'd announced she was pregnant before the wedding had taken place.

Bard eased himself into a blue recliner so new it still had a large tag hanging from one of its arms. Across the living room from the recliner was an equally new, gigantic flat-screen television. Bard motioned to me to take a seat.

From my spot on the sofa, I could see almost the entire first floor of the tiny house. The interior surprised me. In all my previous visits, the house had seemed like an increasingly shabby museum, flash frozen at the time of Abby Ramsey's death. The wallpaper faded, the upholstery grew worn, and the same knickknacks sat in their places year after year.

Now there were colorful fall gourds in a pottery bowl on the round oak dining table and new curtains at the kitchen windows. There were new coasters on the coffee table, though it already had so many rings from the glasses and cans that had rested on its surface, it was like locking the barn door after the horse escaped.

"What brings you here, darlin'?" Bard asked.

He didn't seem drunk. He seemed hyper-alert, though his complexion was florid. A network of broken blood vessels etched a cobweb pattern across his nose. Even when his drinking was at its worst, Bard was a functioning alcoholic.

"I want to ask about yesterday morning. Sonny says he came here to pick up Kyle to haul your traps."

There was a slight hesitation before Bard answered, "If he says that's what happened, it did."

"Around what time would you say he got here?"

Bard didn't speak for so long, I thought he'd admit it hadn't happened, but then he said, "Around ten." He sat forward in his seat. "But tell me, what makes you such a curious kitten?"

The question I'd dreaded. Instead of answering directly, I asked, "When's the last time you talked to Sonny?"

"Last night."

"Did he tell you about—"

"The horrible phone call he got? Indeed, he did. Sicko, whoever made it."

I took a deep breath and told a giant lie. "Sonny's asked me to help him figure out who called him." I gambled that if Bard asked Sonny about it, he'd go along with my version rather than admit the truth; he was lying to his wife so she sent her sister after him.

Bard looked amused. "If you're trying to find

out who made the call, why are you asking if I saw Sonny *after* he got back from the hospital?"

"Just being thorough." Bard was all but laughing at me by that point, but he didn't seem hostile, so I continued. "Sonny said he saw both you and Kyle here, but Kyle was feeling ill, so Sonny went out on the *Abby* alone."

"Sounds right. He's been helping me out since I had rotator cuff surgery. Too many years of lobsterin' come home to roost. I'm near useless on the boat." He held his right arm out, like an old dog offering an injured paw.

"Is Kyle home?" I asked. I wondered if he, too, would corroborate Sonny's story.

Bard heaved himself out of the recliner and went to the bottom of the stairs. "Kyle!" he bellowed. "Julia Snowden's asking for you."

Silence. Bard turned back to me with a shrug. "Since that boy moved back home I never have any idea if he's home. He comes and goes as he pleases."

Not unusual behavior for a twenty-one-year-old. Bard, Sonny, and the departed aunt had done their best for Kyle, but there was no question their best was a long way from good and Kyle had a rough go of it. He'd played football in high school like Sonny, but not nearly as well. He'd done a semester at University of Southern Maine, but college life didn't take. He'd stayed in Portland, waiting tables, washing dishes, nothing with a future in it. He'd come back to Busman's Harbor to be his father's sternman, which he could've done right out of high school.

"Kyle didn't seem sick when I saw the two of you at Gus's this morning."

"There's sick and there's sick," Bard reminded me.

So it had been that kind of sick. I'd spent a lot of Monday mornings tracking down college-age workers at the clambake who'd overdone the partying over the weekend.

"Anything else? Have I helped you investigate?" Bard asked.

"Yesterday at the marina, Lorrie Ann said if Sonny had been on the *El Ay*, none of this would have happened. She yelled it in public, and she probably repeated it when she was interviewed by the cops."

"Don't worry about what Lorrie Ann said, Julia. You're young. I've seen more of these types of accidents than you have. People say things when they're grieved. They want to believe if they, or someone else, had done something different, the result would have been different." He waved his good arm around, taking in the universe. "When it's time for the sea to claim you, there's nothing you can do about it. It's tragic, but it's true. Once Lorrie Ann comes to her senses, she'll stop blaming Sonny. It'll all turn out to be nothin'."

"And the phone call?"

Bard dismissed it, too. "Terrible prank by a buddy, it will turn out to be."

Terrible buddy, if that's really what happened, I thought.

Chapter 11

It was dusk when I walked back to Mom's house. I hadn't accomplished much. Lorrie Ann had refused to talk to me, and Bard had supported Sonny's story, while assuring me there was nothing to worry about. I wished I believed him. I'd discovered nothing that would satisfy Livvie and nothing I could use to goad Sonny into telling her the truth, whatever it was.

I was intrigued by the changes to Bard's house. Had Livvie had a hand in livening up the decor? Doubtful. In ten years of marriage to his son, she'd never done so. Which left only one possibility. One of the Ramsey bachelors, Bard or Kyle, had a woman in his life.

As I passed the fire department-town offices-police complex, a familiar white taxicab pulled up to the front door. I stood at the edge of the big parking lot and stared with pleasure at Chris's bowed head as he and his passenger conversed. His door opened and he unfolded himself smoothly from his seat, went to the back of the cab, opened the trunk, and extracted a rolling carry-on bag. Then he opened the rear door and bent to help his passenger.

A glamorous young woman swept out, clothed in the kind of expensive black jacket I recognized from my Manhattan days. She had short black hair that curved smoothly toward her chin. Though she was tall, Chris still bent his head downward as they spoke. He had the kind of ease with people that created instant intimacy. Women loved this about him, and I had to guard against the visceral jealousy that punched my chest as I watched them. *It means nothing,* I reminded myself. *He picked me.*

I could tell from Chris's posture he was concerned about this woman. I couldn't catch what he was saying, though as he ended the conversation, I lip-read, "I'm sorry," and "Take care."

She swept into the police station and he slammed the passenger door. "Chris!" I called as he came back around to the driver's side.

He broke into a grin of such genuine pleasure it dispelled even the tiniest of green monsters. "Hey, beautiful." He lowered his voice as I came closer. "That was David Thwing's business partner, come to identify the body and try to pick up the pieces of the business. She seemed devastated. I felt for her."

I'd been so concerned about the missing Peter Murray and Livvie's concerns about Sonny, I hadn't thought much about the friends and family of the late David Thwing. "That's tough," I agreed.

"I don't think she has a clue about the business.

From what she said, she's the chef, he was the businessperson."

We stood for a moment, silently contemplating Thwing's partner's troubles. I wondered if she'd proceed with the plan to open a business in Busman's Harbor now that Thwing was dead. A day and a half ago, competition from David Thwing had loomed as a threat to my business and my freedom. Due to the circumstances surrounding his death, I hadn't spent a moment enjoying the relief that would've come if the threat had been removed any other way.

"Coming over later?" Chris asked.

I hesitated for a fraction of a second. I'd left Le Roi in the little house on Morrow Island with plenty of food, water, and kitty litter. He'd be mad. He was the island cat and needed to patrol his domain. But he'd be fine, and for the human, me, it wasn't hard to choose a warm bed over a trip over a cold ocean.

"I'm cooking curried fish and vegetable stew," Chris added.

"Wow. You sure know how to seduce a girl."

"Is it working?"

"Sure. I'll be along," I said. "I have a couple of stops I need to make."

"Fine." Chris bent to kiss me. "I'll see you when I get there."

As we broke the kiss, my childhood friend Jamie came out the police station door. Chris gave him a friendly wave, got in the cab, and drove off. Jamie came to my side and we watched Chris's taillights disappear.

Jamie, headed off duty, was dressed in civilian clothes, a gym bag in his hands. He was handsome as ever. The short hair required by the police couldn't disguise his blond, surfer-dude good looks. In fact it emphasized the dark lashes surrounding his sky-blue eyes.

"That was crazy on the pier yesterday," I said to him.

"It's crazier now," he responded. "Yesterday, we didn't know it was murder."

"Is it absolutely certain it was murder?" I asked, remembering Sonny's theory about how being pulled overboard by the trapline had caused the blows to Thwing's head.

"Oh yeah. He was dead when he went into the ocean. No water in his lungs."

"What time did he die?" I asked. I'd seen Thwing at nine o'clock and spotted the empty boat at a little after three.

"Don't have an exact time. The medical examiner's office is examining the 'fish activity.'" Despite his status as a police officer, Jamie wrinkled his nose in disgust.

I realized belatedly the parking lot where we stood was filled with official-looking vehicles. There hadn't been so many when I'd made my statement to Binder and Flynn earlier in the day. I saw all sorts of insignias, though I couldn't read them from where I stood.

"Who's here besides the state police?" I asked.

"Who's not here? DEA, Maine Drug Task Force, Customs, Coast Guard. It's like an ant farm in there. Only ants know who's in charge."

Really? "I understand why the state cops and Coast Guard are here," I said, "but what's with the DEA, Drug Task Force, and Customs?"

"Julia—" Jamie went on alert, a cop again, not the boy from next door.

"No, I get it. DEA and Task Force mean drugs, Customs means from over the border. But what does it have to do with David Thwing and Peter Murray?" Because drugs would be a whole new angle.

"Jule-YA!"

I knew from long experience that when Jamie stretched my name out, with the emphasis on the second syllable, we were done. The door was closed. I'd get nothing out of him.

"So how are you doing, anyway?" I asked, to keep the conversation going.

"I'm *great*," Jamie answered, a bit too enthusiastically.

I wondered how long we could keep this up. Jamie's family lived next to mine. He'd waited for the school bus with Livvie and me, played thousands of frenzied games of tag. When he was older, he'd worked at the Snowden Family Clambake every summer. When I'd returned to Busman's Harbor in March, I'd had a chance to turn my junior high crush on Chris Durand into something real. But I wasn't the only one with a crush.

Livvie had explained that Jamie had long harbored feelings for me. I'd gotten my heart's desire, the object of my school-age fantasies, which meant Jamie hadn't gotten his.

"I'm seeing someone," Jamie said.

"That's great." I meant it. Jamie in a relationship had the potential to wash all the awkwardness away. He wasn't my choice, but I loved him like a cousin and I wanted nothing more than for these freighted conversations to end and for us to resume being us. "Do I know her?"

He didn't answer and I didn't press. Maybe it was too new to talk about. Besides, Busman's Harbor was a small town. Plenty of people would vie for the opportunity to tell me soon enough.

"See you soon," I said. "Bring your friend around."

"See you soon," Jamie answered.

It took less than a second for us to realize we were both headed in the same direction. "'Bye, Julia."

I stayed planted where I was, which he took as a signal he should go on ahead. Man, I'd be glad when this awkwardness was behind us.

While I stood outside the police station waiting for Jamie to get a head start, Quentin Tupper emerged from inside.

"Helping the police with their inquiries?" I asked.

"I understand that's your fault."

I smiled tentatively to see if he was joking. "All I

told them was you sailed from Morrow Island to your house and may have seen something that would help them understand what time Peter's boat drifted into the narrows. It couldn't have been that bad."

"It was awful. They grilled me for *hours*." He grinned. "Where're you headed?"

"Mom's."

"My boat's at the marina. I'll walk with you."

We set off up the steep hill toward my mother's house. "They didn't really grill you for hours," I said.

Quentin laughed. "More like twenty minutes. Your cops were there, Binder and Flynn, asking the questions. And some fed who scowled through the whole interview, like your guys weren't doing it right."

"They're not my cops."

"They're more yours than mine. Or anybody else's in this town."

I ignored him. "What did they ask?"

"Where I was at what time. What I saw. Pretty simple."

"Did you get any sense they're close to solving Thwing's murder?"

"They know more than they're saying," Quentin said. "But no, I don't think they have it tied up with a bow." We walked a little farther. "I'm teasing, you know that," he said. "I was happy to do my civic duty."

Quentin didn't care to intertwine his life with

other individuals, but he did have a strong sense of fairness and justice.

"Did you tell them about the lobster buoys you found?"

He stopped walking for a moment, though I couldn't tell whether it was to catch his breath on the hill or because of my question. "No. I completely forgot about them. Besides, they didn't ask."

"Did you track down the owner of the buoys using the license number?"

"I told you, Julia. I forgot. I've been busy."

"Doing what?" Quentin had built his entire existence around the principle of doing nothing and answering to no one.

He started walking again. "Doing nothing isn't as easy as it looks."

I didn't challenge him. Maybe it was true. If I didn't straighten out my job situation, I might find out. "Did Binder and Flynn ask anything about the trouble between the Busman's and Coldport lobstermen?" I asked.

"Not a word. I don't think they're interested in our little harbor feuds."

"They should be. Most of the guys at Gus's think Coldport was behind whatever happened."

"So the law enforcement experts at Gus's have decided they know more than a building full of professionals?" Quentin laughed and we walked a little farther. "Did you take the apartment over Gleason's, by the way?"

"No." I hadn't called about the apartment. In fact, I hadn't given it a thought all day.

"Good. It's not right for you."

"Actually, it's perfect for me." *Then why was I hesitating?*

"If you didn't take the 'perfect' apartment, does that mean you're going back to New York?"

"I don't know." I hadn't given a thought to that option, either, or to the call to Owen Quimby, HR director, I needed to make in three short days.

"If you stay, you could always live at my house over the winter," Quentin said.

"You're leaving?" I wasn't surprised. Quentin had houses all over and never stayed anywhere long.

"Sailing the *Flittermouse* south to the Caribbean as soon as the hurricane season is over. No point in spending the winter here." He looked at my face and quickly added, "No reason for me to spend the winter here."

Quentin's huge, sparsely furnished stone house sat the end of a long driveway on Westclaw Point. The other houses on the road were used only in the summer, which made the road the town's lowest priority for plowing. I could live there, but I knew what would happen. I'd end up staying at Chris's so often, I might as well move in with him.

We arrived in front of my mother's dark yellow house with its familiar mansard roof and cupola on the top. We lingered on the sidewalk. "Thanks for the offer," I said, "but I can't stay at your house."

"Yeah," he responded. "Good decision. It's not right for you."

That aggravating saying of his. Even making allowances for Quentin being Quentin, his certainty about what wasn't right for me was getting on my nerves.

"Have you decided what you're doing about Windsholme?" he asked.

The image of the family mansion—scarred by fire, soon to be further destroyed by the elements—flashed into my mind. "No, Quentin. I haven't decided anything about anything."

Chapter 12

Quentin and I parted on the sidewalk in front of Mom's house. It was dark and the cooling air carried the smell of wood smoke. People were stoking their wood stoves and fireplaces for the evening.

Mom's house was dark, too. Not a single light shone from the interior. She hadn't left on a porch light in the front or the back to welcome her home. I let myself inside. My note sat on the kitchen table where I'd left it. I picked up a pen, underlined *Call me* three times and added a series of exclamation points.

Mom, where are you? I dialed her cell. Straight to voice mail. I felt a little flutter in my chest. Not a complete freak-out, but genuine worry. As far as I knew, no one had seen my mother in at least two days, maybe longer. I considered calling Livvie, but I hoped she and Sonny were in the middle of an important, truth-telling conversation.

I fished my keys out of the junk drawer, left the

back porch light on for Mom, and went out to the garage. Across the street, lights were on at the Snuggles Inn. Fee and Vee must have arrived back from Campobello in the late afternoon as scheduled.

I drove halfway up the peninsula, then turned off the two-lane highway onto the access road for Busman's Harbor Hospital. My plan was to check on Mrs. Gus and see if Gus needed a dinner break. But once I'd parked the Caprice, I headed straight for the emergency room entrance. I must have been more worried about my mother than I realized.

The receptionist was gray-haired and round-faced, and looked slightly familiar.

"Has a Jacqueline Snowden come in here?" I asked.

The woman blinked her surprise. "Why, no. I don't believe so."

"Can you check?"

She tippy-tapped her keyboard, then looked back at me. "No. She didn't come in through emergency. And she hasn't been admitted to the main hospital, either."

The next question was harder to ask. "Has a Jane Doe been brought in? I'm looking for a woman in her fifties, blond hair, petite. Kinda looks like me."

"Why, I know what your mother looks like, Julia Snowden! If they brought her in, I would certainly identify her. Is something the matter?"

"No, no, no." What torrent of rumors had I just started? I groped for a way to make myself sound less crazy. "She's not home and my sister is worried.

Probably the pregnancy hormones. My sister's. Not my mother's. Or mine." I was sputtering. "Honestly, there's nothing to worry about, Miss, Mrs. . . ."

"Barkly. Melody Barkly. I was your assistant Brownie leader. At the Y."

I tried to remember those ancient Brownie days and came up with nothing except the sensation of a sash sliding off my shoulder as I ran around the Y gym with my classmates. I nodded gamely, pretending recognition. "Wonderful to see you. I'll reassure my sister that my mother's not here at the hospital. Can you tell me what room Mrs. Farnham is in?"

I got off the elevator on the second floor and turned down the tan-painted, antiseptic hallway toward Mrs. Gus's room.

Her door was partially closed, but as I came up to it, I could see the end of a hospital bed, and hear the murmur of feminine voices.

"We're so sorry," Viola Snugg muttered.

"So, so sorry," her sister Fiona agreed.

I knocked softly and pushed the door open.

The lights were low and the sisters sat in plastic chairs on either side of the prone figure in the bed. Mrs. Gus was still unconscious, hooked up to so many machines it was hard to see her.

"Julia!" Vee jumped up from her chair.

"I came to see if Gus needed anything," I said.

"We sent him to the cafeteria," Fee said. "The poor man needed a break."

"We came the moment we heard. Dropped our bags in the front hall and hightailed it here," Vee explained. "We have a guest at the inn. No prior reservation. Thank goodness she wasn't expecting dinner." At their B & B, the Snuggs only served breakfast.

"What happened?" I asked. The machines hooked up to Mrs. Gus were whirring and wooshing, binging, bonging, and booping. She'd always been slight, but sinewy. All the toughness had been stripped away from the figure on the bed, leaving a wraith of a woman behind.

"She collapsed," Fee said, smoothing Mrs. Gus's long white hair back from her brow. I'd never seen it loose before. "This morning she got up, started her baking and then dropped to the floor. Gus heard the thud and called the ambulance right away. Otherwise . . ." Fee couldn't bring herself to say what would have happened "otherwise."

"Do they know what caused it?"

A look passed between the sisters. Vee said, "Not yet."

"Can I get you ladies something? Coffee, snacks?" I offered.

"We're fine, dear," Fee said. "You go along."

"I could stay—"

"No, no. Gus will be back soon. Then we'll go home and get ready for tomorrow."

I hated to leave them, but I'd been dismissed. I knew better than to argue with the Snugg sisters. I wondered what Fee and Vee would have to apologize to Mrs. Gus about. Going off and leaving her behind? But it was just as well. The situation would have been even more terrible if Mrs. Gus had collapsed on their road trip.

I pulled my cell out of my pocket as soon as I walked out of the hospital. No message from Mom or anyone else. I got in my car, about to head to Chris's cabin, when my phone *brrupped*. Mom.

"I have a note from you to call urgently?" Her voice was clipped, the way it got when she was irritated. Or overtired.

"No one's seen you in two days. Livvie's worried." I hoped all this scapegoating wouldn't get back to Livvie, who wasn't worried at all.

"Why would she be worried? Is it a problem if I leave my house occasionally?"

"Where were you?" I tried to keep my voice curious, not anxious or accusatory.

"As I said, I was out."

What was she, fifteen years old? "Okay, don't tell me."

"Julia, I'm a grown woman," Mom responded wearily. "I don't have to report in to you or your sister about every move I make."

I decided not to pry further. "Did you hear about Peter Murray?"

"Yes, terrible. And Lieutenant Binder and Sergeant Flynn are in town investigating that man's death. Thwing, I think he's called."

Wherever my mother had been, it hadn't been far. She'd picked up all the local news.

"Okay, you're home now. The next time you take off, could you maybe tell someone?"

My mother didn't promise anything of the sort. "'Bye, Julia."

"'Bye." As I turned the key in the Caprice's ancient ignition, my cell phone *brrupped* again. Chris.

"On my way," I said, nosing the car out of the parking lot.

The moment I opened the door to the cabin, the smell of Chris's stew enveloped me—curry, onion, and garlic. I sat in my usual place at the kitchen island. Chris put a steaming bowl in front of me, along with a piece of crusty bread. I took a taste. It was hearty and warm, the perfect meal for a fall evening. The curry and a subtle flavor of coconut milk complemented the fish and the smokiness of the chunks of sausage I found in the bowl. I loved the different textures of the vegetables, chickpeas, squash, cauliflower, and kale.

"Another recipe of your mom's?" I asked.

"No, this one is all me."

"How did you learn to cook?"

"Taught myself. Not without a few disasters along the way. I was single, the winters were long. I decided to try cooking and found I really liked it."

I laughed. "I don't believe you. Slaving in your kitchen alone, no one to appreciate you."

He laughed, too. "All right. I wanted to impress women and there's nowhere on the peninsula in the winter to take a date."

"That's the Chris Durand I know." I was happy to take advantage of the hard work he'd put into impressing those other women.

While we ate, I filled Chris in on the events of the day. One of the things I loved about him was he never asked questions like, "Why'd you talk to Lorrie Ann? Why'd you go to Bard's?" He knew exactly what I was doing and accepted it, even though my activities in past murder investigations had put me in real danger. He always treated me like I was an adult who knew what she was doing.

"Why is Sonny lying?" I asked as I finished my story.

He stood and pulled another beer from the fridge. "How the heck would I know? We're not exactly buddies."

Although Sonny was three years younger than Chris, they'd been friends in high school and teammates at football. But they'd long ago stopped being friends. For a decade Sonny had been a husband and father and Chris had been single, so maybe they'd drifted apart. I sensed it was more than that, though neither of them would talk about it.

"The DEA and Customs are involved in Thwing's murder case," I told him.

Chris moved his dish to the sink. "You don't say." His voice had a wary edge to it.

"That must be what Binder meant when he said he might not be able to control the direction of the investigation."

Chris was noisily rinsing dishes. "Uh-huh," he said quietly. He turned back to the sink.

Drugs, smuggling, and boats. Any time we got

within a hundred miles of the topic of what he might have done during his disappearances over the summer, he shut down out of anger, and I shut down out of fear. Fear of knowing the truth, fear of how angry he'd be if I demanded he tell it to me. No matter how much we tried to ignore it, no matter how often we said to each other the past was in the past and we had moved on, we hadn't.

I picked up a dishtowel and moved to his side at the sink, plucking dishes from the rack as he washed them. We had a well-practiced rhythm that normally represented something solid, even domestic. But all I could sense was the space between us.

"Quentin thinks I should get Windsholme buttoned up for the winter. To, you know, at least preserve the ability to rebuild it. He says if I don't, I'll have pretty much made the decision."

Chris turned, up to his elbows in soap. His eyes met mine, grateful for the change of subject. "It's worth considering if you can find the money. It seems a shame to lose that part of your history."

I gestured around the first floor of the cabin. "Is that why you bought this house from your parents? To preserve your history?"

Chris scoffed. "I bought it because they needed to get out of here and needed the money from the sale to do it. The kind of shape it was in, nobody else was going to buy it. When the right time comes, I'll sell it."

Really? I was starting to get attached to the cabin. Sometimes, as we puttered around the old house, I imagined the second floor finished and as gorgeous as the first. I'd daydreamed at times about living there.

Later, I read as we listened to the Red Sox on the radio. Chris picked up an acoustic guitar that had been gathering dust in a corner of the living room and strummed a little. His fingering was stiff, as if he hadn't played in a long time, but I could tell he knew what he was doing.

What else didn't I know about this man? There was the big what else, of course—where had he disappeared to during the summer? But how many small things were left to learn? Was I really considering giving up my career and my life in New York to stay here with a man about whom I knew so little?

But staying in Busman's Harbor wasn't just about Chris. It was Mom, Livvie, Page, my new niece or nephew, and even, I had to admit, Sonny. It was also Gus, and Fee and Vee, and all the laughing, happy families at the clambake in the summer. And, I had to make sure I didn't romanticize my memories of my job in New York. I'd been overworked and lonely at times. I'd lived on airplanes and often had to give people bad news about their businesses and their dreams. Did I really want to go back to that life?

The ball game went into overtime. Chris gave up and went to bed. Through the open framing of the cabin's second story, I watched him move around the master bedroom, completely unaware he was on stage. I wished I could be as sure of everything in my life as he was.

Chapter 13

Before sunrise, Chris and I left the cabin and headed for Gus's. Keeping the restaurant open was important to Gus and we wanted to support him. The strain of the previous evening was gone, though as I drove along in the Caprice, following Chris in his truck, I worried what turn of phrase, change of topic, or unexpected situation might bring the tension roaring back.

When we arrived at the restaurant, Vee and Fee were already inside, setting up for the day.

"I thought you had a guest staying at the inn," I said.

"We told her she had to eat breakfast here," Vee answered. She'd put on one of Gus's white aprons, which went with her upswept masses of white hair. "Time to make the pancake batter," she said.

Chris was visibly relieved. "I'm way behind closing cottages."

"You go, I'll stay." I grabbed an apron and helped Fee set tables.

We'd barely set out the last of the plastic syrup dispensers when a dozen or so lobstermen trooped into the restaurant. Bard Ramsey was with them, his blue sling tight against his flannel shirt. Kyle and Sonny were absent.

Bard gave a curt nod. "Hi, darlin'," he said as he passed me. The lobstermen were uncharacteristically quiet, faces grim. This was more than a social breakfast.

They moved as a group to the back of the dining room, pushing tables together and gathering chairs. Bard sat at the head of the table without hesitation, as if it was his right, which it was as the highliner. The others sat along the sides. I brought over a fresh pot of coffee and poured each one a mugful.

"I hauled a line of traps yesterday," one lobsterman said. "Not a bug in them. Not a one." Lobstermen often called their prey "bugs."

"Inside the harbor or out?" another asked.

"Outside."

"Somebody got there before you," the other concluded.

"Ayup," the original lobsterman agreed. "If I set traps inside the harbor, there's nothin' in 'em. Go much outside and I'm provoking those Coldporters. Can't win fa losin' in the lobstah game."

I took their orders. Lobstering was strenuous work and they all wanted huge breakfasts. As I told Vee what they'd ordered, I thought about what they'd said.

The year had been a great one for lobsters, but

not for lobstermen from mid-coast ports like Busman's Harbor and Coldport Island. Record catches in Maine had driven lobster to its lowest price in years. It was easy to believe the lobstermen were always complaining. If the catch was high, the price was too low. If the price was high, it was because lobsters were scarce.

But the last few years had been unique. People might argue the reason why, but everyone agreed the Gulf of Maine had grown warmer. As it did, the lobsters moved north and east. Lobstering boomed in Down East Maine, while on the mid-coast, lobstermen worked harder and used more bait and fuel to trap their catch. The price was set based on the catch throughout the state, so Busman's lobstermen got the same price as their brethren Down East who had a much easier time trapping lobsters. In addition, as ground fish disappeared and the great fishing banks were closed down, more fishermen turned to lobstering, crowding the harbors with traps. In October, as the lobstermen followed their prey to the deeper water outside the protective harbors, it was predictable that territories would overlap and collide. The Coldporters claimed the area beyond the mouth of Busman's Harbor was theirs. The Busman's guys maintained that in colder weather they had to trap outside the harbor to survive.

The restaurant filled up and I got busy elsewhere. When I returned to the table with the lobstermen's breakfasts, they were still talking about Coldport.

"My lines were cut. I lost eight traps and God

knows how many lobsters. I can't afford this, not this year," said the man with the beard whom I'd noticed the day before.

"I say we go over to Coldport Island and make those guys feel the pain." The same young guy who'd been agitating for confrontation yesterday put it back on the table.

"What are you suggesting?" the man with the beard asked.

"They've stolen our lobsters, messed up our lines, lost our traps. I'm suggesting we go over there tonight—"

"And what? Vandalize their boats?" one of the older men responded. "They'll come here the next night and attack ours. I'm already out lobsters and traps. I can't afford for anything to happen to my boat."

"Do what you want. I'll do it my way," the younger man retorted.

"Now wait a minute." Bard had been quiet up to this point, but now he broke in. "We stick together. We're loyal to the group. We move as one. No retaliation until we find out, for sure, what happened to Peter Murray. Let the police take care of it. If those Coldporters had anything to do with it—"

The aggressive young man wasn't buying Bard's talk of restraint. "We know those Coldporters have blood on their hands. They'd kill their own mothers—"

"Now just a damn minute." A newcomer, a middle-aged man with slicked-back hair, stepped up to the table. "Say what you want about us Coldport Islanders, but don't be talkin' about my ma."

This is why I hated it when people had these discussions in public. I wished we'd been enforcing Gus's "no strangers" rule.

The young lobsterman jumped out of his chair. "What are you gonna do about it?"

I held my breath. Would there be a fight? It was one Coldport Islander against a dozen Busman's men. I tried to signal to Vee or Fee in the other room, in case we had to call the police, but they were unaware, busy chatting with customers.

"Interesting you think us Coldporters had something to do with what happened on Murray's boat. The way I hear it, Bard Ramsey's son had a beef with the fellow who died, and everybody in Busman's Harbor knew it." The Coldport man looked directly at Bard. "And your son was supposed to be on the boat when it all went down. Who knows, maybe he was. Maybe he killed the both of them."

"Why, you . . ." Bard jumped up. He was tall, and despite his recent enforced time off, well muscled. Even though he had one arm in a sling, the Coldport man backed up a step.

"You want a war?" the man said. "You'll get one. But you don't want one, Ramsey, do you? You're too comfortable. You've got it made, rakin' in the dough, while me and all these guys"—he gestured around the table—"fight over your leavings. It'll all come back to bite you, wait and see. So says Hughie B. Hubler. Remember that name."

Hughie B. Hubler threw some bills on his table and stalked out. The young lobsterman sat down, but Bard didn't. He looked at the clock in on the archway to the dining room. "I've got to go," he said. "Remember, we do nothin' until we hear something about Peter. Then we decide."

His departure seemed weirdly abrupt. There was something off about it. I looked at the clock. It was 7:45 AM. I felt like I'd already put in a full day.

The lobstermen left and the restaurant quieted. Fee and I were clearing tables when the Snugg sisters' B & B customer arrived. The young woman from Chris's cab the day before came down the stairs slowly and stood, waiting. Despite her expensive haircut and sophisticated black dress, her heart-shaped face and big, round eyes made her appear childlike.

"C'min, C'min. Make yourself at home," Fee called. She set a mug on Gus's chipped Formica countertop. "We've got breakfast for you here. Coffee?"

The young woman sat on the stool as directed. "Julia, this is Genevieve Pelletier. She's staying with us at the inn for a few days."

I put the syrupy plates I'd cleared into a rubber dishpan and wiped my hands. "Julia Snowden. Welcome."

"Thanks." Her voice was little-girl breathy, which exaggerated her youth. She couldn't have been older than mid-twenties, which I thought made her an odd business partner for David Thwing.

She scanned the menu board behind the counter and went with an eastern omelet. Good choice. There was none of Mrs. Gus's homemade bread, so to go with the eggs, Vee toasted some store-bought I'd found earlier in Gus's walk-in.

I sat on the stool next to Genevieve. I wasn't going to lose this opportunity to speak to one person available to me who had known David Thwing.

"I understand you were David Thwing's business partner."

Her brown eyes darted from side to side. They were surrounded by thick, dark lashes, which emphasized their large size and round shape. She probably thought Fee and Vee had told me she was Thwing's partner. I doubted she'd ever connect me with her handsome cab driver from the day before. With her city clothes and taxi-taking ways, she didn't seem like a small-town girl.

"Yes," she said. "The police needed someone to formally identify his body. The nice lieutenant let me do it from a photograph. But even so, after spending time in the water, the body was . . ." She shuddered.

"I'm so sorry you had to go through that. He didn't have a family member who could identify him?"

"David was all work. He had no family. No girl-friend. No time for any of that."

Fee delivered the omelet. Genevieve picked at

the edges as we talked. She didn't seem to have much of an appetite. I felt a surge of the same protective instinct toward her Chris had shown and the Snugg sisters seemed to feel. I wondered if she always brought that out in people, or if it was just in her present circumstances.

"How did you and Mr. Thwing become business partners, if you don't mind my asking?" I wondered if she'd answer. If she recognized my name as her potential chief competitor in the harbor, she might think I was prying.

"I love to talk about how I met David. I've told this story so many times." The Snowden name didn't appear to have registered with her. Genevieve put down her fork and gave up all pretense of eating. "David discovered me. Right here on the coast. I worked summers at a little clam shack out on the harbor in Round Pond."

Less than forty minutes from Busman's Harbor by road, even closer by water. I'd been completely mistaken about her. I never would have taken her for a mid-coast girl.

"Our next-door neighbors owned the clam shack. I worked there from the time I was about twelve. At first I refilled the napkin holders and bussed the picnic tables, but by high school I was the main cook. The food they offered was delicious—whole belly clams, Maine shrimp, haddock, French fries, and the best onion rings on the planet—but I got bored to death with deep-frying things. I started to experiment, doing daily specials. It was a game between the owner and me. At the dock, he'd buy me the freshest seafood he could find and I'd figure out what to do with it." Her cheeks turned an attractive rose color, and her face, so sad and stunned when she'd entered the restaurant, was happy and animated.

"Word spread about my specials. At first around our peninsula, and then farther. We had long lines every night in the summer. We bought more food, put in more picnic tables. I added a second special every night, and then a third. It was a miracle we pulled off the prep work in that little hut, but we did."

She slowed down to catch her breath. "That winter, I studied all the great seafood chefs, read cookbooks, tried out recipes. I applied to go to culinary school for after high school graduation. The following summer was even more insane, and we got some write-ups in the press. People came from hours away. One day David Thwing was standing at the clam shack window. He ordered one of everything on the menu, even though he was alone. He took all his plates to a picnic table and sat there sampling the food. When he was done, he asked to have a word with me."

I tried to remember if I'd ever heard anything about this cooking phenom from the next peninsula, but came up empty. Undoubtedly all this had happened during my long years away.

"The lines were still around the yard and up the street, so I told him he'd have to wait. He sat at his table for hours, while different groups of people joined him, ate and left. He talked to all of them:

why did they come? What did they like? How had they heard about the clam shack?

"When we finally finished serving for the night, he told me he wanted to buy a restaurant in Portland and set me up as the head chef. In Portland, Maine! I was too young to appreciate what he was really offering. To me it was big city, bright lights. And making my living cooking. He told me he'd find the right place. He said I should get ready to move at the end of the season."

Vee refilled Genevieve's coffee and put a steaming mug in front of me. I looked at her gratefully.

"It must have been a challenge," I said. "To move from working in a clam shack to running a restaurant." In my job in venture capital, I'd worked with a lot of people running a business for the first time, but none of them had been seventeen-year-olds.

"It was hard at first. I had to learn how to run a restaurant, how to be a boss. I had no idea how competitive the food business was in Portland. They say there are more restaurants per capita in Portland, Maine, than there are in San Francisco.

"David never treated me like a high school girl. He consulted me on all the decisions—location, decor, menu, everything. He brought me to Portland to do the hiring, though I'd never worked with anyone but my neighbor and his kid. David believed in me that much. We called our place Le Shack to reference my clam shack roots, but also to indicate an upscale spin. In the end, the food won out. By the end of the next summer, we were as much of a sensation in Portland as I had been in

Round Pond. David started talking about a second location. Bar Harbor was next. Then Ogunquit."

"You had a steep learning curve," I said. The food business was difficult. I had been brought up in it, and yet when I'd taken over the clambake last spring, I'd still felt overwhelmed. Labor costs were high. Margins were slim. Making a restaurant profitable was like landing a small plane in a fierce wind.

"I'd taught myself to be a chef. Then I learned to be an executive chef, in the sense that I was running several kitchens and had chefs with far more experience working for me. But I never was an executive chef, really, because I never learned the business side. David took care of all that." All the happiness she'd shown while telling her story drained out of her. She dabbed at her eyes with a folded paper napkin.

Gus's outer door banged open, distracting us both as we turned to look at the source of the noise. A pair of gray pants appeared on the stairs, followed by a blue sport coat and finally by the good-looking face and crew-cut head of Sergeant Tom Flynn as he descended into the restaurant.

"There you are," he said to Genevieve. "You were supposed to be at the Snuggles. We told you to let us know if you went anywhere."

"That was our fault, Sergeant," Vee called from behind the counter. "We didn't have time to feed Genevieve at the B & B, so we asked her to come here."

"Great. Thanks." Flynn brushed Vee off and

turned his full attention to Genevieve. "We're ready for you. Come with me."

Without a word, she picked up her expensive leather bag and followed him out.

After they left, I washed dishes using Gus's old-fashioned conveyor washer. Flynn's behavior toward Genevieve had been odd. He'd expected to find her at the Snuggles, and seemed angry she wasn't there. If she was in town to identify the body and provide background about David Thwing's life, why did she have to account to Flynn for her every move?

Could they be looking at Genevieve as a suspect? There was something about her little-girl act that didn't ring true for me. In my former job, I'd known plenty of successful entrepreneurs. One thing they all had in common was drive. And the food scene in Portland was a competitive jungle. Someone as naive as Genevieve Pelletier pretended to be couldn't have survived, much less thrived.

A soft hand clamped my shoulder. Fee stood behind me. As always, she was simply dressed, her short hair more chopped than styled. I wondered what it had been like, growing up the "plain" sister, compared to the glamorous Vee. Fee's back was bent even more than usual.

"How's the arthritis?" I asked. Working at Gus's must be difficult for her.

Fee smiled, stood up a little straighter, and said she felt fine. "I've had a new medication for a few months. Much, much better." She paused. "You seem like you have somewhere else you need to be. You go along. Vee and I can handle lunch."

"Really?"

"Go," she commanded, in a tone that left no room for argument.

Fee was right. I did have somewhere else I needed to be. Le Roi the cat had been cooped up in the house on Morrow Island for a day and a half. No doubt he was furious with me.

Chapter 14

I drove my car from Gus's to Mom's house. No surprise, her car wasn't in the garage. I decided not to fret about it. She'd made her feelings clear. I returned my car keys to the junk drawer in the kitchen and walked down to the town pier to pick up our Boston Whaler and head out to Morrow Island.

After a bumpy boat ride out, I turned the key in the lock of the little house by the dock. It was already unlocked. *Strange, I was sure I locked it.* A sharp chill caught me as I stepped inside. The unseasonably warm day hadn't penetrated the house, and last night's temperatures lingered.

"Anybody here?" My voice echoed though the empty house.

"Here puss, puss, puss." Le Roi hadn't run to greet me. I imagined him upstairs, sacked out in the square of sun on my bed, ignoring me, for spite. But when I looked in my bedroom, he wasn't there. "Puss, puss, puss." I was sure I'd left him in the house.

I returned to the kitchen where a quick glance at his bowls told me Le Roi had eaten, so he'd definitely been inside when I left. "Puss, puss, puss." I didn't take long to search the house, which was maddeningly quiet and still.

I called him again. No response. How could he have gotten out? I mentally reviewed the list of people who had keys and might have come out to the island, unlocked the door, and let him escape. Sonny and Livvie. Unlikely. My mother still had a key as far as I knew, but she hadn't set foot on the island since my dad died. Clearly, I hadn't locked up, even though I'd thought I had.

I opened the door to the outside and called the cat. He usually came like a dog when summoned, but not that day. I went back inside and filled his bowls, hoping he'd shimmy out of some indoor hiding place, but no dice. I opened the outside door again. "Puss, puss, puss."

Searching the whole wooded island would be ridiculous, but I did have some idea of Le Roi's favorite places. I checked the kitchen in the clambake pavilion and behind the bar. Finding no sign of him, I continued up the great lawn toward Windsholme.

Even in the bright, late morning light, the old mansion looked sinister and ruined. As I got closer, I spotted an unmistakable hole on the bottom of the orange hazard fence. "Oh, Le Roi." There was no question he had made it. He and I were the only mammals on the island.

Concerned he was somehow trapped inside, I eased myself through the fence and followed. The mansion's center, where the massive, winding staircase had climbed for three stories, was a charred ruin. The two wings of the house—the kitchen and dining room with bedrooms and servants rooms above on one side, and the ladies' withdrawing room with bedrooms above on the other—were still intact.

I entered by the French doors in the dining room and made my way gingerly into the house. "Puss, puss, puss." I was amazed at how well this part of the building had survived. The hand-painted wallpaper, though smoke-damaged, could probably be restored. Slowly, testing each piece of floor before I put my weight on it, I went through the swinging door into the butler's pantry, and then onto the balcony ringing the second floor of the two-story kitchen. "Puss, puss, puss." Nothing.

I'd reached a dead end. I couldn't cross the ruined great hall, so I retraced my steps, calling for Le Roi as I went. I was at a huge disadvantage. The cat could get so many places I couldn't. I walked across the front porch to the other wing and entered through the French doors into the ladies withdrawing room. "Puss, puss—"

"Hello."

I screamed and jumped three feet in the air, turning like a corkscrew. Quentin Tupper was in the doorway behind me.

"You scared the crap out of me!" I yelped.

"Sorry. As I tied up at the dock, I spotted you walking around up here."

Focused on Le Roi, I hadn't even noticed the *Flittermouse* arrive.

"Cat lost?" he asked.

"How did you . . . ? Oh." He'd heard the *Puss, puss.* "I can't find him."

"I'll help you look." We moved through the rooms together. "See, I told you this place wasn't in such bad shape," Quentin said. "It's only the area up the main stairs and the roof that's destroyed. You should repair it."

"Isn't there some kind of expression about the center not holding? Anyway, we've been through this. To what end? It's too expensive."

He put a hand on my forearm to stop me. "Julia, you know I'll lend you the money. Windsholme is an architectural treasure. It should be saved."

"Maybe." Quentin had invested a good sum in the Snowden Family Clambake Company. I wasn't sure I wanted to take any more of his money. "Puss, puss, puss," I called.

He could afford to lend me the money, of course. He could probably write a check to restore Windsholme without breaking a sweat. But we couldn't afford to repay him. His investment in the clambake, yes. All we needed was to string together a few years of decent weather, a decent economy, and, I could admit it finally, no competition from David Thwing. Windsholme was another story. It didn't generate income. Paying off Quentin would be impossible.

A ringed plume of a tail, sticking straight up, appeared, it seemed, out of nowhere. "Meow!"

"There you are." I took him in my arms. No mean feat with a twenty-pound, wriggling cat. "Bad boy. How did you get out of the house?"

Le Roi, wisely, said nothing.

"Why are you here, anyway?" I asked Quentin as we walked down the lawn.

"I got so caught up in the hunt for this guy, I forgot to say." Quentin reached over and ruffled Le Roi's fur affectionately. "I came to check out Windsholme for myself. Get a sense of the amount of damage. Part of my plan to talk you into restoring it. Do you mind if I look around some more?"

"Help yourself."

As I opened the door to the cottage, the cat jumped from my arms and ran to his food. I had to take him to the mainland. I'd slept at Chris's every night and spent my days in town. It wasn't fair to Le Roi.

But where would I take him? The thought of Le Roi loose in the construction zone that was Chris's house sent a shiver down my spine. "Mom's house it is," I said to Le Roi. Le Roi spent his summers ruling Morrow Island and until now had spent his winters in an isolated house at the end of a dirt road on the mainland. I wasn't sure how he'd feel about being a town cat, but there weren't any other options.

"I'm done." Quentin came through the kitchen door.

"What do you think?"

"What great architecture. It's a shame your family stopped using it. I'm sure Windsholme can be salvaged."

I scrunched my forehead over my nose in my best skeptical look.

"Think about it," he urged.

I walked Quentin back to the *Flittermouse*. The buoys he'd found the day of David Thwing's murder were piled in a corner of the deck.

"You haven't tracked down the owner of the buoys yet?"

Quentin jumped to the deck and pushed one with the toe of his boat shoe. "Nope. Too busy."

"You? Too busy doing what, exactly?"

He smiled back up at me. "You figure out your life yet?"

Touché. "Nope."

"Let me know if I can be of service."

After Quentin sailed off, I dug Le Roi's carrying case out from the storage space under the eaves.

"Here puss, puss, puss."

Le Roi was as determined not to go into the carrying case as I was determined he would. I didn't want him running free on the boat, not with his love of swimming. As I lowered his enormous body into the carrier, he put all four catcher's-mitt-sized paws on the sides and pushed back with all his might. He'd gotten heavier in middle age, like his namesake, Elvis, The King, but he still felt like one giant muscle. Finally, after a scene that left both of us panting, he was in his carrier and all I had to do was get it to the dock.

Chapter 15

In town, I lugged the carrier holding Le Roi, who felt like he weighed fifty pounds, up the hill to Mom's house. I'd thought I was in great shape from working at the clambake all summer long, but evidently I was wrong. I staggered into the kitchen and released Le Roi, who took off like a shot into the bowels of the house.

A gleaming, chrome cappuccino machine sat on the counter. I looked twice to make sure it was really there. What a strange thing for my mother to have.

I left Le Roi food and water. In the garage, I found a bag of kitty litter Mom had bought to supply traction in the driveway during ice storms.

To cover my bases, I called Mom's cell. Straight to voice mail, as I expected. I sat down at the kitchen table and wrote her a note explaining why she now had a cat. *Temporarily*, I emphasized.

The presence of the elaborate cappuccino machine was far more alarming than my mother's unexplained absences. She had a born Boston Brahmin's dread of ostentation combined with the habits of the thrifty Yankee housewife she'd become. I'd never known her to drink fancy coffee, much less own a fancy coffeemaker. Or any showy kitchen appliance for that matter.

I pushed the troubling chrome monster from my mind and grabbed my keys from the kitchen drawer. I wanted to check on Livvie.

Livvie, Sonny, and Page lived on Barbour Cove, a spit of land on the bayside of Eastclaw Point. It was a ten-minute drive from downtown Busman's in the off-season, a cul-de-sac ringed by modest ranch houses, a rich mix of young families and retirees.

Livvie threw open her front door before I was halfway up the walk. She stood, strong and straight in the doorway, wearing a pair of jeans and a flannel shirt open over a T-shirt. Was it possible she looked more pregnant than when I'd seen her the day before yesterday? She wore a ponytail bound at the nape of her neck to tame her luxuriant auburn hair.

The first thing I noticed when I stepped into the house was the rich aroma of Livvie's pumpkin cookies, fresh out of the oven. The second thing I noticed was the gigantic flat-screen TV dominating the living room. "Wow, what is that?"

"It's called a television," Livvie deadpanned. But

then, perhaps a bit defensively, said, "Our old one died."

I recognized it as the same model Bard Ramsey had. And on the opposite wall from the new television was a spanking-new leather couch. Livvie followed my eyes as I took it in, but said nothing. One of the problems with working with family was we all knew pretty closely how much money each of us made. Bard was probably throwing some money Sonny's way for his help on the *Abby*, though I didn't think it could be much, because Bard and Kyle had to live off the lobstering proceeds, too. True, Bard was a highliner, but boat maintenance, fuel, and equipment were expensive. I doubted there was a lot to spare.

In the winter, Livvie usually made ceramics for a local pottery outfit to sell during the season, but she and Sonny had decided she'd skip it this year because of the toxins in the clay and glaze, so that bit of income wouldn't be coming in. With a new baby on the way, it seemed like time for Livvie and Sonny to be cutting back, not buying brand-new stuff.

In the kitchen, dozens and dozens of big, dark orange cookies sat on cooling racks. "Get a little carried away?" I asked. Livvie baked when she was stressed.

"Swim team bake sale."

That took me back to the smell of chlorine and the loud echoes in the pool area of the Y, where I'd spent so many of my childhood Saturday mornings. Livvie had been a champion freestyler. Best in class as soon as she was old enough to compete, state champion two times in high school. "How does Page like it?"

"Loves it."

"She's always been a fish."

"Help me fill these?" Livvie pointed to a big blue bowl of cream cheese filling she'd been mixing. So the cookies were to become whoopie pies. Whoopie pies, sweet filling between two cake-textured cookies, were the official snack of the state of Maine, where they'd been invented. Some people in Pennsylvania disagreed with that version of history, but I was sure they were mistaken.

Livvie handed me a rubber spatula and we worked side by side, piling a thick layer of filling on the flat side of a cookie and then placing another on top, sandwich-style. The recipe she used was our grandmother's on our father's side, and the task made me nostalgic. To me, these delicious treats meant fall.

"I'm glad Page loves the team, but it makes the afternoons awfully long," Livvie said. "She doesn't get home from practice until after six."

I looked more closely at my beautiful sister. She had puffy circles under her hazel eyes and her pregnancy glow had been replaced by a waxy pale-ness. Her worries about Sonny were taking a toll. And I wondered if maybe I wasn't the only one having a problem adjusting to the slower pace of the off-season. With no winter job to go to, Sonny helping Bard, and Page tied up after school, the days would be emptier than usual for Livvie. At least until the winter forced Sonny's dad's boat out of the water and the new baby arrived.

"Sonny told me about the phone call he got from the hospital the morning David Thwing was killed." Livvie kept her eyes on the task at hand, not looking at me.

"That must have been upsetting for you to hear." I followed her lead and concentrated on filling the pies. "Do you have any idea who would do such a thing?"

"None. It's so awful. Whoever it was must have wanted to hurt Sonny."

"Or they really wanted to keep him off the *El Ay*. Did he tell you where he was the rest of the day?"

"Nope. Despite a rather loud 'discussion.'" She finished stuffing the last pie on her cooling rack and picked a pumpkin cookie off mine. As usual, I was slower in the kitchen. "We try not to fight in front of Page. It upsets her. But sometimes it can't be helped. She was upstairs doing homework, but I'm sure she heard us."

I had an awful thought. "You don't think he's cheating on you?" She wouldn't be the first pregnant woman that had happened to.

Livvie laughed. "Sonny? Cheat at cards, yes. Cheat on the size of a lobster a tenth of an inch, maybe. Cheat on me? Never."

I admired her sureness. It was the same certainty I had with Chris when it came to other women. Both our men were confounding us with different kinds of secrets.

"What was he doing on the *Abby* that's worse

than lying to police so he ends up being a murder suspect?" I asked. "You don't think—?"

"My husband killed his best friend? No. Or that Thwing guy, either."

I wished I had her certainty. As we worked, I ticked through the ledger. Sonny's hot temper. Sonny's over-the-top, seemingly personal hatred of Thwing. Sonny's dogged loyalty. I had no doubt Sonny would hurt anyone who threatened Livvie or Page. Or me or Mom. Or Kyle. Or Bard. Or maybe the Misses Snugg? As the circle in my mind grew, the cold pit of dread in my stomach expanded.

What was I actually thinking? That my brother-in-law might have murdered someone? I didn't want to believe it. In addition to the devastation it would cause my sister and niece, the truth was, after all these years with that aggravating man, I loved him. He was my family.

When the whoopie pies were finally all stuffed, Livvie put one on a plate for each of us and poured us each a glass of milk. I bit into mine, rolling the flavors across my tongue. The sweet of the pumpkin contrasted with the tang of the cream cheese—the perfect dessert.

When we finished, Livvie began silently packing the cooled cookies in plastic tubs.

I gave her a hug. My poor sister. I longed to lift the weight off her shoulders.

Livvie returned my hug. "I love you, too. I'm going to take some of these whoopie pies to the Murrays. Come with me? I'm not sure Lorrie Ann will see me if I come by myself. She hasn't returned any of my calls."

I shook my head. "I know she won't let me in. I visited yesterday. Belle invited me inside, but Lorrie Ann asked me to leave."

Livvie was resolute. "Let's see how she reacts to the two of us."

I looked at my sister. She was asking for my support. "Sure," I said. "Let's give it a try."

Chapter 16

I drove Livvie into town in the Caprice. She said Sonny would pick her up when he returned from lobstering. In addition to the large container of whoopie pies Livvie had packed for the Murrays, she put three smaller plastic storage boxes on my back seat.

"What?" she asked, catching my expression. "One each for Mom, you and Chris, Bard and Kyle. I've put the rest away for the bake sale."

"Mom would have to be at home to eat hers."

"Don't start with that again."

On the ride, I asked her what Peter Murray was like.

"You know Peter," she said. I did, sort of. He and Sonny were the odd couple. The big football player and the tiny wrestler. Blustering, take-no-prisoners, in-your-face Sonny, and quiet, conflict-avoiding Peter.

"He's always been in Sonny's shadow," I said. "I don't feel like I know him much at all. For example, was he a good lobsterman?" I remembered the peeling paint and worn roof shingles of the Murray house.

Livvie laughed. "Good heavens, no. He was a dub, for sure." A dub was a lobsterman who consistently returned to the harbor with a small catch. "Sonny thought Peter had no talent for lobstering. Wondered how he fed his family."

"And Lorrie Ann, what's she like?"

Livvie sighed. "I would have liked us to be friends. Our husbands were best friends. But we've never warmed to each other."

"You don't like her?"

"She's fine. We're just not friends. And unlikely to be, with what's happened."

"Were she and Peter happily married?"

"Devoted. Sonny used to tease that Peter had found the only woman in the harbor shorter than him. But privately, to me, Sonny would say Peter had found his perfect match. She's bossy, and Peter needed someone to tell him what to do." Livvie was quiet for a moment, then spoke again. "When you saw Lorrie Ann yesterday, how was she handling things?"

"She was fine, but I don't think she'd accepted her situation."

There were no cars parked at the Murray house beyond Lorrie Ann's ancient SUV sitting in the short driveway. "Where is everyone?" Livvie asked. She, too, expected the house to be crowded with lobstermen's wives.

Lorrie Ann answered the door in her bathrobe,

hair uncombed. Over the last twenty-four hours, the enormity of what had happened to her husband must have sunk in, and from the looks of things, it had sunk her with it. The cries of an unattended baby echoed down the narrow staircase. Despite the noon hour, PeeWee and Mavis were still in their pj's, staring at the blaring television.

Livvie didn't ask permission; she barged in. "Get Toddy," she directed me. "Upstairs, second door," she added unnecessarily. I only had to follow the sounds of his wails.

From his crib, Toddy lifted his arms to be picked up. He was a sodden mess so I took him directly to his changing table. As I fumbled for dry diapers, Livvie's conversation with Lorrie Ann floated up the stairs.

"Have these kids had anything to eat?" Livvie asked. Her tone was kind, but all business.

"Some muffins?" Lorrie Ann didn't sound too sure.

I managed to get Toddy changed and dressed, though my diapering experience with Page was nearly a decade in the past.

I carried Toddy downstairs and found Livvie in the kitchen heating canned soup on the stove and toasting bread. Lorrie Ann sat at the table crumpling a tissue.

"Where's your mom?" Livvie asked her.

Lorrie Ann's chin quivered. "We had a terrible fight. She walked out. Yesterday, just after you left." She glared at me like I'd been the instigator. But nothing had happened during my visit that should have precipitated a fight. Unless it was the mere fact that Belle let me in. I couldn't imagine that was it. Stress levels in the house were no doubt high, but it had to have been a heck of a disagreement for Belle to walk out on her daughter and grand-children in these circumstances.

"Do you know where your mother is?" I asked. The last thing the world needed was another disap-pearing mother.

"She's with a friend." Lorrie Ann sniffed. "I've been holding it together, really I have. The police were here again this morning."

"I'm sure you have," Livvie reassured her. "Did the police"—Livvie lowered her voice so the chil-dren wouldn't hear, which was hardly necessary given how loud the TV in the living room was—"have any news?"

"None. There was a state cop. He asked *me* a lot of questions."

"Lieutenant Binder? Sergeant Flynn?" I prompted.

"Flynn," Lorrie Ann answered. "Mostly he asked about money. How much does Peter make lobster-ing? How much do we owe? I explained things were hard because on top of everything else, we've been responsible for Mom since her hip replacement."

"Was that all he asked?" I wanted to know.

"He asked a lot about Sonny."

"Sonny?" Livvie turned the burner off under the soup. "What kind of questions did he ask about Sonny?"

"How did he and Peter meet? Were they friends? Had they ever been in business together?"

"Business together?" Livvie's voice rose.

"I don't think they understand lobstering," Lorrie Ann said. "I explained Sonny was just helping out. Or was supposed to help out."

The kitchen went silent for a moment. Then Livvie called the older children for lunch.

I put Toddy in his high chair. When PeeWee and Mavis were slurping away, and Toddy was gumming some cut-up toast, Livvie inclined her head toward the living room and I followed her.

"I'm going to stay," she said. "I'll call some friends to see if we can get twenty-four-hour coverage over the next few days. Can you go to the store? The pantry is empty."

I nodded. I would be grateful to get out of there.

"Milk, eggs, bread, hot dogs, peanut butter," Livvie whispered.

I indicated I'd got it and slipped out the door.

When I arrived back at the Murray house, Livvie stepped out onto the porch and grabbed the grocery bags. There were two cars parked along the street and the sound of female voices came from inside when Livvie opened the front door.

"Marshaling the troops?" I asked.

Livvie smiled. "I only had to ask. Everyone wanted to help, but Lorrie Ann had told each of them not to come."

"Why would she do that?"

"I dunno."

"Does her behavior seem odd to you?" I asked.

"What's odd if your husband is lost at sea and a stranger's body's been hauled up with your boat?" Livvie responded.

I had to give her that one. "When I was here yesterday, I thought Lorrie Ann was in denial," I said. "She was doing laundry, acting like nothing was wrong."

"So it hit her today."

"You know her better than I do. Do you think she seems sad?"

Livvie frowned, a rare crease in her forehead. "No. Now that you ask. She's acting more anxious than sad. She's a nervous wreck. Jumps at every little noise."

"That's what I thought, too."

"It's probably the waiting," Livvie said. "Dreading the call saying they've found Peter's body. She can't mourn properly until he's pronounced dead."

Livvie looked toward the door. "I need to get back inside. Where're you headed?"

"Mom's. I brought Le Roi back from Morrow Island earlier today. I want to make sure he's settled in."

Livvie rolled her eyes. "Le Roi at Mom's. Do you think that's a good idea?"

"It's not a good idea. It's a temporary necessity." I realized as I said this I hadn't called the rental agent to see if the owner of the apartment over Gleason's allowed pets.

"The whoopie pies are in your backseat," Livvie

reminded me. "Would you drop Bard's off at his house?"

"Sure. Call me if you need me."

Obedient sister that I was, my next stop was the Ramsey cottage. I climbed out of the Caprice and fetched a container of whoopie pies from the backseat.

The doorbell echoed inside, but I didn't hear movement. Bard's truck was in the driveway, so I tried again.

Heavy footsteps lumbered down the stairs and the sea-green front door flew open. Kyle Ramsey stood in the doorway.

"What?" he demanded. Then he mumbled, "Oh, it's you."

"Livvie sent you and your dad pumpkin whoopie pies." I thrust the plastic container toward him.

It seemed as if it took him a few seconds to figure out who Livvie was. "Thanks," he slurred.

His eyes were red, and I could tell even from where I stood that he needed a shower. I remembered his disheveled appearance at breakfast the day before. Though he'd seemed with it then, he certainly wasn't now.

So this was what Sonny meant when he said Kyle was "under the weather" and couldn't haul traps on Monday. He wasn't hungover from alcohol, as I'd guessed based on what Bard said. It didn't take a genius to know what was wrong. Abuse of prescription painkillers was a problem everywhere, and nowhere more than in northern New England with our high seasonal unemployment and proximity to an international border. The victims could be seen walking around town, glassy-eyed, nodding off. No family I knew was completely untouched. And then there was the collateral damage of the money needed for the drugs, which led to house-breaks and even armed robberies. Sometimes it felt as if we'd been invaded by a siege of stumbling, dangerous zombies. Now Sonny's family had been hit as well.

"Your dad around? I see his truck."

"Can't drive it, can he, with his arm." Kyle swung the door toward me.

I put my foot out and stopped it. "Know where he is?"

"Off with his girlfriend." Kyle pushed the door toward me again.

"Know when he'll be back?" I'd been right about the feminine touches in Bard's house. Bard had a girlfriend.

Kyle didn't even bother to answer that one. "Tell Livvie thanks for the cupcakes." His mouth went slack and the belligerence seeped away, replaced by a sadness that seemed to go to his core. "Livvie's always been good to me," he mumbled, closing the door completely.

I got back in the Caprice feeling crushed. Poor Bard. Poor Sonny. Poor Kyle. Yes, Kyle had lost his mother young. Yes, he'd been brought up by an aunt who resented getting saddled with her sister's children, and who counted the days until she could get out of town. And Bard had drunk heavily for a lot of those years. But Bard and Sonny had tried to do their best by Kyle in their own limited ways. The Ramsey men loved and supported one another, anyone could see that. Kyle's addiction must be breaking Bard and Sonny's hearts.

Where did Kyle get the money to feed his habit? During the good lobstering months, his work as Bard's sternman probably kept him in cash. But in months when lobsters were scarce, like now, and were made even scarcer by the troubles with Coldport, I didn't think Bard would be inclined to pay Kyle much. Nothing at all on the days he missed work on the *Abby*. What did Kyle do to support his habit?

It was too depressing to think about.

I started the Caprice and headed up the hill to Mom's house, pushing away the sad thoughts.

Chapter 17

As I pulled into Mom's garage, I spotted Genevieve Pelletier on the front porch of the Snuggles Inn. I crossed the street to say hello.

She held a smartphone tightly to her left ear, occasionally pulling it away so she could shout something into it. "We'll stay closed in Portland tonight and tomorrow out of respect, but we'll open on Friday. The other locations should keep to their normal hours."

She listened, nodding so her sleek black hair fell forward across her face. Then she said, "I don't know. The police haven't released his body. Our corporate attorney is looking for any family at all." She clamped the phone back to her ear, then shifted it again when she talked. "You're right, of course. Whether or not family turns up, we'll do a memorial ourselves."

She spotted me on the walk. "Got to run," she

said into the phone. Then she gestured for me to join her on the Snuggles' deep porch.

The outdoor furniture had been put away. Sonny had done the task for the Snugg sisters, lugging the heavy oak rockers and glider to their overstuffed two-story stable-cum-garage. Genevieve sat on a Victorian dining chair she must have carried from inside. I settled for a plastic milk carton.

"Business," she said, semi-apologetically, gesturing toward the smartphone. "It keeps going no matter what. Columbus Day weekend is coming and Portland will be full of tourists. We can't afford to lose the takings."

"I thought you didn't know anything about the business side."

She smiled. "I know we don't make money when we're closed."

I smiled, too. "Actually, I do know something about running an eating establishment. My family owns the Snowden Family Clambake."

Her eyes registered zero recognition, so I added, "We'll be your competition in Busman's Harbor. That is, if you go ahead with your plan to open here."

"Oh," she said vaguely. "David said something about some guy."

"My brother-in-law, Sonny. He's attended the hearings on our behalf."

At that moment, Sonny appeared, as if he were a genie and I'd conjured him simply by saying his name. He walked up the steep hill from the marina, head down, steps deliberate. Genevieve spotted him, too, and raised her hand to wave. I thought for few seconds they knew each other. Sonny continued until he was in front of the Snuggles. When he got closer, Genevieve, as if realizing a mistake, lowered her arm.

Sonny looked past her, straight at me. "Hey, Julia. Know where Livvie is?"

"At Lorrie Ann's. She's got her cell if you need her. She's expecting a ride home."

"Her phone's going straight to voice mail," he groused.

"It's a little crazy over there."

"Thanks." If Sonny had questions about why it was crazy at the Murrays' or what Livvie was doing there, he didn't ask them.

"Sonny, this is Genevieve Pelletier, David Thwing's business partner. Genevieve, this is my brother-in-law, Sonny Ramsey."

Both of them needed a moment to take in this information. Then Genevieve said, "Nice to meet you."

"Sorry for your loss. Mr. Thwing was a . . ." Sonny's eyes widened as he realized the verbal trap he'd created for himself. ". . . a person," he finally finished.

Fortunately, Genevieve didn't appear offended by Sonny's tongue-tiedness. "He certainly was," she replied.

"Got to go." Sonny turned and booked it across the lawn.

"Wait!" I caught up to him when he reached the sidewalk. "Where are you going?"

He stared at a crack in the cement. "Police station."

"What, again?"

"Same questions, same answers."

I kept my voice low, as he had, so Genevieve wouldn't hear. "Sonny, tell them the truth, please. Tell them where you were on Monday after you went to your dad's."

"Thanks, Julia. I never thought of that."

"Sarcasm doesn't become you. Neither does lying."

Sonny rubbed a big hand over his freckled brow. "Are we done here? Because I'd hate to be late to my interrogation." He rumbled off down the sidewalk.

I turned back to Genevieve, who grinned. "So he's the one who gave David such a hard time."

"The very one."

"Funny, I thought I knew him. He must look like someone I know. I just can't figure out who."

"Now that you know who I am," I said, "I have to ask. Will you go ahead with your plans for Busman's Harbor?"

Genevieve's big eyes narrowed. "The location here was David's pet project. I don't know much about it yet. But it's my decision. I own the business one hundred percent now. I'll be the one to decide whether we go ahead or not."

"I understand." I'd sensed in Genevieve a steely resolve, a backbone strong and straight as a knife, and I'd been right about that. Plus, she'd just revealed a motive for killing David Thwing. With him dead, she owned their string of five restaurants outright. I said my good-byes and walked across the street to Mom's house.

Inside the house, I called for Le Roi, but he didn't come. No doubt he was miffed about being shut up in a new place and abandoned. In the kitchen, I eyed the shiny new cappuccino machine. It looked like more trouble to figure out how to use it than it was worth, so I put the kettle on for tea instead. I fixed myself some toast and jam and headed to my office upstairs.

As I passed my mother's room, I noticed a rubber plant knocked over on the floor. Dirt was scattered across her peach-colored rug. Uh-oh. This was not a good start to the Mom-cat relationship. "Le Roi!" I bellowed. But if I sounded angry, why would he come? "Le Roi," I said more softly.

No sign of him. I righted the plant, returned what dirt I could to its pot and vacuumed the rest.

At my desk, I fired up my computer, searching the Web for stories about Genevieve and Thwing.

There were lots of stories about Le Shack—in glossy magazines like *Portland* and *Down East*, in newspapers like the *Portland Press Herald* and even some national press. The *New York Times* included praise for Le Shack in its "Twenty-four Hours in Portland, Maine" column and *Food & Wine* included it in a nouvelle seafood story. I'd read most of these articles while doing competitive research when Thwing first came to town. I dug deeper.

The stories that featured the restaurant's history or Genevieve's personal background were identical to what she'd told me, which didn't surprise me. Her meteoric rise made for fascinating reading, and would be catnip to any journalist.

Going back in time, I found local articles about Genevieve's summers at Bob's Clams in Round Pond. Not all the stories mentioned her by name, but they all mentioned the people lining up for food every day of the season. I found a photo of Genevieve standing in the window of the clam shack between Bob Harris, the owner, and his son, Evan. Her hair was hidden under a kerchief, but she had the same wide-open eyes. They were all giving the camera big smiles, basking in their success.

I expected to find stories in the local press after Genevieve left Round Pond, on the "local girl makes good" angle, but there was nothing. Perhaps there'd been some resentment when she moved on? Likewise, there was nothing about Genevieve prior to her summers at Bob's Clams, which also surprised me. If she'd played on a sports team or been in a school play, or participated in any activities at all, she would've made the small-town paper.

I switched focus to David Thwing. He was much older than Genevieve—the news stories about the murder said he was forty-four—and he had enough money to finance Le Shack, which I was sure was an expensive undertaking. The stories about his murder focused on the same biography Genevieve had given me, owner of Le Shack and four other coastal Maine restaurants. But that only accounted for five years. He must have done something before.

I couldn't find much. He'd owned a few businesses, a string of convenience stores, a chain of storage facilities. No prior interest in the food business that I could find. And as Genevieve had said, no social life—no marriage announcements or appearances at fundraisers or parties.

I felt stymied. The articles about Genevieve and Thwing all read like some PR agent's gloss. But if I couldn't get to the real story about Genevieve and Thwing's partnership, the police could. Flynn had acted so oddly toward Genevieve at Gus's this morning. Perhaps she was already in their sights. Perhaps I could push it along.

Chapter 18

As I searched the Web for information about Thwing and Genevieve, the shiny cappuccino machine called out to me from downstairs, demanding I think about it. It made a mockery of every value I was raised with. It was showy, even show-offy. Worse, it was unnecessary. Mom had a perfectly serviceable coffeemaker.

I called Livvie on her cell. "Did you give Mom an espresso machine?"

"Julia, what on earth are you talking about?" In the background, I heard conversation punctuated by laughter. The gathering at the Murray house had moved from intervention to wake.

"There's an expensive coffeemaker sitting on the counter in Mom's kitchen and I thought with all the new stuff you've bought—"

"Hang on a second. I'm going out on the porch." I waited while Livvie moved outside. "It's none of your business, Julia, but since you seem so hung up on it, I'm going to tell you. Bard bought us the TV. And the couch."

Bard? I couldn't recall a gift of any size he'd given Livvie and Sonny throughout their marriage. And where was he getting excess money all of a sudden? Especially while he was injured and in the midst of a war with Coldport Island.

"Okay," I said. "Sorry. I didn't mean to pry."

I ended the call, but my discomfort about the cappuccino machine lingered. I went downstairs to look at it again. It had enough chrome on it to outfit a 1955 Chevy. It stuck out like a sore thumb in my mother's perfectly serviceable, but un-flashy kitchen.

What was it doing there? I dialed Mom's cell again, and it went straight to voice mail. Again.

I noticed the swinging door from the kitchen to the dining room was open a bit, caught on the Oriental rug. Most of the money and possessions from my mother's once wealthy family were long gone by the time she was born. What little was left of the china, crystal, and silver that had passed to Mom from the mother who died when she was a child was in the corner cabinet and sideboard in our dining room.

I pushed through the door. The normally latched, glass doors of the corner cabinet were wide open. In it, on a shelf holding twelve delicate, etched crystal goblets, was the cat.

"Le Roi!" I yelled. Then instantly regretted it. He was asleep, stretched out in a V shape against the two back walls of the cabinet. The goblets were between him and me. The last thing I wanted was for him to move. How he got in there without breaking anything I would never know. And what pinhead had left the doors open?

I crept forward. He opened one eye, but returned to sleep. Gingerly, I moved the glasses two at a time to the dining room table. When they were all moved, I scooped up Le Roi and dumped him on the floor. "Bad cat."

I returned the glasses to the shelf and firmly latched the doors. As I turned to go, I looked again at the dining table. A silver bowl of seasonal gourds served as the centerpiece. Exactly like the one on the dining room table at Bard Ramsey's house. Except Mom's bowl was sterling and Bard's was pottery, but otherwise, exactly the same.

I had a sudden, horrible flash of intuition. My mother was dating Bard Ramsey!

Bard was apparently giving gifts of appliances. And Kyle had confirmed he had a girlfriend. Was that why Mom was never around? Was she off somewhere with Bard?

The thought of having the Ramsey men more involved in our lives made my heart sink. Not that there was so much wrong with Bard. He was a leader, and had been apparently sober the last few times I'd seen him. But in comparison to my dad? I couldn't even . . .

I thought about calling Livvie back, but she'd seemed annoyed by the last call. I pushed back my horrible thoughts, grabbed my tote bag, and headed to the police station.

* * *

At the police station, the door to the multipurpose room was propped open, a wooden wedge stuck under it. The place was a beehive, with more uniformed and plainclothes agents than I'd ever seen buzzing around. My friend Jamie dashed by, rolling his eyes at me as he went. I suspected the local cops weren't enjoying this invasion.

The civilian receptionist directed me to the folding table where Binder and Flynn sat, both staring into laptops.

"Julia." Lieutenant Binder leapt to his feet as soon as he spotted me.

"Ms. Snowden." Flynn rose more slowly.

I greeted the men and took a seat in the metal chair across from them.

"What brings you in?" Binder asked as he sat back down. His voice was neither wary nor warm.

"The Thwing investigation."

Binder smiled. "I figured that part out. But what specifically? Do you have new information?"

I didn't. My goal was to make sure they used the information they had. "No. I'm concerned about all these out-of-towners." I gestured around the crowded room. "They might not pick up on the local angles."

Flynn raised both brows. "Such as?"

"Maybe you've heard the lobstermen in town are involved in a so-called gear war with Coldport Island."

Binder picked up a ballpoint pen and held it

horizontally between his index fingers. "We're aware."

"Don't you think that might be the reason Thwing and Peter were killed? Lobster wars have turned deadly before."

Flynn sat up even straighter. I was surprised it was possible given his normal military bearing. "Ms. Snowden, we work in a state with a shoreline longer than California's. I assure you, the Maine State Police Major Crimes Unit knows what goes on between lobstermen."

"It's just that no one seems to be following up."

"We're investigating every possibility." Binder waved toward the dozen or so agents doing paperwork or talking on cell phones. "There's double the number of agents in this room out in the field. Everything is being considered, including the trouble with Coldport Island."

"What about Genevieve Pelletier?" I asked.

Flynn looked up sharply. "What about her?"

"She's not some innocent girl. With Thwing gone, she owns the entire five-restaurant chain. That seems like motive to me."

"She's not a suspect," Flynn said in a tone that didn't allow for argument.

I didn't let him deter me. "She's not the naive chef who doesn't understand the business she pretends to be."

Flynn went pink in the face. "That's not a crime." He shifted in his seat. "Le Shack is a highly successful business. The Snowden Family Clambake narrowly avoided bankruptcy this year. Thwing was poised to compete with you. Your brother-in-law was badmouthing him all over town. As I see it, Sonny had a stronger motive to kill David Thwing than Ms. Pelletier did. So did you, for that matter."

The breath whooshed out of me. "Are you kidding? Am I a suspect?"

Binder held his hand up, signaling Flynn to back off. "Of course not."

"You're so worried about whether we're considering every suspect. I'm reassuring you we're being thorough," Flynn said.

I didn't miss the sarcasm, but I also didn't let it deter me. "Do you really think Sonny killed Thwing, along with his own best friend?"

Binder looked me straight in the eye. "He'd be better off if he told us the truth." He inclined his head toward the noisy room. "We're not the only agency working this case. I can't control what these other officers think, or even what they do. And I'll tell you this, they know your brother-in-law is lying about his involvement."

I caught that. Not lying about where he was. Lying about his *involvement*.

"Well, while they're looking into people who are lying, tell them to look at Genevieve. I know she's covering something up."

I marched out of the room, back straight, determined to prove them wrong. Genevieve was lying. There were two places I could go to get more information it, Portland and Round Pond. Round Pond was closer.

Chapter 19

The drive from Busman's Harbor to Round Pond was a pretty one on a late afternoon in the fall. Visitors might have gone all the way up our peninsula to Route One, but the locals knew the back way, a pleasant, winding drive past farms and woods to Damariscotta.

Main Street, Damariscotta, had always seemed like the perfect downtown to me. It had a great bookstore, an old-fashioned movie theatre, and fabulous restaurants and art galleries, all in quaint two-story brick buildings. It was a tourist town, but had much more of a year-round population than Busman's Harbor. People bustled in and out of the stores.

I turned down Route 129 toward Round Pond. The Bristol peninsula was one of the most scenic places in a scenic state, and it dazzled in the fall. I wished I were on a casual visit to the lighthouse perched dramatically above the crashing surf at Pemaquid Point, but I was a woman on a mission, headed to the east coast of the peninsula and the breathtaking harbor at Round Pond.

Round Pond was a perfect bowl of dark blue water on the Muscongus Sound. Like Busman's Harbor, it was mostly buttoned up for the coming winter. The pleasure craft were gone. But it was also a working harbor. Screaming gulls surrounded the lobster boats as they unloaded their catch at the dock. The lobstermen of Muscongus Bay had their own history of territorial wars with neighboring harbors, but things had been quiet there for a long while.

I'd gambled Bob's Clams would be open so late in the season. Genevieve had said she and Bob were neighbors, so I hoped I could track down their homes if the clam shack was closed. I was relieved when I came around a bend in the harbor road and found the shack sitting almost squarely in front me, the front window open for orders. Bob must have been counting on leaf-peeping tourists to eke out the last few pennies of the season.

The heady days of Genevieve's gourmet cooking were over. The dishes on the menu, lettered in dark red on a white-painted board, were typical, as Genevieve had described—fried clams, scallops, Maine rock shrimp, haddock, hand-cut French fries, and onion rings. I recognized Bob Harris working inside, slightly balder and heavier than in his photo with Genevieve, but otherwise the same. A small woman worked at his side. Though there'd been no mention of her in any of the articles, I assumed she was his wife. Their gently rounded shapes and steel-gray hair reminded me of matched salt and pepper shakers.

I ordered the fisherman's platter—in other words, everything on the menu. It would be more food than I could eat in three meals, but it would keep them busy cooking for a while and I could hang around and talk.

"Good season?" I asked.

"Not bad," Bob answered, which in Maine-ese means stupendous.

"Us, too," I said. "Julia Snowden. My family runs the Snowden Family—"

"I know the place." Bob moved away from the fryer and his wife seamlessly stepped in. He came to the window and looked over his glasses at me. I wondered if he'd bring up the murder on Morrow Island in June, or any of our other troubles, but instead he said, "Nice operation." The highest form of compliment. "I'm Bob. This is my wife, Mil."

"Nice to meet you." I looked around, as if taking in the name on the hand-painted sign for the first time. "Isn't this the place Genevieve Pelletier got her start?"

"Hmpff." Mil dropped a plastic basket filled with fried seafood in front of me. It smelled heavenly. "Cocktail or tartar?"

"Both, please. And ketchup for the fries."

Bob watched silently while I ordered a soda and paid Mil for the meal.

"You asked about Vieve," he said. "I heard about David Thwing getting murdered. It's all people around here can talk about. Happened down your way, didn't it?"

"I was the one who spotted the empty boat."

"Doesn't explain why you would drive all the way over here to ask questions."

I hadn't been as casual as I'd hoped. I went with a straightforward approach instead. "My brother-in-law was supposed to be on the boat with Thwing and the owner. The owner's wife, and maybe some law enforcement types, think my brother-in-law was involved somehow. So I thought—"

"You could offer them another suspect," Bob finished for me. "If you think Vieve could be involved in some way in murdering David Thwing, you're barking up the wrong tree."

"Hmpff," said Mil, like she didn't agree.

Bob glanced at his wife, then looked at my basket of seafood. "That'll get cold if you don't eat it. Let's go over to the picnic table yonder."

Bob sat across from me. Mil didn't follow and I assumed he wanted to put some distance between her and our conversation. I skewered a forkful of tiny Gulf of Maine shrimp. They were sweet and tender, with just enough breading to enhance, not disguise, their taste. Bob and Mil were pretty good cooks in their own right.

"Like it?" Bob's pride was obvious.

"Delicious."

He took his glasses off. His eyes were a gray, with a darker circle around the irises. "You wanted to know about Vieve."

"Yes."

"So I imagine you've read the magazine stories, how she and Thwing met and so on. That's what brings you here."

I recounted the story for Bob as I understood it. He sat back on the picnic table bench, arms folded.

When I finished, he said, "Now I'll give you the real story, not the PR version." He leaned forward, placing both elbows on the table. I waited, shoveling the food from the fisherman's platter into my mouth as I did, savoring the salty crunch of the fries, the perfect sweetness of the onion rings and the lighter-than-air taste of the haddock.

"It's true Vieve was a neighbor. Her family's owned that place for four generations." He pointed across the lawn at a huge shingled house on the harbor.

"Wowsa." It was a marvel of Maine seacoast zoning, or lack thereof, that a mansion could have a clam shack practically in its backyard.

"Indeed. They're summer people, of course. And since my place is so close, we've always been friendly. Once in a while, they complained about the noise or the trash, but mostly, it's been good. I knew Vieve from the time she was a little kid."

"Boating family?" I asked.

"Of course. Like all the kids around here, full-time and summer, Vieve knew her way around a boat. But it turned out, she wasn't as interested in fishing as she was in fish, and what she could do with them. She was on her own a lot, so she'd come over and play at bussing the tables. 'Help out.' Cute stuff."

"Where did she live in the off season?"

"Connecticut. I forget the town. Her parents are

divorced and I think her stepfather adopted her. But when she started gaining a reputation for her cooking, she began using her real dad's name, Pelletier. She never said why, whether it was trouble at home or she thought it was more chef-like. She got shuffled around a lot, spent most of her time at sleep-away schools."

I nodded sympathetically. Of course, I'd spent my time at boarding school, too, but I didn't say that. The name change explained why I'd found no trace of Genevieve on the Web until the clam shack.

"I gave her a few bucks for helping. She came around more and more. The summer she was fifteen, she started in the kitchen. She was a good fry cook, fast-learner. I thought I'd be lucky to keep her for a couple of summers, maybe even through college. My son, Evan, could take over helping me then.

"But Vieve, who'd always been an unsupervised kid without much direction, got a fire in her belly. On her breaks from school, she had her mother send her for cooking instruction. New York, Paris. She came back the next summer with a goal. The 'specials' were her idea. It's a myth of her making I bought the seafood and challenged her to pre-pare it. She charged the fish to her mother's credit card. Picked it out herself. We always made plenty of money to pay it back." He rubbed his eyes. A tired gesture, though he seemed to have plenty of enthusiasm about the subject of Genevieve Pelletier. "She was so full of life, I let her do it. I couldn't argue about the results. Lines all around the place."

"And that's it? The rest is the same as the stories in the press?"

"Not quite. The summer after her senior year of high school, Vieve started talking about her plans. Her parents wanted her to go to college, or at least culinary school, but she was eager to get on with her career. She wanted us to open a restaurant together. Said I had the management know-how, she had the cooking skills. I figured she was right, we would be a great team. The same people who came here to the clam shack would come to a restaurant. We had enough local trade, I thought we could make it through the winters. So I started looking for a place. I signed a lease on a building on Main Street in Damariscotta. She picked out the decor and fixtures, developed the menu and set the pricing. I did everything she asked. I took a second mortgage on my house to pay for the improvements to the space."

"Then David Thwing came along."

"He'd been sniffing around the harbor all summer for something to sink his money into. He was going to buy a commercial fishing boat from a friend of mine, then backed away. He was going to buy a tour boat somewhere else. Then he fetched up here. I never liked him. Weird way of walking. Eyes darting all around."

I knew what he meant. That'd also been my impression during my single, brief interaction with David Thwing.

I pushed the food away. I couldn't eat another bite. Even if I hadn't been full, I could see where this story was going, and it was enough to kill my appetite.

"Vieve went off with Thwing. Mil and I tried to run the restaurant in Damariscotta ourselves. The leasehold improvements were already done, but it was six ways from wrong. The prices we had to charge were too high for the food we were capable of cooking, and after all the renovations, the overhead was too high to support the right prices for our kind of food. Then came the stock market crash. The recession. We were done before the next season began."

Bob rubbed his eyes and put his glasses back on. He was stoic, but I could see the pain of that time. My family had almost lost our business, too. The loss of a family business was like a death.

"So now it's just Mil and me, back at the shack, which we barely held on to along with our house. I'll be paying that second mortgage 'til I die. Our son, Evan, went off to Maine Maritime. He has no interest in the business. When you've seen a train wreck like that at an impressionable age . . ." Bob didn't finish.

"Was the relationship between Thwing and Genevieve platonic?" I asked. He had been thirty-seven to her seventeen when they'd met, but it wouldn't have been the first time that line was crossed.

"Strictly business," Bob answered. "At least while she was still here. To tell the truth, I think she was in love with success and he was in love with money. I never blamed Vieve for what she did," Bob went on. "She got a better offer, plain and simple. David Thwing could give her everything she ever dreamed. There was nothing in writing between her and me. Not even an employment contract, which, now I look back, was stupid. But she was a minor, not quite eighteen. Who knows if it could even be enforced?"

Bob shifted his weight on the hard picnic bench. "Mil, though. Mil has some bitterness in her," he continued. "She dreamed of retirement someplace warm. It'll be a long time, now, if ever. That's why I thought it was better to talk over here."

A car with an Ohio plate pulled up to the clam shack and Mil stuck her head out the window. Bob gestured to my two-thirds-full basket of seafood. "Want me to wrap that up to go?"

I couldn't say no.

Chapter 20

It was dark by the time I started back down the peninsula toward Busman's Harbor. As I'd suspected, Genevieve's little-girl act was just that. She had the kind of single-minded ambition that left a lot of victims in its wake. She might not have had a legal obligation to Bob and Mil Harris, but she had certainly had a moral one. To walk off and leave them stuck with that loan was reprehensible.

But was it enough to interest the police? Nothing about Bob's story indicated Genevieve had the slightest inclination to kill David Thwing. In fact, the opposite. He was her patron. If anything, it was the Harrises who had a motive. I couldn't picture gentle Bob killing anyone, though I wasn't so sure about the taciturn Mil. It was all too far-fetched, and I felt silly for wasting the afternoon.

As I drove along, I considered. If Genevieve was out as a suspect, the best lead I had was the person who'd called Sonny Monday morning. Whoever it was hadn't wanted Sonny on the *El Ay*. Which meant either they'd known something was going to happen, or they'd been planning something and wanted Sonny out of the way. Which meant whoever they were, they knew something I needed to know. Halfway down the peninsula, I pulled off the highway onto the access road for the hospital.

In the emergency room, Melody Barkly had been replaced by a woman in her twenties I didn't recognize. She had a stud in her eyebrow, a crease in her forehead, and the evident assumption, before she even raised her head to look at me, I was going to be a pain in her neck.

"Fill out the form, return it to me," she said, handing me a clipboard without looking over the high counter separating us. The waiting room was quiet, except for a mother with a coughing child in her lap and a guy holding his swollen hand.

"I'm not here about—"

"Whatever you're here for, first you fill out the form." She looked at me then, as if my lack of cooperation merited eye contact.

I put the clipboard back down on the counter. "Sorry, I wasn't clear. I'm wondering who helped my brother-in-law, Sonny Ramsey, the day before yesterday, in the morning around eight? He received a prank phone call from inside the hospital."

Instantly, her officiousness melted away. "Oh, that was me. I normally work mornings, but I'm covering for someone tonight. That was so creepy! I felt bad for him. He was shaking like a leaf. Has he figured out who it was?" She stood up, setting her elbows on the counter. Her nametag read, BRITTANY B.

"No he hasn't. He's quite upset about the incident, and he's asked me to help him figure out who called him. I was hoping you could supply some information. Do you remember the number of the extension he was called from?"

Brittany's eyes narrowed. "If he asked you to help him, how come he didn't give you the extension number?"

I stuck my hand in my tote bag and flailed around a bit. "He did. And he wrote the number down. But I can't find—"

Brittany B. took pity on me. "Maybe I did write it down. I wanted to follow up on my end because it's somewhat myster—here it is." Triumphant, she held up a little piece of white notepaper. "4927."

"And you're sure it isn't the number of any department or doctor?"

"No. It's not listed in the hospital directory." She tapped her keyboard, then turned her monitor so I could read the list of names and departments paired with extensions. The list was alphabetical by person, not numerical by extension, so I had trouble understanding what numbers were used and which were skipped.

"What happened when you dialed 4927?" I asked.

"It rang and rang. You can try it again from the phone over there if you like."

I stepped over to a house phone at the other end of the high counter, picked up the handset, and dialed the extension. As Brittany said, the phone on the other end kept ringing until I hung up. No outgoing message, no prompt to leave a voice mail, nothing.

When I moved back to her station, Brittany B. was giving her "Talk to the hand, fill out the form" speech to someone new, so I waited until she was done. "It just rang," I confirmed. "No voice mail or anything. Can you think of any reason an extension would be live, but not assigned to someone?"

"I wondered, too," she answered. "In the olden days, in the waiting room for each service there was a receptionist who had an extension. But now with budget cuts, you do your paperwork at centralized reception in the lobby, and most waiting rooms are unattended. The nurses and technicians call patients in for tests or whatever."

"So these receptionist extensions are still active, even though no one sits at the desks?"

Brittany frowned. "Maybe. The docs might use them once in a while, like if they get a page."

"So how do I get a list?"

"I don't think there is one. I'd send you to talk to the switchboard, but no people work there anymore, only computers. You'll have to look for the phone attached to the extension."

Great. But it was important to know who had called Sonny, so I thanked Brittany. "If you find an unattended phone, you can call me." She jotted her extension on a piece of scrap paper. "I'll read back the number that shows up on my phone."

I wended my way from the ER to the lobby and looked at the directory for the hospital and the related healthcare facilities in the annex that shared the same exchange. There were departments related to tests—ultrasound, X-ray, MRI—and departments for every body part—eyes, ears, feet, and so

on. I took the elevator to the top floor of the main
hospital building, planning to work my way down.

The structure of most of the suites was the same,
a waiting room off the main hallway, with the service itself in a warren of offices or labs behind. As
Brittany had said, few of the waiting rooms had re-
ceptionists. Some were sleekly modern, others old
and beat up. I discovered it was the run-down ones
that had live phones sitting on the empty reception
desks.

The first unattended phone I discovered was in
the ultrasound suite. I picked it up and got a dial
tone. I called Brittany's extension. "Can you see the
number I'm calling from?"

"Yup. 4113."

"Do these numbers make any geographic sense?
Like do the numbers go up or down or maybe indicate a certain floor?"

"I think they might have, years ago. Before I
worked here. But the numbers have been reas-
signed so often, nowadays they're totally random."

"Do patient rooms have the same exchange?"

"Nope. Just the services."

Thank goodness. I thanked Brittany B., hung up
the phone, and moved on to the next suite.

I tried every waiting room in the hospital and
moved to the annex. After three more failures, I
reached the physical therapy suite. The waiting
room was busier at that time of day than any of the
other services, filled with people arriving for physical therapy after work. A woman in exercise
clothes emerged from the inner door, called several people's names and checked them off on her

clipboard. As people entered through the open door, I glimpsed a large, windowed room that looked more like a gym than a hospital suite.

No one took the slightest notice of me as I picked up the phone on the empty reception desk and dialed it. Brittany's extension rang until I hung up. I was about to leave when I decided to try her one more time. Brittany answered right away. "Sorry, I was busy. You got it! 4927. Where are you?"

"PT service. Thank you so much."

I looked around the PT waiting room. There were people of every age and shape, some of them nursing obvious injuries and others looking perfectly normal. I didn't recognize a soul. But then, of course I wouldn't. Someone had called Sonny from this room at 8:00 AM on Monday morning. It was now after six o'clock on Wednesday. Could I get Binder interested in following up, maybe asking for a list of people with Monday morning appointments? If that didn't work, all I could do was come in the morning and hope whoever had made the call had a regular 8:00 AM therapy appointment.

I headed back to the main hospital. I wanted to check on Mrs. Gus. As I walked, something nagged at the back of my mind. PT. PT. Yes, Bard Ramsey had told me the day before he was in physical therapy for his shoulder.

But would Bard do such an awful thing to Sonny? And wouldn't Sonny recognize his own father's voice?

Chapter 21

Gus sat quietly at his wife's bedside when I entered her room.

"Hi," I whispered. "Any change?"

He didn't rise to greet me, unheard of for him. "They say she's 'lightening up.' Sometimes she moves her fingers, opens her eyes for a second," he said.

"That has to be good, right?"

He shrugged. "Not as good as if this hadn't happened."

"What did happen, Gus?"

"One minute she was there, starting her pie crust and the next minute she was on the kitchen floor. There was an open bottle of her arthritis pills on the counter. The people from the ambulance team said to bring it with me, otherwise I would have never thought of it. She kept her pills in the kitchen, took them in the morning."

Mrs. Gus collapsed right after taking her arthritis medication? This was new information. "Has she ever had a reaction to her medication before, even a slight one?" I asked gently. I was there to support, not interrogate him. "Or was the medication new?"

"She's been taking arthritis pills forever. After I brought the pills along to the ER in the ambulance they took them off somewhere." Gus waved a hand toward the inner depths of the hospital.

"I'm so sorry this happened to Mrs. Gus. And to you."

"Thanky." Gus reached a liver-spotted hand toward the bed and took his wife's hand in his own. He stared at her face with naked tenderness and sighed deeply. As his curmudgeonly armor, the "Gusness" of Gus, dropped away, I thought of slipping out. But I didn't want to leave yet, so I lingered, shifting uncomfortably from foot to foot, trapped in their private moment.

Gus let go of his wife's hand, pressed a misshapen knuckle under each eye, and turned back toward me. "How's my restaurant?" he asked, his voice gravelly with emotion.

"It's fine," I reassured him. Gus didn't need anything else to worry about. "The Misses Snugg ran it this morning. I helped."

"The restaurant is important," he said. "Take care of it."

"We will. Please don't worry. Fee, Vee, Chris, and I will handle it. We know how important it is. You and Mrs. Gus have put your lives into it."

"Yes," Gus answered, "but that's not what I meant. The restaurant is important to the town."

* * *

I sat with Mrs. Gus while Gus went off to find something to eat in the cafeteria. It was strangely peaceful in her room, with the machines bonging out a mysterious rhythm. A nurse came in, checked her temperature, and adjusted the flow of her medication.

"Are you a relative?" she asked.

"A friend." I wondered where Gus's children were. He and Mrs. Gus had a son and daughter, both middle-aged and prosperous with families of their own. Both lived out of state. It would be so like Gus not to "bother" them with news of their mother's coma. He must have been hoping it would all turn out all right and he'd never have to tell them.

"You can talk to her," the nurse urged.

"Can she hear me?"

"We don't know," the nurse answered. "Hearing and touch are the last senses to go and the first to come back. She may not understand what you're saying, but it can't hurt."

When she left the room, I moved closer to the bed and took Mrs. Gus's hand. "Mrs. Gus, I'm so sorry this happened to you. Gus misses you, and so do your friends Fee and Vee. The whole town is missing your pies." I stopped. Was I putting too much pressure on a sick woman? If I were lying unconscious, would I want someone nagging me to get up and turn out pies? I knew so little about her. Not even her real name. A woman in her seventies deserved an identity that was more than her marital state followed by her husband's first name. "Come back to us," I finished, "if you can."

I heard the masculine clap-clap of several pairs of leather-soled feet coming down the hallway, followed by a familiar voice conversing with the nurse. Lieutenant Binder entered Mrs. Gus's room, followed by two men in sports coats.

"Ms. Snowden."

I stood. "I'm staying with Mrs. Gus until Gus gets back. He's in the cafeteria," I explained.

Binder nodded. "This is Special Agent Williams of the Drug Enforcement Administration and Sergeant Crisp assigned to the Maine State Drug Task Force."

Williams shook my hand, but Crisp merely nodded. As I tried to get my head around their presence, a white-jacketed doctor entered the room. He was about my age with black hair, parted and slicked back and the kind of dark-rimmed glasses that were so old-fashioned they looked cool. His name tag said, DR. PARK, PHARMACY.

"Is this the daughter?" he asked the officers, as if I were a mannequin who couldn't speak for herself.

"No," Binder answered for me. "We're waiting for—"

Gus walked into the room.

"Mr. Farnham." Binder spoke before Gus could react to the law enforcement officers standing around his wife's hospital bed. "We need to talk. Perhaps we could go to the family conference room?"

Gus kept his composure. He cocked his head in my direction and said, "I want her there."

"Of course," Binder responded before the others could object.

I followed the men down the hospital corridor, matching my stride to Gus's. I worried about the conversation that was coming, and vowed to support Gus any way I could.

We gathered around the laminate-topped table in the conference room. Binder made the introductions. Special Agent Williams and Sergeant Crisp each slid a business card toward Gus. I swept them up and put them on the table in front of him so he could remember who was who.

The room was cheerfully decorated, but was nonetheless uncomfortable, like a cloud filled with all the bad news ever delivered there hung overhead. What kind of bad news were these officers bringing?

Dr. Park began. "Mr. Farnham, these gentlemen are here because lab tests have confirmed your wife did not have a reaction to her medication. There was a foreign substance mixed in the capsules with the medicine."

He let that sink in.

"You mean she was poisoned?" Gus's voice shook.

Binder spoke up, "She may have been deliberately targeted, but our current theory is she got ahold of some tainted medication manufactured outside the United States that included the substance that caused her condition."

Gus looked from one man to the next. Binder and Park at least appeared sympathetic. Williams and Crisp were stone-faced.

Binder continued. "Mr. Farnham, the label on the pill bottle you brought to the hospital didn't have your wife's name or a pharmacy name on it. It had the generic name of the drug, the dosage and a logo that's not registered to any pharmaceutical company known in the U.S."

Gus's eyes widened. "I didn't notice. It was a normal, brown pill container. My wife was on the kitchen floor, barely breathing. When the ambulance came, one of the EMTs told me to bring the pills along, so you'd know what she took."

"That was the right thing to do," Dr. Park said.

"Do you know where your wife got the pills?" Binder asked. Williams and Crisp sat forward.

"I assumed they came from the big pharmacy up on Route One. Are you saying they didn't?" Gus put his hands on the table. "She's been taking arthritis medication forever. The truth is, my wife took care of all that stuff—prescriptions, insurance, Medicare. I don't know anything."

"Have you ever known her to get her medication from somewhere other than a pharmacy?" Park asked. "Say over the Internet?"

Gus shook his head. "The Internet? She barely uses it. Once in a while she sends an e-mail to the grandchildren. I can't imagine she'd order drugs over the Internet. No."

Special Agent Williams took over. "Perhaps she had a supplier here in town? Someone with a boat?"

Gus's great white eyebrows shot up. "You're suggesting my wife had a drug dealer? It was arthritis medication."

"Was she taking a painkiller?" I asked.

"A non-steroidal anti-inflammatory." Dr. Park cleared his throat. "But it was a powerful medication not sold in the U.S. and not yet approved by the FDA."

"But that's not why it hurt her?" Gus was clearly bewildered.

"Correct," Dr. Park answered. "It wasn't the active medicine in the capsules that caused her to become unresponsive. It was a tainted filler material that was added."

"Now that you know what caused her condition, will that change her treatment?" I asked.

Park looked away from me. "I'm sorry, no. There's nothing to do but wait.'

Special Agent Williams said, "Mr. Farnham, we'd like to search your house for other tainted medications and any clues as to how Mrs. Farnham obtained the arthritis drugs."

"Search my house?"

"It's urgent," Binder said gently, but forcefully. "We have to find out as much as we can, in case there are any more tainted drugs out there. We don't want anyone else to get hurt."

Gus saw their logic. "Give me a minute to say good night to my wife."

Dr. Park left the room with Gus. Williams and Crisp bolted to the hallway to make calls on their cell phones. Binder stayed with me. "You okay?"

"I'm shocked. Is that why all those extra people are here—the DEA, Customs—because of the bad drugs?"

Binder looked through the glass wall at Williams

and Crisp pacing in the hall outside, cell phones to their ears. "No. They're not here because of Mrs. Gus or even because of a possible epidemic of tainted drugs. We didn't know about this until today. They're here because David Thwing was one of the largest smugglers of oxycodone in Maine. They've been on his trail for nine months."

We sat in the conference room while I absorbed what Binder had said. My mind was reeling. Mrs. Gus had been poisoned. She'd bought her arthritis medication from some place, not a pharmacy. Medication she didn't have a prescription for that wasn't even sold in the U.S.

And David Thwing was an international smuggler of a highly addictive prescription painkiller. It cast a whole new light on what might have happened on that boat. Did this mean Peter Murray was involved in drug smuggling? Go-along, get-along Peter, who seemed like he was barely capable of planning his kid's birthday party, much less a drug-running franchise?

If you had asked me before that night, who, out of all the people I knew, would have been the least likely to cross paths with a drug smuggler, I might have said Mrs. Gus. It didn't make any sense. Was there some major trade in smuggling anti-inflammatory drugs for little old ladies? I couldn't imagine. And how was it all related to David Thwing and the oxycodone?

One happy thought did shine through in all this. "If Thwing was a drug smuggler and the feds have been after him for nine months, that pretty much lets anyone in Busman's Harbor out of it, right? He was probably killed by a supplier or a rival."

Binder shook his head. "We still have no idea what happened on that boat or why. Nobody is off the hook. Your brother-in-law is still very much in their sights. Can't you persuade him to tell us where he was?"

"If you believe I can, you don't know as much about Sonny and me as you think you do." The essence of my relationship with my brother-in-law was that neither of us could tell the other a damn thing.

I couldn't comprehend any of it. I didn't know anything about drug smuggling. But I suspected—in fact, had suspected for a long time—I knew someone who did. The idea of it freaked me out, but it was finally time to have the conversation I'd put off way too long.

Chapter 22

I called Chris as soon as I got in my car. I managed to get one word out, "Babe?"

"What's wrong?" he asked. "You sound shaky. Where are you?"

"I'm in the parking lot at the hospital. I was with Gus. A lot has happened. I'll explain when I get to the cabin."

His voice morphed from concerned to alarmed. "Is Mrs. Gus okay?"

"She's the same."

"All right. Come along. You're sure you're okay to drive? I could come get you."

I nodded, then realized he couldn't see me and said, "I'm fine."

When I walked through the door, Chris sat in the comfy chair in front of the fireplace, listening to the Red Sox. He jumped up, turned off the game, crossed to the kitchen, and took me in his arms. I held my face against his hard chest. I loved that place, took such comfort from it. I was terrified of where this conversation was going to take us.

Chris spoke first. "What's wrong?"

"Binder, a DEA agent, and a Maine Drug Task Force guy were at the hospital. They said what happened to Mrs. Gus was because of tainted medication." Chris put a hand on each of my shoulders and stepped back so he could see my face. I kept talking. "She didn't have a prescription for her medication. It isn't even approved in the U.S." My eyes teared up. I could barely get the words out. "The DEA agent asked if she maybe had a drug supplier here in town. Someone with a boat." I worked to keep the quiver out of my voice.

Chris didn't say anything.

"Do you know anything about this?" I asked quietly. When he didn't respond, I said more forcefully, "We have to talk about it."

"No. We don't. We have a pact about last summer. We both agreed to move on." His voice had a sharp edge.

"It's not working."

That did it. "It would if you'd stop talking about it!" he yelled.

"It's not working for me." We never talked about it, but it never went away. "There's more. Binder told me David Thwing was a major smuggler of oxycodone."

Chris's hands dropped off my shoulders, and he took another step back, doubling the distance between us. "Are you asking if I smuggled oxycodone? Is that what you think of me? Look around you,

Julia." He swept his arm, taking in the half-finished house. "If I'm a drug smuggler, *where did all the money go?*"

"Well, maybe not a very good one."

He didn't laugh. The tension didn't break. We stood, breathing heavily, a few feet apart. If there'd been even one room with a door on it anywhere in the cabin, I would've gone there and slammed it behind me. But the only option was the first-floor powder room, and I wasn't going to sit in there. I grabbed my keys and my tote bag. "Call me when you're mature enough to discuss this." I stomped toward the kitchen door.

"Call me when you're mature enough to let it go!" he shouted back, right before I slammed it.

I drove down the peninsula to Mom's house way too fast. My stomach roiled and tears cascaded down my face. I parked the Caprice next to Mom's Mercedes in the garage and took a few minutes to pull myself together. I was furious and scared, hurt and sad.

When I got to Mom's house, the lights were out, but there was a clean dish, glass, and silverware in the dish rack, so I knew she was home. My note explaining about Le Roi was still on the kitchen table, but unfolded and obviously read.

I crept up the back stairs and lingered in the hallway outside her room. The light was off, early for her, but when I pressed my ear to the door I could hear her even, slow breathing. One less thing to worry about.

I moved down the hall, entered my childhood bedroom, and threw myself on the bed. I'd slept in that room all spring and summer, but the twin bed and rose-covered wallpaper still made me feel like a child.

"What a total mess," I said out loud. Over the course of our relationship, Chris and I had had disagreements. We'd had miscommunications, too, more than our share. But we'd never had a fight like this one. Up to now, one of us had always backed away or given in, accepted a "compromise." I'd accepted the compromise that I wouldn't ask Chris where he'd disappeared to during his absences over the summer, and he wouldn't do whatever it was anymore. I could no longer live with my choice.

"*Brr-rup.*" Le Roi landed heavily on the bed next to me, purring loudly. He always knew when the humans around him needed comforting. He kneaded my rib cage with his immense paws, still vocalizing. I got up and found a pair of pajama bottoms and a T-shirt in a dresser drawer. Le Roi, still on the bed, regarded me as I changed.

"Don't worry," I told him. "I'll find us a place to live." When I returned from the bathroom, he hadn't moved. Evidently, his plan was to spend the night with me in the twin bed. "Shove over," I said, getting under the covers.

I stared at the familiar ceiling, trying to work out what I'd learned.

David Thwing was a major drug dealer. Though I never would have guessed, it made sense. My own experience had taught me that even in the age of ubiquitous credit cards, an eating establishment generated enough cash to provide efficient money laundering. His locations and cuisine provided excellent excuses for meeting boats and unloading goods.

Perhaps his desire to compete with the Snowden Family Clambake had nothing to do with a moneymaking "dining experience," and everything to do with an excuse to own a remote island or piece of shoreline with a deepwater dock. It both cheered me and depressed me to think David Thwing might not have made a study of our clambake business and identified a boundless business opportunity.

And what about Genevieve? Did she know about Thwing's real business? If my trip to Round Pond had proved anything, it was that she was an ambitious and ruthless businessperson. Could she really be unaware of the source of her partner's seemingly unlimited funds? Was she in it herself, or simply the beneficiary of Thwing's illegal and predatory trade? If she was in it, that would explain Sergeant Flynn's keen interest in her whereabouts. Why he kept her so close.

Were Mrs. Gus's troubles a coincidence of timing, or related? Try as I might, I couldn't connect the wholesale import of oxycodone with the fulfillment of an elderly woman's prescription. And if Peter Murray and David Thwing had gone out to pick up

Mrs. Gus's drugs, how had the pills wound up in her house on Tuesday morning? Neither Thwing nor Peter had made it home.

The more I thought, the more confused I became. I knew only two things. Someone had made sure my brother-in-law hadn't gone out on the *El Ay*. Whoever it was didn't care how cruel they had to be to achieve their goal. The other was Sonny was lying, still, about where he'd been and what he'd been doing the day of Thwing's murder, and the police knew it, too.

I rolled over. Le Roi was sacked out beside me. I reached over him and set my alarm for 6:00 AM. If Sonny wouldn't tell the police where he'd been, I'd have to force it out of him myself.

Chapter 23

When my alarm went off, my eyes flew open, adrenaline surging through my body. *6:00 AM? What the—? Oh, yeah, Sonny.* For my plan to work, I had to be on the *Abby* before he got there. I dressed warmly and hurried out of the house.

A line of sunlight appeared on the horizon as I jogged to the marina and climbed aboard the Ramseys' boat. The *Abby* was large, a forty-foot fiberglass body with an inboard diesel engine, embodying Bard's status as a highliner. High rails encircled its bow, offering a little protection to the crew from rough seas. The side rails sloped downward as they embraced the wider stern to make hauling traps up onto them easier. There was an open shelter housing the helm, where all the electronics hung from the ceiling or sat on the bulkhead—Fathometer, depth sounder, LORAN navigational locator, GPS, and a VHF marine radio. The roof of the shelter supported the antennas for the equipment. It was

not your grandfather's little wooden lobster boat.
Or at least it wasn't mine.

Below deck, there was a small cabin, intended as
a place to sleep on overnight fishing trips, but used
by the Ramseys for storage. I wasn't counting on
Sonny not discovering me for long—just long
enough. I squeezed into the jam-packed cabin to
wait. The harbor was deadly quiet, though I knew
it wouldn't be for long.

It was dark in the cabin, but soon I heard the
good-natured shouts of the lobstermen and sternmen preparing to go out. Radios crackled and
diesel engines revved. Boats leaving the marina
created a wake that slapped the *Abby*'s stern.

Then silence. Just when I'd begun to fear Sonny
wasn't coming, there was a thunk and a grunt on
the dock, followed by heavy footfalls I would have
recognized anywhere as Sonny's. I listened for a
second set of footsteps, indicating Kyle was aboard,
but none came. He must again be "under the
weather." Sonny was going out alone. Exactly what
I wanted.

With all the trouble in the harbor, I was afraid
he'd take time to search the boat, but he seemed
more intent on getting out to sea quickly. I heard
and felt the pulse of the motor, followed by the
rustling of the lines. The *Abby* moved away from
the dock.

I thought we might stop at the lobster pound to
pick up fuel and bait. Those necessities were put
"on account" and later deducted from the value
of the catch. But we kept chugging along, no stops.

Sonny opened up the engine, pushing the *Abby* swiftly through the water of the outer harbor toward its mouth. I wasn't sure where Bard set his traps. A highliner like Bard would know where the good bottom was, strewn with the medium-sized rocks called cobble that offered lobsters plenty of comfortable crevices for their homes.

The engine was loud, my position in the crowded cabin uncomfortable. As we came out of the harbor into the North Atlantic, I felt the chop increase. When we'd gone farther than I expected, Sonny throttled down the engine. I hadn't thought nearly enough about how I'd let him know I was aboard. The last thing I wanted was to startle him. He might react defensively before he realized who I was, punching me in the face or throwing me over the side. I crept to the cabin door and watched him lumber to the back of the boat to get the gaff he'd use to pull his dad's orange and bright blue buoys out of the water. In a moment, he'd turn and see me.

I stepped out from the cabin. "Sonny!" I called loudly so he could hear me over the idling engine.

He dropped the gaff and stepped backward. For a moment I thought he'd go head-over-heels over the low stern wall.

"Julia!" he sputtered. "What the hell?"

"I'm sorry." I stood on the deck, feet planted wide, getting my sea legs. "I wanted to see where you went." I scanned the horizon. We were well out to sea, but not so far I couldn't see the mouth of a harbor in the background, surrounded by a little village. "Which is where? Sonny, isn't that—?"

"Coldport."

"What're you doing here?" I tried to sound calm, but my high-pitched voice betrayed me.

"It's not what you think. If what you think is that I came out here to vandalize some Coldport Islander's traps." With Sonny and me, arguments usually accelerated from zero to one hundred miles an hour in seconds, but his tone was even. He didn't yell or react defensively, like he normally did.

"What on earth are you doing in Coldport Island waters?" Whatever it was, it couldn't be good, if it was worth lying to the police about.

Sonny stared at me for a minute while he appeared to make a decision. "See for yourself." Sonny shrugged and the suspenders on his orange oilpants rippled on his big shoulders. "You might as well help. We'll get done faster and get out of here. There's gear in the cabin."

Since he hadn't thrown me overboard or turned around to take me home, I figured helping him do whatever he'd come to do was my best course of action.

I went back below deck and found an orange oilskin jacket, oilpants, black boots and gloves. They must have been Kyle's and from when he was heavier. The jacket came down to my calves. I didn't even try the boots.

When I got back up on deck, Sonny looked at me and burst out in a hearty laugh that broke the tension. I held a droopy sleeve out to him and he rolled it up, securing it tightly with an elastic strap he pulled out of the pocket of the jacket. Then he did the other one. I pulled on the gloves.

Sonny bent over the side rail and with one fluid motion, he hooked a orange and bright blue buoy, Bard's colors, and found the line to his father's traps. He attached the line to a pulley that hung from the boat's roof on the starboard side, then started the mechanical hauler that powered the pulley. The first trap in the string of six churned to the surface. Sonny wrestled it onto the *Abby's* side rail and bent to retrieve the next one. "Don't just stand there," he ordered.

I opened the trap. It was large, four feet long, and made of bright yellow plastic-coated wire. Like all lobster traps, it consisted of two "rooms," the kitchen with the bait bag and a telescoping entrance to let the lobsters in, and the parlor, where they moved after they'd eaten, to await their fate.

With a practiced motion, Sonny picked the first of three lobsters out of the trap, measuring it with a metal gauge. Legal lobsters were between 3.25 and five inches on carapace, or from the eye socket to where the body met the tail. The first lobster was undersized. He was so close to legal, Sonny measured him on both sides.

"Sometimes the sides are different lengths, short on one side, legal on the other."

This one was no dice. Sonny dropped him tail first back into the sea to grow for a few more seasons. The second lobster was quite large, maybe eight inches. Sonny didn't bother measuring him, simply picked him up and dropped him over the side. "'Bye, old man. Go off and make some babies."

The third one was a keeper. Like most lobsters, his shell was green, the same color as the suit David Thwing had worn the day he died. Though billboards and signs all over Maine, as well as our license plates, showed bright red lobsters, they only turned that color when they were cooked. Rarely, lobsters could be blue, yellow, calico, half one color, half another, and even albino, but most were green, like this fellow.

Sonny put him in a compartment of a metal sorting tray. He handed me the pliers-like tool used to put rubber bands on the lobster's claws. I nodded gamely. It had been fifteen years since I'd done it. Like most kids in town, I'd tended a couple of traps from a skiff as a teenager, but that was my last experience.

I picked the lobster up awkwardly. The gloves made him hard to hold. Sonny wasn't wearing any, but his hands were always a mass of little cuts. I was determined to keep the gloves on.

I grasped the lobster in one hand as firmly as I could and blew on his claw to get him to close it. As I brought the bander to the claw, the *Abby* shifted, rising over a swell. I hit the claw with the tool. It detached from the lobster's body and flew into the sea.

Sonny looked up from hauling the next trap and grunted. "A cull." The lobsterman's name for a one-clawed lobster. "Band him anyway and put him in the tank."

I took the gloves off and tried again, muttering, "It's all in the wrist." By some miracle, I succeeded and dropped the lobster into the aluminum tank.

"You know what to do," Sonny said.

Unfortunately, I did. I threw the flotsam and jetsam that remained in the first trap back into the sea—seaweed, snails, small fish, even a very annoyed crab. I hoped against hope there wouldn't be an eel, because, frankly they were disgusting. Then I pulled the bait bag from the trap and prepared to refill it, the most disgusting job of all.

Lobstermen used all kinds of bait, but the most common was herring. Old, ripe, herring. I opened the bait barrel and stepped back, as if I could dodge the horrible smell. I held my breath and scooped the bait into the bag and retied it to the trap, closing it up. I moved the trap to the rail on the back of the boat, ready to be re-submerged. By then, Sonny had taken the lobsters out of the second trap and I prepared to band the legal ones.

We repeated the steps for all six traps on the line, then Sonny returned them to the water. As they thundered over the stern back into the sea, it was easy to imagine a person's foot getting caught in the line and it dragging him under the boat, just as it at first appeared David Thwing had been.

Sonny piloted us to the next line of traps and we started again. Eventually, we developed a rhythm. I pre-filled extra bait bags I found on board, while Sonny steered us along. At the next stop, he threw back two female lobsters covered with eggs after carefully notching their tails with a V symbol, so they would never be taken, not even when they were eggless. The lobstermen took good care of the fishery. They knew it was their future, and they'd seen so many other fish stocks collapse around them.

We worked on, with only a short break when Sonny shared the lunch Livvie had packed for him. I felt badly taking one of his two sandwiches. I was sure he needed the fuel, but I was light-headed from hunger. We were always in sight of Coldport Island, surely in their traditional waters, yet no one had emptied Bard's traps or messed with his buoys or gear. In all, we pulled two hundred traps, and got around a hundred and seventy-five pounds of lobster. Not a great haul, but respectable for this time of year. I was sore everywhere and my hands were a mess.

Chapter 24

At a little after one o'clock, Sonny flipped the radio on. The air was suddenly filled with the chatter of lobstermen. "Headed to the co-op," one after another said, finishing up their day.

A co-op was a lobster pound jointly owned by a group of lobstermen, usually from one harbor. It collected the catch, stored it temporarily, and sold it to the wholesalers. While Coldport Island had a co-op, Busman's Harbor's lobster pound was privately owned. Which meant the lobstermen from Coldport shared the profit from their catch and Busman's lobstermen did not.

Eventually, the radio went silent for a while. Sonny turned the *Abby* toward port. But not Busman's Harbor. Coldport.

"Where are we going?"

"We're selling the lobsters."

"In Coldport?"

"Yup."

"All of them?"

"All we got today."

"But why?"

Sonny drew his red eyebrows together, squinting at me, like he knew I could figure it out if I thought hard enough.

"That's why Bard's traps don't get bothered," I said. "Because he's cutting the Coldporters in." In return for lending his major highliner boost to their co-op's profits, they tolerated Bard lobstering in their traditional waters.

Sonny nodded. "As long as they get their piece, they keep quiet about it."

If there was a profit, all the owners of the co-op got a bonus at the end of the season. The more lobstermen, the more lobsters, the greater the profit.

"Don't the Busman's Harbor lobstermen suspect something when you never sell lobsters to the pound there?"

"Dad's got eight hundred traps in all, the legal limit. Four hundred in Coldport waters. The other four hundred are in Busman's. I haul those and take the lobsters to the Busman's pound. Dad does so much better than the other lobstermen, they don't notice. At least they haven't so far."

The puzzle pieces fell into place. "You were here the day David Thwing died," I said. "That's why you turned off the GPS and the radio. You were working Bard's traps near Coldport Island and selling at their co-op."

Sonny didn't respond, which I took as a yes.

"So being suspected of murder is better than

having everyone in Busman's Harbor know you're selling to the Coldport co-op?"

Sonny didn't say anything. But maybe, in his mind at least, it was. Lobstermen prized loyalty above all other virtues. Being a traitor might be regarded as worse than being a murderer, particularly if the victim was somebody "from away" nobody cared about anyway.

I remembered Bard at Gus's, arguing against retaliation against Coldport Island. His advice was compromised. If he were viewed as working against his own harbor for the other side, Bard would become a social pariah, as would Sonny and Kyle.

We pulled up to the dock at the Coldport co-op. There were no boats around and I was sure Sonny had picked this time of the day for that reason, though I figured everyone on the island had to know Bard's secret. But I could also believe no one in Busman's knew. There wasn't much reason for the insular, territorial lobster gangs to mix with others, and there were plenty of reasons not to, even socially. Highliners like Bard, on the other hand, did seek out equals from other harbors. They needed peers to talk to.

A sinewy man with hooded eyes, his black hair worn in a ponytail, helped us unload the lobsters. He didn't introduce himself to me, and he and Sonny skipped the hellos.

"Surprised to see you here today," the man observed. "Things are pretty tense."

"Doin' my job and keepin' my head low," Sonny responded.

"That's worked up to now. But there were cops on the island yesterday asking about you." Sonny stared at the man as he continued. "Not everybody likes it that you and your dad come and go as you please. A few of the dubs think you're catching lobsters that would be theirs if not for the arrangement with your dad."

"Let 'em prove it," Sonny said.

When we were done, the man weighed our catch. As he did, he looked over Sonny's shoulder at the harbor beyond. "What the . . . ?"

I followed his gaze to a mooring where thick, black smoke rose from a lobster boat.

"What the . . . ?" Sonny repeated the man's words.

The boat went up in a fireball. Flames shot thirty feet in the air as the wind spread the dark smoke. The guy from the co-op shouted something into his phone and then a siren wailed, calling volunteers to the fire station.

It was a new fiberglass lobster boat, a big one.

There weren't any boats moored close enough to be in immediate danger. Within five minutes, the Coldport town fire engine pulled up to the dock. Firefighters attached the hose, but the burning boat was too far away. The water from the hose fell ineffectively into the harbor.

"Can you tell whose boat is it?" Sonny asked the man.

"Ayup. It's the *Gilded Lilly*. Belongs to a fellow

named Hughie B. Hubler. Never could figure out what a dub like him was doing with a big, fancy boat."

Hughie B. Hubler. The guy from Gus's who'd said Sonny had the best motive for murdering David Thwing.

Sonny whirled to face me. "We're getting out of here."

"Sonny, wait. We saw it go up. Someone might want to talk to us."

"We're going," he insisted. I could see it was pointless to argue.

We sped away as fast as a lobster boat like the *Abby* could carry us. A Coast Guard fireboat sped by us going the other way. I held on and kept my mouth shut.

A few miles from Coldport, Sonny changed course, heading toward Westclaw Point. Now what? Surely we were headed home. But as we approached the narrows, Sonny cut the engine and grabbed his gaff again.

"Aren't we done?" I moaned. I was so tired and achy, I could barely face the idea of more lobstering.

Sonny pulled a buoy over the side. Not his dad's orange and bright blue ones, but neon green and navy. Exactly like the ones Quentin had found floating in the water the day Thwing was killed.

"Those aren't yours," I pointed out.

Sonny nodded. "They're Peter's. A few of us have been hauling his traps. You know, until they figure out what happened to him. Lorrie Ann's gonna need the money."

The traps had lobsters in them, some of them legal-sized, though not nearly as many as Bard's. Sonny and I found our rhythm again and pulled, emptied and returned ten strings of Peter's traps into the sea.

I was tremendously relieved to have discovered the truth about where Sonny had been the day Thwing was murdered. But unless Sonny came clean with the state cops and the feds, they'd continue to suspect him.

"Sonny, you have to tell Binder and Flynn what you were doing the afternoon David Thwing died," I said as we worked.

He straightened up, wiping his brow with his forearm. "Who says I do?"

"Surely being suspected of murder is more dangerous than confessing to working with a harbor gang that isn't your own."

"They'll need some evidence to arrest me for killing David Thwing, which they won't find. All they have are a few idle threats I made at town meetings, and the accusation of an hysterical woman that I was supposed to be on that boat."

He had a point. The police wouldn't come up with evidence, because he hadn't been there. And someone had made sure of it.

"Really, Sonny, who do you think telephoned you that morning?"

"Honestly, I don't know. I can't figure out why anyone would do that to me."

"You definitely didn't recognize the voice?

Could it have been someone you know, disguising his voice?"

Sonny shrugged. "It could have been. I was out of my mind."

What the caller had said was awful, but was it so awful he couldn't even recall the voice?

Sonny saw the question in my face. "It wasn't the first time," he said.

I was shocked. "It wasn't the first time you got a terrible call like that?"

Sonny shook his head. "The last time I got a call like that, it was real. Livvie lost our baby." He didn't look at me as he said this, but gazed out over the stern at the horizon.

I felt like I'd had the wind knocked out of me. "If Livvie had a miscarriage, I would know."

"It was five years ago." Sonny voice was low. I had to lean in to hear him. "Your dad was near the end of his life. We decided not to tell anyone on your side of the family. You had all you could handle emotionally."

I could see, from the pinched lines at the corners of his eyes, he was telling the truth, and there was still a lot of pain in it. I wanted to throw my arms around my bear of a brother-in-law. Poor Sonny. And poor Livvie. At a time when I'd thought my father's illness was as much as I could bear, she'd had to bear more.

I wiped a tear from the corner of my eye with my wrist. My hands reeked of fish. "Sonny, I'm glad you told me about the miscarriage, even at this late date. Back when it happened or anytime later, who else did you tell?"

Sonny gazed at the horizon. "My dad," he said. "And Peter."

So at least two people knew how deeply the information that Livvie was miscarrying would affect Sonny. Peter had no reason to make the phony phone call. He could have telephoned Sonny and simply said he didn't need him to help on the *El Ay*.

Would Bard do such an awful thing to his son? What would the motive be? Whatever it was, at the moment I wasn't feeling so positive about the Coldport-lobster-selling, possibly-phony-phone-call-making, possibly-innocent-mother-seducing Bard.

After an hour and a half of hauling Peter's traps, Sonny took a bandana out of his pocket and wiped his brow. "Had enough?"

"Plenty."

We took Peter's lobsters to sell at the Busman's Harbor lobster pound. Sonny pocketed the cash.

"Have you been taking the money to Lorrie Ann?"

"Nah. She doesn't want to see me. I give it to my dad and he takes care of it."

I flashed for a moment on the new TVs, furniture, and possibly cappuccino machines Bard was passing out. No, those were bought before Peter Murray died. Bard's extra money came from lobstering undisturbed in Coldport waters.

Chapter 25

Sonny maneuvered the *Abby* into her slip. He hosed down her deck, washing away the bits of old bait and non-lobster sea animals that had come up in the traps. I wiggled out of the enormous oilpants.

"I came to help." Kyle stood on the dock, in better shape than he'd been in the day before when I'd seen him at Bard's house, but obviously high. It was painful for me to see him that way. I could only imagine what it did to Sonny and Bard.

"When I needed your help was this morning, when you were supposed to haul traps with me," Sonny said without looking up.

"Sorry," Kyle mumbled.

"Sorry doesn't cut it." Sonny turned his back on his brother and continued washing down the deck.

Kyle, crestfallen, didn't attempt to defend himself. He jumped aboard and picked up a mop. They'd spent years on this boat, knew every inch of it, and fell back into their routine like a choreographed team.

"If you don't mind, I'll be going." Neither brother acknowledged me, though I wasn't sure they'd heard me over the noise of the hose. As I climbed to the dock, I spotted two men in uniform headed toward me, Jamie and his partner, Officer Howland.

I stayed put. I couldn't have passed them on the narrow wooden walkway, anyway. When they got to the *Abby*, they stopped. Jamie glanced at me, then turned toward the boat, clearing his throat loudly.

"Sonny," he said, then corrected himself. "Mr. Ramsey. We need you to come with us to police headquarters, now."

Sonny shut off the hose and stared at Jamie. "What if I don't want to?"

"Then we're to place you under arrest."

"For what?" Sonny demanded

"For arson," Jamie said. "Destruction of the vessel *Gilded Lilly*."

What? "I was with Sonny all day!" I shouted. "Standing right next to him when that boat went up. He didn't do anything. Besides, you couldn't possibly have completed an arson investigation in such a short time. This is ridiculous."

Jamie grimaced. He'd known Sonny for years, ever since Livvie had brought him into all our lives. Officer Howland didn't look any more comfortable. He and Sonny were friends. I wondered what jurisdictional kink, in a police station full of cops from so many agencies, had resulted in having local officers do this job.

"We have a witness who places Mr. Ramsey on

board the *Gilded Lilly* moments before the fire," Jamie told me. "Our witness took photos with his phone of the *Abby* speeding out of Coldport Harbor while the *Lilly* was still on fire."

"Why on earth would I set fire to that boat?" Sonny thundered.

"Lots of things happen during a lobster war," Jamie answered.

"This is bogus," I said. "If you look at the phone photos, you'll see I was on the *Abby*, too. Ask the guy at the co-op in Coldport. We were with him when the fire broke out."

"Julia!" Sonny glared at me.

Was he still determined to keep his crazy secret? "Oh, Sonny, give it up. You're not continuing this charade about Coldport now. You're about to be arrested."

"Shut up, Julia. If you want to help," Sonny said evenly, "call my wife. And have her call a lawyer."

Sonny climbed onto the dock and asked Jamie and Howland, "Are you going to cuff me?"

"No need," Jamie answered. "You're coming in voluntarily."

The cops led Sonny off the dock to their cruiser. I used my cell to give my shocked sister Sonny's message. Before I left the dock, I looked around for Kyle. During the commotion, he'd faded away.

When I arrived at the police station, Sonny was nowhere in sight. I waited, pacing and jiggling, until Jamie walked by.

"You know this stinks," I hissed at him. He raised and lowered his shoulders in that way that said, *Nothing I can do about it.*

I charged into the multipurpose room and found Lieutenant Binder. He was deep in conversation with Sergeant Crisp, the Maine Drug Task Force guy I'd met the night before.

"I need to speak to you. Right now," I said to Binder.

He nodded to Crisp and followed me into the corridor.

"Sonny's being arrested," I said.

"I know," Binder responded.

"It's completely made-up. He wasn't near that boat. I was with him the whole day. Why is this so-called witness on Coldport Island more believable than me? What's his name, anyway?"

"Keep your voice down," Binder commanded. He looked around to make sure we were alone. In a low voice, he said, "The gentleman's name is Hughie B. Hubler."

"That guy has it in for Sonny." My voice rose again. "He was in Gus's yesterday mouthing off about how Sonny had the best motive for killing Thwing."

"Shhh!" Binder checked again to make sure there was no one nearby. "I'm sure your brother-in-law will be released soon. I doubt he'll even be charged. The fire's an excuse to bring him in and question him about the murder."

"But I know where Sonny was Monday after-noon. He was lobstering in Coldport waters on the

Abby. He sold his haul at the Coldport co-op. You can check it out." Sonny might still have qualms about telling people where he'd been, but I didn't.

"That's great, Julia, but eyewitnesses have told us the *Abby* went out twice on Monday. We can't find anyone to confirm the time she first departed, but she returned around noon and left again not long after. We believe Thwing was killed before noon. We also believe it was on that first trip back to the marina that Sonny brought in the drugs."

"What drugs?" I demanded. *How could this get any worse?*

Binder put a hand on my arm. "Julia, we believe Peter Murray was responsible for bringing in the tainted drugs that hurt Mrs. Gus. And we know Sonny was Peter's partner in the drug-smuggling operation."

"What!" Livvie stood three feet away with Cuthie Cuthbertson, attorney-at-law.

I'd found an answer to my own question. It could indeed get worse. It just had.

Chapter 26

Even with everything else that was happening, it was the first time I'd seen my sister since Sonny's revelation that afternoon about her miscarriage. I threw my arms around her and hugged her close.

"Okay, okay." Livvie wriggled free, annoyed with the hug like Page would have been. She had more immediate problems to deal with. "Tell me what's going on." While I'd hugged her, Binder had slipped away.

"Yes, what do you know?" Cuthie Cuthbertson asked. He was short and round, with a head full of brown hair that had been coated in "product" that smelled like Vaseline. Despite his girth, his suit was too big for him. Light blue and polyester, it hung on him like pajamas. Appearances to the contrary, Cuthie was a brilliant criminal lawyer. He'd represented Chris when he'd been accused of a murder he hadn't committed, as well as an innocent employee of ours in the summer.

I told them everything that had happened, including what Binder had just told me. While I talked, Livvie went pale, then pink, then bright red. She was clearly furious. At Sonny? The cops? I suspected both. She didn't ask why I'd been on the *Abby*. She was concentrating too hard on my story, which included an alibi for her husband on the arson charge, at a minimum.

"I'll put a stop to this," Cuthbertson said when I finished. He walked briskly down the hallway.

"I'm staying here." Livvie's voice was clipped. "Can you pick up Page at swim team?"

"Of course. Whatever you need."

When I pulled up at the Y, Page was as delighted to see me, as I was to see her, even given the circumstances. I'd seen her every day all summer on Morrow Island, but between her busy school schedule and my move to the island, it had been close to two weeks since we'd had any alone time.

"Can we get pizza?" she asked before she settled into the car. "Please?"

"We'll see. We're going to Grandma's."

She nodded enthusiastically. "Where's my mom?"

"She's tied up right now." Let Livvie and Sonny explain as much to Page as they wanted. "She's been at the Murrays' all day," I added.

"Oh." Not much got by Page. "PeeWee hasn't been in school since, you know."

"Is he a friend of yours?"

Page sniffed like an English lord, affronted by

the suggestion. "No, silly. He's a kindergartner!" Then she burst into giggles at her ridiculous aunt.

When we pulled into the garage, Mom's car was back. She was in the kitchen, fussing with the cappuccino machine.

"Le Roi!" Page had spent the summer with her beloved cat, and true to form, he ran to her and let her manhandle him in all sorts of undignified ways.

"Page is staying with us until Livvie and Sonny are free," I said to Mom in a tone that didn't invite questions.

Mom nodded. She understood we weren't discussing the reason Sonny and Livvie were tied up in front of Page. Besides, nothing could get in the way of her delight at seeing her granddaughter. She threw her arms around Page and Le Roi and kissed the top of Page's head.

Page squirmed away. At nine, she could hug the cat, but she was getting too big for grandmotherly cuddles. She grabbed her backpack and headed through the swinging door to the dining room to start on her homework. She'd spent so many afternoons at Mom's house during Dad's illness and in the years since his death, even given the fall's new routines, she fell immediately into her old groove.

"Would you like a cappuccino?" Mom had the instruction book propped open on the counter. She was dressed in nice slacks and wore makeup, which was unusual and deeply suspicious. I glanced at her left hand and was relieved to see she still wore her wedding ring.

"No, thank you. I'll have tea." I put the kettle on, not so subtly telegraphing *Isn't this more your speed?* "What's up with that thing, anyway?" I asked when I couldn't stand it any longer, indicating the new machine.

"It's a treat for me," Mom said. "Do you have a problem with that?"

"Of course not." I meant it. Mom deserved the best of everything. But she'd never been one to indulge herself. So who was indulging her? That was the question that plagued me.

She finally got her cup of espresso and frothed milk made. I had to admit, it smelled kind of great. Page wandered into the kitchen looking for a snack. I gave her one of Livvie's whoopie pies and took one for myself, suddenly aware I'd eaten nothing all day except the sandwich Sonny had given me on the *Abby*.

From beyond the kitchen's swinging door, I heard the sound of the front door opening and closing.

"What were you thinking?" Livvie yelled.

"I told you to stay out of it!" Sonny commanded. They were in the front hall, on the other side of the kitchen door, out of our sight.

The skin over Page's pretty nose pinched. She sat heavily next to my mother and took her hand, desiring the physical contact she'd so recently brushed away.

"How can I stay out of it?" Livvie demanded. "I'm in it. What if they arrest you for real next time? That will affect Page, me, and the new baby. Why are you still lying? To them? To me?"

"They're not going to arrest me." Sonny shouted. "If they could've, they would've."

Page was pale and trembling. I was a little queasy myself. Livvie and Sonny didn't fight, at least not like this. They bickered, sure. And Sonny was a yeller, though not at Livvie. As a couple, they always had each other's backs.

Now they faced an unimaginable chasm. If Sonny truly was a partner with Peter Murray in a drug-running operation, not only had he taken a huge risk and broken the law, he'd lied to Livvie about it. I knew my sister well enough to know that was what hurt the most. Could she forgive him? Would she?

Mom asked Page quietly if she wanted to creep up the back stairs and watch the TV in her sitting room. Page shook her head, craving the comfort of family.

Sonny's voice dropped. "Livvie, you have to trust me," he pleaded.

"Trust you? How can I trust you when you didn't even tell *me* the truth?"

There was a lot more shouting. I tried not to listen. Page and I played tic-tac-toe on a napkin, both of us desperate for a diversion.

"I'm outta here!" Sonny finally yelled. "Call me when you've calmed down."

"I'll calm down when you stop lying to me," Livvie shouted back.

The front door slammed and I heard the cough of an ignition catching, a sound I'd recognize anywhere as Livvie's ancient minivan. The rattling engine disappeared down the drive, followed by

Livvie's soft footsteps and barely muffled sobs as she headed upstairs.

Page and I both stood to go to her. My mother put a hand on each of our arms. "Give her some time." She pulled a deck of cards out of the junk drawer and shuffled them, dealing us hands for Old Maid. Page played her cards stoically. My chatty niece had gone silent.

Chapter 27

Twenty minutes after Sonny left, the house phone rang, its shrill sound shocking in the silence.

"Oh, Lord, who is that?" Mom asked.

I picked it up, worried about cops or even reporters, but afraid to leave it if it was news from or about Sonny.

"Julia, it's Vee," the grandmotherly voice said. "Genevieve has offered to cook us dinner tonight, as a thank you. Fee and I thought your family might like to join us."

I glanced at the clock. 7:30. At the mention of food, my stomach rumbled, in spite of the whoopie pie. I didn't want to leave the house, but I knew we needed to eat, or at least feed Page, and the warm familiarity and happy memories of the Snuggles Inn seemed like just the place.

"Mom, it's Vee, inviting us for dinner."

Mom, looking strained, nonetheless nodded her assent.

I told Vee yes and went upstairs to check on

Livvie. I found her asleep in the guest bedroom. She lay on her side. Her belly was, if anything, more pronounced than it had been a day ago.

I showered the saltwater off and slipped into a pair of black slacks from my New York life that were still in the closet. I threw a clean white blouse over them and headed down the back stairs.

Mom, Page, and I crossed the street to the Snuggles, bearing a bottle of wine of unknown label and origin Mom had dug out of her pantry. It was the best we could do in a pinch. Fee saw us coming and opened the front door. As I stepped into the Snuggles' familiar Victorian foyer, the smells emanating from the kitchen were a heavenly concoction of brine, wine, and garlic, and my stomach growled in response. I hoped no one else had heard it. I kissed each of the Snugg sisters on a powdery cheek.

"Genevieve's made a delicious hot lobster dip for us," Fee said. "It's in the parlor."

Page beelined to the coffee table in the front room and inhaled two crackers with dip. She was normally a polite kid, especially around the Misses Snugg. She must have been starving. It was eight o'clock. She was a growing girl who'd been swimming all afternoon.

"I'll take this to the kitchen." I held up the wine bottle.

Genevieve stood at the stove, her back to me. The blunt cut of her dark hair grazed the collar of her tailored white shirt. She was in her familiar black, this time well-cut slacks and a vest. The string of one of Vee's frilly aprons cut across her hips and was tied at her tailbone.

"Thanks for inviting us," I said, offering the wine.

She took it from my hands, glancing at the label. "Oh, good. Perfect for cooking." She put the wine on the countertop next to the stove. "The Snugg sisters thought your family could do with a nice meal. I just hope it isn't awkward."

Because my brother-in-law was suspected of involvement in the murder of her business partner?

I didn't respond directly. Instead, I asked, "What are you making?" I looked into the simmering pot.

"One of my mussels dishes. For the first course."

"Can I help?"

She pointed to Vee's aprons hanging from a peg at the entrance to the back stairs. She set me chopping apples and pears for what she called her autumn salad. She diced and chopped, too. She was five times faster than me, and cut up an onion, celery, several tomatoes and a pepper for the mussels in the time it took me to finish the fruit. In our matching black and white outfits, we looked like caterers.

"It must have been so difficult for you when you heard about . . ." I hesitated, unsure about whether to use the name "David" or "Mr. Thwing." I finally went with, "the death of your partner."

Genevieve put water on to boil for pasta. "Shrimp and lobster scampi for the main dish," she explained, showing how to chop fennel for it. She didn't reply to what I'd said.

"Where were you, when you heard?" I tried again.

This time Genevieve looked up from her cooking. "Just ask me whatever it is you're trying to ask," she said levelly.

"I went up to Round Pond to see the Harrises," I told her.

She stopped what she was doing and looked down at the countertop. "I see. I'm sure they didn't have anything good to say about me."

"Mil didn't." Looking back over the conversation, Mil hadn't said anything much beyond *hmpft*. "I think Bob takes a more nuanced view."

"It's one of the greatest regrets of my life. I don't know what to say, except I was seventeen and a stranger arrived from out of town and dangled in front me everything I had ever wanted in my life. I was too young, too eager. I jumped."

"When did you begin to suspect the stranger's capital came from drug smuggling?" I gave up all pretense of chopping and focused completely on her.

"Just now. I found out yesterday." Her great eyes opened wide. "You believe me, don't you? It's important you do."

I didn't. She'd been in business with David Thwing for seven years and never realized she was fronting a massive drug smuggling operation? My interview with the Harrises proved she wasn't the naive thing she pretended to be.

I was saved from responding by the sound of the doorbell, followed by excited chatter in the front hall. Genevieve swept through the swinging door ahead of me. "You're here!" she cried.

Lieutenant Binder and Sergeant Flynn stood in the doorway. Binder's eyes widened when he spotted me, and then he recovered and extended a hand forward, offering another bottle of white wine.

So that was what Genevieve meant when she said she hoped it wouldn't be awkward.

Everyone talked at once. Then, the hellos out of the way, for a telling moment, no one said anything at all. Binder and Flynn had no more been expecting us than we had been expecting them.

My mother's uncompromising manners came to the rescue. "Lieutenant, Sergeant," she advanced on them, hand extended, voice warm. "How nice to see you." Her breeding didn't allow for awkward pauses, even when dealing with the people who had just threatened to arrest her son-in-law.

"Jerry, please. We're off duty."

"Tom," Flynn said, barely moving his lips.

Vee sailed in behind her and invited everyone into the dining room.

The survivability of the dinner was built on four foundations: my mother's and the Snugg sisters' impeccable upbringings, Binder and Flynn's professionalism, the presence of a nine-year-old, which ensured the conversation couldn't veer off course, and Genevieve's incredible food.

I left Vee's apron on and kept my role as kitchen helper. Genevieve and I brought out the first course, mussels served in the sisters' fine china soup bowls. The aroma of tomato, onions, and thyme wafted through the room. I dug in.

The flavor was amazing. There was sausage,

which I recognized as chorizo, that put off a nice heat that contrasted with the brininess of the mussels. The bite of mustard came through, along with smokiness from the chorizo and smoked paprika.

The table fell silent, and not from the awkwardness of the evening. We were too immersed in the food to converse.

Page was seated next to me. I was afraid she might balk at the mussels, but she was a true Maine kid, raised on everything from the sea. She finished her bowl and started to ask for more. I put my hand gently on her arm and whispered, "There's lots more food coming." Her eyes grew wide.

When the mussels were gone, Flynn jumped up to help Genevieve and me clear the table. He was like an eager puppy around her, over-piling the delicate dishes and then nearly dropping them on his way through the kitchen door.

Next came the salad I'd helped with. The pears and apples were served over greens, along with dried cranberries, pine nuts, and crumbled Gorgonzola. In the dressing, I tasted sweet and citrus, thyme and rosemary. I could have made a meal of the salad alone.

Genevieve didn't serve our wine or Binder's. She paired each course with a wine she'd purchased specifically for it. For the salad, it was a Chilean chardonnay, crisp and not at all oaky.

As she poured, I watched Tom Flynn watching her. My attempt to make her a suspect had been silly and futile. For one thing, the cops wouldn't be here, eating and drinking, if she was. For another, Flynn couldn't tear his eyes off her. I was sure he was smitten.

The wine helped, and somehow we stumbled through the salad with talk about the weather, and the Red Sox post-season performance, always reliable Maine topics. My mother enumerated the fall nature walks in and around the harbor as if Binder and Flynn were in town on a sightseeing trip.

After the salad, Flynn and I helped clear again. In the kitchen, I watched in wonder as Genevieve poured the pasta into a big bowl and assembled the shrimp and lobster scampi in a matter of minutes.

During the main course, my mother asked Binder about his boys. "First and third grade," he told us. "Luckily, they both love their teachers this year."

"And tell us about your wife?" Vee asked. Thank goodness, because I was dying to know in that way you do when you like someone and want to know about his or her spouse.

"Name's Hailey. She's state police, too. Motorcycle officer."

I never would have guessed.

From Flynn, the ladies extracted the information he was from Providence, as I'd recognized from his accent. His brother was a city cop, as was his dad, who would retire as a captain in the spring.

"Why did you leave Rhode Island?" It was the

first question Genevieve had asked of anyone all night.

He stared into his plate and mumbled something about it being a small state.

"I won't be able to help out at Gus's tomorrow," I told Fee and Vee, changing the subject to let poor Flynn off the hook. "I have something I need to do."

"Oh dear," Fee said. "We hoped you and Chris would take care of the restaurant in the morning. We promised Gus we'd sit with Mrs. Gus so he could look at long-term care facilities. I don't want to let him down."

"I'm not sure about Chris." I wasn't sure about anything related to Chris. I hadn't seen or heard from him in twenty-four hours.

"I'll do it," Genevieve volunteered. "It would do me good. I'm used to a busy restaurant."

The Snugg sisters and I looked at one another. There was no question Genevieve was capable. Fee nodded. "It's settled. Vee and I will come over in the morning and make sure you're set up."

The scampi was a triumph. The lobster added a richness beyond the shrimp's, and the fennel gave it a delightful crunch.

By the time we were done, Page was slumped over the table, eyes closing. Flynn jackrabbited out of his chair to help clear, and I started to make our excuses for leaving. But then Fee and Vee brought out coffee and Vee's homemade apple pie, and Page found her second wind. Vee's pies, like all her baking, were terrific, though good apple pie depended on good apples no matter who was cooking. These were perfect, firm, not mushy, and tart. Vee's pies had a light, flaky crust, while her friend Mrs. Gus's crusts were sturdy and sweet, made from a recipe she'd vowed to take to her grave. I wondered if I'd ever eat a piece of Mrs. Gus's pie again.

Page ate half of her dessert, then closed her eyes, her forehead moving toward the tablecloth. I shook her awake gently. She was far too big to carry, so I pulled her up to stand as Mom said our good-byes.

At Mom's house, I helped Page upstairs, found a pair of not-too-too small pajamas in a bureau drawer and tucked her into her pink princess bed after making her brush her teeth. Le Roi, with his unerring sense about which human in the house most needed comforting, ran into her room and jumped on the bed. After he settled himself at her side, I turned off the light and was closing the door when she called me.

"Aunt Julia?"

"What, honey?"

"I know my dad's in trouble. How bad is it?"

I sat on the side of her bed. "I don't know."

"That's okay," she reassured me, turning on her side and snuggling into the covers. "Everything's going to be fine. Because my dad would never, ever do anything wrong."

Oh Page, I thought, as she drifted off, *I wish I had your certainty.*

Chapter 28

I said good night to Mom, whose own eyes were puffy with fatigue, and headed to my bed. The combination of the wine, the rich food, and the drama of the day—not to mention my 6:00 AM rising and hauling lobster traps—had taken its toll.

After I settled into bed, I heard noises coming from the bathroom. Thinking Page might be having trouble sleeping, I crept into the hallway. The toilet flushed, water ran, and Livvie stepped out, turning off the light as she did. She'd removed the jeans, sweater, and socks she'd slept in earlier. She stood in a T-shirt and underpants, looking ridiculously young, like the girl who'd been pregnant with Page a decade before.

Her eyes were still swollen from crying. I put my arms around her and hugged tight. She followed me to my room and sat on the end of my bed. The scene felt nostalgic, a call back to all the holidays and spring breaks during the years when I'd been away at prep school or college and Livvie had been home, raising hell and driving my parents crazy. Both accomplished in the company of Sonny Ramsey, the love of her life.

"Not sleeping at Chris's tonight?" she asked.

"Big fight," I explained, rolling my eyes.

"What a couple of sad cases the Snowden sisters are. What was your fight about?"

I propped my pillow against my headboard and leaned back. "The usual."

"The usual, you can't commit, or the usual, he won't fill in the blanks of his life?"

A couple of sad cases, indeed. "The latter."

"Oh."

"And you?" I asked.

"Don't pretend you didn't hear the whole fight. The funny thing is, I'm not even angry that he may be, somehow, mixed up in whatever happened aboard the *El Ay*. Or even in some crazy business with Peter. I'm furious because he lied to me. He's still lying to me. And lying to the cops."

"What did he tell you?"

"He admitted he was in Coldport the afternoon of the murder."

"Hauling Bard's traps in Coldport waters and selling the lobsters at Coldport's co-op," I confirmed.

"At least you can stop wondering where Bard got the money for the TV and couch he gave us." Livvie scooted up beside me to rest her back against the headboard, too. "Sonny hasn't admitted he and Peter were smuggling drugs, if that's even true. I find it so hard to believe, because Kyle has a problem—"

"I know about Kyle. I'm sorry. I'm sure it's hard for Sonny."

Livvie frowned. "Kyle sits up in his room at Bard's all day. He's silent. You don't even know he's there, until he comes downstairs and its obvious he's heard every word you've said." She was quiet for a long moment. "But that's one of the reasons I find it so hard to believe Sonny would smuggle drugs. His family has been hurt by them."

If anything, Kyle's problem made it more likely Sonny would want to kill Thwing, whom he already hated. Perhaps Sonny sensed, or even knew, there was something sinister about Thwing. I'd always felt his hatred of Thwing seemed personal.

Kyle's addiction wasn't the only thing my sister had kept from me. Sonny's story about her earlier miscarriage had crushed me. For what she'd been through, yes, but also that she'd been so alone. Not for the first time, I wished I'd been home more when my father was dying.

Livvie and I sat silently for a minute. "So what do you think is going on with Mom?" I asked.

She rolled her eyes. "This again."

"She's never here. There's a brand-new chrome cappuccino machine sitting in her kitchen and she came home today wearing makeup. I think she's seeing a man."

Livvie laughed. "Listen to you, Nancy Drew." It was wonderful to hear her laugh.

"I think it's Bard."

"Don't be absurd." Livvie laughed again. At least I was good at amusing my distraught sister.

"Think about it. His house has all those feminine touches nowadays. Kyle says he has a girlfriend. And he's giving people gifts. You got a TV and a couch. Would the mother you grew up with buy herself an expensive cappuccino machine?"

"No. Not my mother," Livvie agreed. "But would it be so terrible if Mom were going out with someone?" She paused, but not long enough for me to answer. "Would it be so terrible if it were Bard?"

"You're kidding."

"No, really. Bard's not so bad. He's been in AA now for two years, doing really well. He's a good man. A good dad. Something terrible happened to him. He lost his wife, suddenly, when his boys were young. He did his best."

"How do you feel about Mom dating anyone at all?" I asked.

That slowed her down. Her shoulders slumped and she got a little misty-eyed. "No one will ever replace Dad for her. Or for us. But it's been five years. She needs to move on."

Our mother's life had been stuck in neutral since Dad died. She hadn't just lost the great love of her life. Up until Dad got sick, she'd been an integral partner in the Snowden Family Clambake business, spending every summer on the island and running the gift shop. She'd taken delight in going through wholesale catalogs and ordering the merchandise every spring, and in telling the trinket-buying tourists the story of Morrow Island and Windsholme.

She hadn't set foot on the island from the day of Dad's diagnosis. She'd lost her husband, her job, and her place in the world. A string of devastating losses.

Livvie eased off the bed and moved toward the door. "If Mom is with Bard, it would be only fair. We're both with men she didn't approve of, at least at the beginning. Now she's giving us a taste of our own medicine."

"She started it," I reminded Livvie. My mother, descendant of a genteel and formerly wealthy summer family, had married the boy who'd delivered groceries to her island in his skiff.

"Family tradition," Livvie agreed.

"I'll remind you of this conversation in a few years when Page starts dating."

"Argh. Thanks, pal." She hesitated in the doorway.

"Will you and Sonny be all right?" I asked.

"Yes," Livvie answered. "I'm not sure how right now, but I can't imagine my life without Sonny." She shifted her weight onto her left foot. "Will you and Chris be okay?"

I answered honestly. "I don't know."

Chapter 29

I awoke at first light to the sound of voices floating up the back stairs. Sonny, Livvie, and Page were in the kitchen, eating breakfast and packing lunches. In other words, getting ready for a normal family day.

I lingered upstairs so they'd have time together. It must be difficult enough for Sonny and Livvie to face each other, without adding me to the mix.

Listening carefully, I heard brittleness in Livvie's voice, an abruptness in Sonny's. It would take them time to find their way forward. I was surprised at the level of investment I felt in their relationship. After all these years, I counted on Livvie and Sonny to be a couple. Page seemed completely back to normal. She jibber-jabbered at her parents as they went about their morning.

At last, I heard the *ka-thunk* of the minivan's sliding door, followed by the sound of the old engine receding down the drive. I glanced at my phone.

7:00 AM. I sprinted to my car and drove to Busman's Hospital.

I'd done a lot of thinking about the call Sonny had gotten from the PT room. It had come a little after eight on Monday morning. On Wednesday morning, at Gus's, I'd seen Bard Ramsey leave abruptly at 7:45, announcing he had "someplace he needed to be." I felt sure that place must be physical therapy. I hoped the appointments were scheduled at regular times and intervals, like 8:00 AM Monday, Wednesday, and Friday.

I was certain Bard was behind the call to Sonny. Maybe he hadn't actually made the call, but he'd made it happen. He wouldn't easily admit doing something so horrendous to his own son, so I gambled if I confronted him, at the scene of the crime, so to speak, I'd have the upper hand.

The 7:00 AM people were already inside the therapy room when I arrived. If someone had made the call when therapy was in session and the waiting room was empty, he could have used the phone without anyone overhearing.

At about twenty minutes before eight, the next group of PT patients began trooping in. I held my breath, wondering if Bard would arrive, and how he'd react when I confronted him.

A few minutes later, a familiar face entered the room, leaning on a cane and limping slightly. My old dentist, Gil Garretson.

"Julia! How nice to see you!" He sat down next to me. "What're ya in for? Me, broke my ankle," he continued without taking a breath. "Walked off a curb and came down on it wrong. Can you believe it? One minute I'm leaving Gleason's Hardware and the next, I'm flat on my back staring up at the sky. It was embarrassing, I can tell you. If it was winter at least I could say I did it skiing, not buying a replacement hinge for my screen door. Like that's a dangerous assignment. So how are you? When did you get back to town? Who are you using as your dentist? I still have your files, so you should make an appointment with Marie and—"

My parents had called him, "Garrulous Gil Garretson." He was notorious for loading up your mouth with cotton, Novocain, and equipment and then asking you a question. No wonder he never waited for answers. Most of his victims couldn't talk.

I leapt in front of his conversational freight train. "Sorry about your ankle. How long have you been coming to PT? I bet you see a lot of the same people every day. Do you ever see my brother-in-law's father, Bard Ramsey? I'm supposed to pick him up, but maybe I have the wrong day, or the wrong time." I figured I'd get as many questions in as I could, because there was no telling when I might get another chance.

"I've been coming here for four weeks. Yes, we are quite a close group. Right, Rosa?" he shouted at a young woman across the room, not waiting for her answer. "I see Rosa every time she comes. And Bard, of course. All the time. He's Mondays,

Wednesdays, and Fridays, so he should be here any minute. Usually it's his son, the younger one, who brings him. Scruffy-looking kid. But who am I to judge? My daughter lives in a yurt in California. A yurt, I tell you. It's a big round tent. She gave birth to her youngest right there on the yurt floor. But what can I do about it? She's allegedly an adult. Kids, right?"

I nodded my agreement. Dr. Garretson's daughter was at least a decade older than me, but hey. *Kids.*

The dentist went on without missing a beat. "Me, I'm here every day. Not for sessions, mind you, but on my off days they let me use the equipment on my own. My wife insists on it. Drives me here herself. I'm in a hurry to get this rehab done. I can't work 'cause I can't stand without the cane. Can't drill teeth with one hand, eh, eh. Sometimes my wife forgets to pick me up, though."

I have never felt pity the way I felt it for Mrs. Garrulous, stuck at home with this guy and his relentless palaver. She must be ready to put her head in the oven. "Dr. Garretson, do you remember if Bard was here on Monday of this week?"

"Of course he was. Why wouldn't he have been?"

As he talked, a line of physical-therapy-weary patients came out of the exercise room, rubbing various body parts and moving as fast as their ailments allowed.

A young woman with a clipboard came to the

door and shouted, "Eight a.m. group! Check in with me. Let's keep moving."

"That's me," Gil said, pushing himself up with the cane.

I jumped up. "Can I help you?"

"Nope. Thank you. I can do it on my own. You should have seen me before. I'm a thousand times better now. Guess Bard's not going to make it today. Sorry you came all this way to give them a ride."

Dr. Garretson moved haltingly toward the PT room door.

"Wait," I called. "You said them. Give *them* a ride. Did you mean Bard and his son Kyle?"

"No. Why would the kid need a ride? Delivers them to the room here and takes off. The daughter usually picks them up."

Daughter? "Bard doesn't have a daughter."

"Not Bard's daughter. Her daughter. His girlfriend's. Belle. Her daughter drove them home after almost every appointment. Lorrie Ann Murray. I'm sure you heard—terrible tragedy." Dr. Garrulous seemed poised to speed off down that conversational boulevard, but the attendant tapped her clipboard and he limped off toward the PT room.

Mom wasn't dating Bard! I was shocked by how relieved I was. As Livvie had insisted, Bard wasn't so bad. Dad had been gone for five years, but I wasn't ready for Mom to move on. Pretty selfish. Of course, now I was back to square one on where the espresso machine had come from. Was there some other Cappuccino Casanova waiting in the wings?

Bard's girlfriend was Belle. What did this additional connection between the Ramseys and the Murrays mean?

Before I left the hospital, I checked on Mrs. Gus. Her door was angled open, and from the hallway, I spotted Fee and Vee, seated at her bedside. Mrs. Gus appeared unchanged. She laid in the bed surrounded by her slightly fewer machines, her skin the same gray color. Her eyeballs jumped around behind her thin lids, but didn't open. She clenched and unclenched her hands. She even sighed from time to time.

Fee reached for her hand and clutched it in her own. Fee's hand was fleshier and pinker than Mrs. Gus's, but they shared the same twisted knuckles, the same disfiguring pain. Tears slid down Fee's cheeks. She wiped them away with her other hand.

"Oh, Vee, what have we done?"

I stepped into the room. "What have you done?" I asked.

The sisters locked eyes; then Vee gave a small flick of her head. Fee nodded. "We were going to confess anyway."

There was no third chair in the room, so I stood against the wall opposite the bed where they both could see me.

Fee let go of Mrs. Gus's hand and turned to face me fully. "About our seniors' trips," she started.

It turned out they had gone to Campobello Island, at least for the day. And to all the other places they claimed to have been over the last few years. But then, every time, after their touristing, they went over the Canadian border to fill their prescriptions.

"Why would you do that?" I was astounded. "Aren't you all on Medicare?"

"Most of us, but not all our prescriptions are covered," Fee said.

I leaned against the wall and folded my arms expectantly.

"Some of our drugs are expensive, difficult, or even impossible to get," Vee explained. "So, for years, a group of us have been traveling over the border. It's all on the up and up. We see a reputable doctor, then go straight to the pharmacy with our own prescriptions."

"And we do our sightseeing. Have a nice little trip," Fee put in.

I nodded. I was sure they did, though whether it was for enjoyment's sake, or so the seniors didn't have to tell quite so many lies to their friends and families about where they'd been, I wasn't sure. "I don't understand," I said. "Can't you do all this over the Internet nowadays?"

"So many scams," Vee responded. "You pay your money and then nothing comes."

"Or worse, the drugs aren't from Canada. They're from China, or anywhere. Unregulated. No quality assurance," Fee put in.

"We're so close to the border. It's safer to go,"

Vee continued. "Fee's arthritis drug is approved in Canada, but not yet here."

"My pills make me feel so much better. And I have less inflammation, more strength in my hands," Fee said.

"So you talked Mrs. Gus into trying this miracle drug." I had just worked that bit out.

Fee began to sniffle again. "Yes. Only she wasn't well enough to come on the trip with us."

"What did you do?" A chill ran through me. I was afraid for Mrs. Gus, and for the sisters.

They looked at one another again. With another silent nod, something between them was resolved. "There's always been another way. A friendly boat owner picks up prescriptions for people who can't make the trip. People like Mrs. Gus who are too sick or people who can't get the two days off work. So I asked this person to pick up the drugs for Mrs. Gus. He was going anyway."

"But Mrs. Gus didn't have a prescription."

"That was the tricky part. We gave this person a copy of my prescription." Fee started to cry again.

I looked at Mrs. Gus, who lay restlessly in the hospital bed. The sisters had been so foolish. I wanted to shout at them, something about wisdom not coming with age. But what good would it do? They would only feel more awful, and surely the punishment had far outstripped the crime.

"We don't know what went wrong. We realize now it could have been so many things. She's a good deal smaller than Fee, so maybe the dosage was wrong," Vee said.

"Or maybe the drug didn't mix with one of her other medications. And now we've killed her!" Fee put her handkerchief, embroidered with purple pansies, to her face.

"Wait a minute. Have either of you told Gus about this?"

They shook their heads in unison. "We thought he had enough troubles."

"Gus told us that first day he gave her medication to the ER doctor," Fee said. "So we knew they had whatever information they needed to take care of her. We haven't discussed it with Gus since then."

"So he hasn't told you. It wasn't the arthritis prescription that did this to her. The capsules were cut with a poisonous substance. Whoever you dealt with did not pick up prescription drugs in Canada. They bought something cheap and dangerous." I paused, so they could take this in. "Ladies, who did you ask to get this prescription for you?" I moved my head back and forth so I could stare at each of them.

Fee looked away, but Vee stared right back. "We asked Peter Murray. He's the one who does the runs now."

"Have you told this to Lieutenant Binder?" I asked.

They looked at their laps.

"You must."

"Do you think we'll go to jail?" Fee asked meekly.

Visions of these women, so proper and so dear to me, serving mandatory minimum sentences swirled in my head. And what if Mrs. Gus died? Would they be some kind of accessories? But Binder had to learn what the sisters knew about Mrs. Gus's tragedy. For all I knew, he was close to figuring it out on his own.

"Did you give Peter Murray money for this prescription?" I asked. Perhaps if they hadn't paid, hadn't transacted anything, they wouldn't be charged.

"Yes. We got the money from Mrs. Gus and gave it to Peter upfront, like he asked."

"Who delivered the medication to Mrs. Gus?"

The ladies blinked. "Not us," Fee said. "We didn't get home until later in the day, long after she'd taken them."

It wasn't Peter Murray, or David Thwing, that much we knew. Neither of them had returned from the voyage. There had to have been a third person involved. The police believed that third person was Sonny. Perhaps one day Mrs. Gus would wake up and tell us who had dropped the brown pill bottle at her house. Until then . . .

"Grab your handbags," I said. "You're going to see Lieutenant Binder. I think, to be on the safe side, you should call an attorney."

"Old Farber did our wills and whatnots," Fee said.

Old Farber was so old, he had a son called Old Farber. "Perhaps he can recommend someone." I held Cuthie Cuthbertson in reserve in case Sonny needed his services. "Let's get going."

As we walked down the hospital corridor, I asked

the thing I'd dreaded asking. "Before Peter Murray, who went to Canada to pick up the prescriptions?"

Fee stopped walking. "Julia, do you really want to know?"

And of course, the moment she said that, there was no need to say the name.

"He's at Gus's," Vee said. "Showed up this morning looking for you and we set him to work helping Genevieve. In case you want to talk to him."

Chapter 30

I said good-bye to the Snugg sisters when they reached their elderly Subaru. They promised to go straight to police headquarters and meet with Lieutenant Binder.

I drove toward town, feeling depressed and discouraged. I loved Fee and Vee, and while they'd done something very, very foolish, I didn't want any harm to come to them. My cell phone rang. I picked it up without looking at the display, hoping it was Chris.

"Julia. Owen Quimby." The HR director at my old firm, calling for my answer. Would I keep my job and return to New York, or stay in Busman's Harbor?

"Hi Owen. I'm in the middle of something. Can we talk later?"

"We agreed today would be the deadline."

"We did say today," I agreed. "But I have until five."

"I don't think we set a time." Owen sounded reluctant. "I have a great candidate for your job if you aren't coming back. I don't want to keep him waiting all weekend."

"I'll be back to you by five." I hung up the phone. My relationship with Chris was the strongest reason I had to stay in town, and I didn't know what the state of that relationship was.

I drove straight to Gus's. Chris's pickup was parked on the street. He was still there.

I entered through the kitchen door. It was the quiet time between breakfast and lunch. Genevieve looked up from cleaning the grill. "I'll give you two some alone time," she said. She took off the apron and slipped out.

Chris's back was to me. He turned around when Genevieve spoke. As soon as the door closed behind her, he strode across the dining room floor and enveloped me in his arms. "I'm sorry," he said. "I'm a jerk."

In that instant, all my doubts melted away. I snuggled in deep and then kissed him on the lips. "I'm sorry, too," I said.

We homed like pigeons to "our" booth. When we were settled, I said, "You know the thing we never talk about?"

"Vee called me from their car."

Oh, really? Perhaps they hoped to soften the blow of having ratted him out. "You can see it never would've worked to keep it secret," I said. If I was hurt about anything, it wasn't about having my worst fears realized. It was that apparently everyone in town knew except me.

Chris ran both hands up over his brow through his light brown hair. "I never brought in illegal drugs. You have to believe that." He paused. "That's not technically true, of course. It was all illegal. But I never brought in anything to resell like this oxycodone the cops told you Thwing smuggled. I never did anything like that. Every single drug I picked up had a prescription from a doctor and had a specific person waiting for it. I didn't even take extra money to cover my fuel costs."

"Then why didn't you tell me?"

"Whatever I might have thought about what I was doing, it was illegal. Punishable by years in prison. So when you and I got serious, I decided I had to get out. Partly because you were asking so many questions, and partly because my being gone for days at a time caused so much trouble between us. I decided the less you knew the better off you'd be."

"Can you help me understand what happened to Mrs. Gus?"

Chris placed his clenched hands on the table and stretched his fingers open, palms up. He was opening up to me. "When I got out of the business, I walked away. I didn't look for someone to replace me. I told my regulars I was done."

"How did that go?"

"People were disappointed, but they understood. A few weeks later, I heard through the grapevine Peter had agreed to make the next run. I caught up to him at the marina, and asked if it was true. He said it was, so I gave him some tips. I told him my rules. Only prescriptions, only intended for a specific person, get your cash upfront. I gave him some routes. I told him"—Chris hesitated for the first time—"how to avoid Customs agents, the Marine Patrol, Coast Guard, the whole array of people who might wonder what a lobster boat like his was doing so far from home. In that sense, he had it harder than me. Sailboats move up and down the whole coast all summer. And that was it. He asked me a few questions, nothing important, nothing I remember. It was August. I was crazy busy with work. I didn't think about it again."

"Did you ever hear Sonny was partnering with Peter?"

Chris looked up sharply. "Why do you ask?"

"Binder told me last night the feds and the Maine Drug Task Force agents believe Sonny was Peter's partner."

"Then yeah. I did hear rumors."

"Why didn't you tell me?"

Chris spread his arms wide. "Julia, we had an agreement not to talk about what I did last summer. There was no way to tell you Sonny was doing the exact same thing."

He had a point. Still, the secret stung. "How many times did Peter go to Canada after he took over from you?"

"Two, I think. Maybe three."

"Did Sonny go with him?"

"Not that I ever heard. As far as I know, he met Peter's boat somewhere at sea so Peter wasn't the one bringing the goods in, in case he was being tracked. Sonny brought the medications into the harbor."

That explained why Sonny had no unexplained overnight absences. It also supported the cops' theory that Sonny brought the drugs in on the *Abby*.

"Did you ever hear anything about Peter and Sonny smuggling oxycodone?"

"No. I thought they were doing exactly what I'd done. Prescriptions for specific people who had them from a doctor. Period."

"Did you ever hear there was anything weird about the prescriptions—bottles with odd labels, wrong medications, people getting sick?"

"No, I swear."

My mind was still a muddle. I couldn't make any of it fit. The prescriptions. The oxycodone. The phone call to Sonny. The poisoning of Mrs. Gus. The murder of David Thwing. "I don't understand what happened."

Chris shifted his weight on the banquette. "I think I do, at least some of it. It's purely speculation based on what I've heard around town and what I've you've told me about the investigation."

"Go ahead," I said.

"Peter was in tough financial shape. Three little kids, a dependent mother-in-law. He saw a chance to expand his operation and bring in drugs that were wanted, but not prescribed. Oxycodone."

"How would it work if he did that?"

"He'd have to find a supplier. It wouldn't be hard. Maybe he'd track one down on his own, or maybe one of his potential buyers on this end would make the connection."

"And the connection was Thwing."

"Yes, and Thwing would change Peter's entire operation. He'd no longer enter Canadian waters himself. He'd meet a larger ship at an agreed upon location at sea. Thwing must have persuaded Peter it was best to pick up everything from the same supplier. Drugs for his prescription customers, too. Most likely the drugs weren't from Canada at all. Maybe they came through there, but were manufactured somewhere else. South or Central America, Europe, Africa, Asia. There's a lot of money in drugs."

"Why was Thwing on board the *El Ay*?" I asked.

"Thwing was probably introducing the supplier to Peter. Someone who needed Thwing to personally vouch for Peter and put up the money, before he'd deliver the drugs to him the first time."

"I get that part. What I don't understand is how Mrs. Gus got the bad medication. If Peter and Thwing were the only people on that boat, and they're dead, who brought the drugs to town? There must have been a third person."

"That's where they think Sonny comes in," Chris said.

I put my head in my hands. "Yes," I admitted. "That's what they're saying." My poor sister. I was sure Sonny hadn't meant to hurt Mrs. Gus, but if he'd brought the tainted drugs into the harbor . . . I couldn't bear to think about it. "But why would he do it? I get why you did what you did. Fetching prescriptions for people who couldn't afford them might seem altruistic. But oxycodone? With a wife and daughter and new baby on the way, why take a risk like that? Sonny's not well off, but with the clambake back on its feet, they have enough to get by."

"I see what you mean." Chris took my hand. "When I fell in love, I had to stop."

I gripped Chris's hand more tightly. "Now that all this has come up, about the drugs from Canada, will the cops come after you?"

"I don't think so. There's no evidence against me. I didn't make any money or keep any drugs. They're not going to catch me in the act, which was my worst nightmare, because I've given it up. I suppose one of my old customers could rat me out, but the cops have bigger fish to fry."

"That's a relief." I let his hand go.

"That's why I gave it up. I never wanted you to worry."

Why hadn't Sonny had the same consideration for my sister?

We sat silently, each absorbed in our own thoughts. Finally, I said, "What are you doing when you finish here?"

"I have to get to the marina as soon as the lunch rush is over. We're taking the *Dark Lady* out of the water this afternoon. I want it done before the storm they're predicting comes in." We looked out the window at the steel-gray clouds sitting low in the sky.

The idea of the *Dark Lady*, the first place I'd ever spent the night with Chris, shrink-wrapped, sitting on a trailer in his driveway made me sad. Another marker of the season passing.

"You?" Chris asked.

"I have stuff to do," I said.

Chris grinned. "Oh, yeah. Stuff. Be careful."

One of the things I treasured most about Chris was he let me be me. In situations like this one, where it was obvious how determined I was, he said, "Be careful," not "Don't do it." Which would have been a waste of breath anyway.

The clack of the kitchen door told us Genevieve was back. Early lunch customers would arrive soon.

He reached for my hand again. "Are we okay?"

I smiled. "We're fine."

Chapter 31

After I left Gus's, I sat in the Caprice for a while. Four nights ago, Livvie had asked for my help because she believed Sonny was innocent. I'd believed it, too. Now I wasn't so sure. I wasn't interested in helping the police prove Sonny was Peter's partner. Or was involved in Mrs. Gus's poisoning, or the murder of David Thwing.

But I also found it unbelievable Sonny would be involved in a smuggling operation with Thwing, whom he hated. Or with oxycodone, especially given Kyle's addiction. It didn't make sense.

So how could Peter have possibly persuaded Sonny to go along with the venture? I thought the buoys Quentin had found might hold the key.

I drove all the way out to the end of Westclaw Point and bumped down Quentin's driveway, which was really a pair of tracks, separated by a mound of grass. I was relieved to see his old wooden-sided station wagon parked at the end of the drive and, as I came across the deck, to see the *Flittermouse* bobbing at its dock.

I knocked at the sliding glass door that provided entry to the granite and glass fortress of a house. Quentin appeared from somewhere in the back and unlocked it. He didn't invite me in, but instead stepped out onto the deck. It was a bit chilly for talking outside. Rough weather was coming.

"What brings you all the way out here?" Quentin asked.

"The buoys you found out by Coldport Island the day Thwing was murdered. They're Peter's," I said.

"How do you know? I never got around to tracking down the license holder."

"I was out with Sonny on the *Abby* yesterday and we hauled some of Peter's traps."

Quentin wrinkled his tanned brow. "You, out on the *Abby*, hauling traps?"

"It's a long story. When you found the buoys, were there any others around?"

Quentin squinted, remembering. We both stood along the rail of his deck. He hadn't asked me to sit down, and I doubt I could have contained my energy. "Yes, there were other buoys," he said. "But they were attached to traps, not floating free. And they were different colors. Orange and bright blue."

The Ramsey colors. "Thanks." I turned to go.

"Hey, wait. Why does it matter?"

Sonny had called Peter a dub, a poor lobsterman. But lobstermen had another derisive term, "copycat." A copycat had no lobstering instincts of his own, but placed his traps near a highliner's, trying to horn in on his territory. If Peter had followed Bard hoping to find his traps, chances were he'd figured out Bard had an arrangement with the Coldporters. That knowledge could have been the leverage Peter used to get Sonny involved in the prescription-drug-running scheme in the first place. Or, Peter could have saved it for when he really thought he needed it—when he had to persuade Sonny to smuggle oxycodone.

I didn't say any of this to Quentin. To him, I said, again, "Long story."

He opened his mouth to protest, but seemed to think better of it. We said our good-byes and I walked to the end of the deck.

"What did you decide about the job?" Quentin called.

I turned around. "Nothing yet." Though I was fast approaching the place where no decision was a decision. Same with the apartment over Gleason's, if it wasn't rented by now. And if we didn't properly secure Windsholme soon, it would probably be destroyed by the winter weather and the option of restoring it would disappear. Why couldn't I make decisions all of a sudden? I'd made them without looking back for years. Was I so worried about making the wrong decisions, I couldn't make any decisions at all?

"The job's not right for you," Quentin said.

Alone in his polished granite monolith of a mansion, I often thought of Quentin as Batman. In fact,

I suspected he cultivated it, naming his sailboat *Flittermouse*—the bat. He had rescued me once, I had to admit, by putting his money in the clambake. Quentin's form of righting wrongs involved writing checks, not physical bravery.

I was tired of his interfering advice, and his withholding—the one-sidedness of our relationship that made my life fair game, while his was out of bounds. What kind of friendship was this? Quentin's kind.

I lost my temper. "Since you're the greatest living expert on what's *not* right for me, would you mind telling me what *is* right? And bear in mind, we're talking about what's right for me, not what's right for you. I can't live like you do. No job. No relationship. A few months in one place and then gone. Empty house. Empty life. Not for me."

Quentin went pale behind his tan and his jaw slackened. I had hurt him.

"I'm sorry," I apologized. "That was uncalled for. I really need a friend right now. You've told me over and over what's wrong for me. Please tell me, what's right for me?"

Quentin raised his head and looked at me with such concern, I couldn't doubt he was my friend. "I only mean, when it's right, you'll know it instantly. You won't have to struggle so hard to decide."

"Thanks," I said. *But what if nothing like that comes along?*

I drove back to town. When I rang the bell at Bard's house, he answered.

"Julia! Darlin'. Come in."

Belle stood behind him, leaning on her walker. She looked gray and worn, like the life had gone out of her.

"Is Kyle here?" I asked.

"Hauling traps with Sonny today."

Good. I wanted this conversation to be private.

Bard sat in his shiny recliner, Belle on the sofa, her walker parked nearby. I remained standing, feeling a little guilty about trying to intimidate two older people, both coping with significant physical issues.

"It's time for you two to tell the truth," I said.

I'd been pleased, but not surprised, to find them together. Bard's house must have been where Belle fled after her fight with her daughter.

"I know you two are a couple." I stated the obvious, gaining confidence as I spoke. "You both attend the eight a.m. PT sessions at the Busman's Harbor Hospital on Mondays, Wednesdays, and Fridays, though you weren't there this morning."

"Belle didn't feel up to it," Bard confirmed. "This thing with Peter is really getting to her."

Belle nodded her agreement.

"The two of you knew Peter was smuggling prescription drugs," I continued.

Bard protested, but Belle said quietly, "Enough. This has gone far enough. A man is dead. My son-in-law is missing and all that's left is to find his body. I'm here in this house, even though my daughter and grandchildren need me more than they ever have. I can't go on keeping all these secrets."

She bowed her head. The room was still. I waited for her to find the words.

Finally, she spoke. "Peter took over picking up the prescriptions from your boyfriend."

"How did he get involved with Thwing?"

"The prescriptions didn't bring in any real money. Peter charged more than Chris did, but if he charged too much, his customers wouldn't be saving money. It wouldn't be worth the bother to get the drugs from Canada. My daughter convinced Peter to distribute the oxycodone."

"Lorrie Ann was involved?" Much as I blamed Sonny for keeping his activities secret from Livvie, I had to admit his behavior was typical. Most lobstermen never would have talked to their wives about such things.

"Involved?" Belle said "She talked Peter into it. He was a nice man, but no backbone. Lorrie Ann always pushed him around." Belle inhaled deeply. "I begged her to think about her little children, and the danger their father would be in. But she wouldn't listen." Belle looked into my eyes. "With this hip, I'm completely dependent on them. For a place to live, transportation. They even help me out financially. So I argued as long as I felt I could, but then I shut up."

"But you told Bard."

"Everything. Right here in this room. The day before all this happened."

"Did Sonny know about the oxycodone?"

"No," Belle answered. "Never. Lorrie Ann and Peter weren't going to tell him, either. Sonny didn't make the runs to Canada. He met Peter at sea somewhere with the *Abby*, picked up the prescriptions, and brought them into the harbor, in case the *El Ay* had been spotted by the authorities anywhere along the way."

Exactly as Chris had described.

"The plan was for Sonny to meet them with the *Abby*, the way he had before," Belle continued. "By that time, the oxycodone would be aboard the *El Ay*. Sonny would be angry, but Peter and Lorrie Ann were confident he'd play along."

They would have relied on Peter's long friendship with Sonny. And if that didn't work, Peter would have threatened to reveal Bard's arrangement with the Coldport co-op.

I turned to Bard. "So you tried to put a stop to it. You called Sonny from the PT waiting room. You disguised your voice and gave him that terrible message to make sure he would be too late to meet the *El Ay*."

"I did not." He spoke forcefully, but also forthrightly, looking me in the eye. I believed him.

I turned to Belle. "Then you made the call." Her gravelly smoker's voice would easily sound like a man's. Especially since, after her first sentence was out, Sonny's brain wouldn't register anything except his fear.

"No, I didn't, either." She looked away from me, gazing into the kitchen. "But I would've if I'd thought of it. No point in two families being torn up by this."

"Why didn't you just tell Sonny what was going to happen?" I asked Bard.

He didn't answer for a moment. Then he said, "I'd talked to Sonny about this prescription business in the past. Whenever I tried to reason with him, I'd get one sentence into it and he'd blow up. Even though he wasn't crossing the border, he was bringing prescription drugs into this harbor in my boat. If he'd been caught, the *Abby* would have been confiscated. We'd fought about it before. I wouldn't have gotten anywhere. You know how he is."

Yes, I did. Stubborn as a mule. "After PT on the day of Thwing's murder, you came home from the hospital. That's when Sonny got here, right Bard?" When I first talked to him about Sonny's visit, I'd thought Bard was lying. But the alibi he supplied was more important than ever. The police believed Thwing was killed before noon. The more of that time period Sonny could account for, the better.

Bard shook his head. "You might as well know. I didn't see Sonny that morning. We were late coming home from PT. Lorrie Ann never picked us up. We had to take a cab. When I helped Belle into her house, we discovered Lorrie Ann was gone. She'd left the kids with a neighbor and a note for her mother to retrieve them. Belle doesn't move around so easily, so I went to get them and then stayed to help out."

This was news. "Lorrie Ann wasn't home Monday

morning? Could *she* have been aboard the *El Ay* with Peter and Thwing?"

"If she was, how'd she get home?" Belle said. "Because she was home by one o'clock. No one else aboard the *El Ay* made it home that day."

It was a good question. "Belle, you said you wanted this to be over. You two need to go to the police," I said.

"It's hearsay," Bard shot back. "Conversations Belle overheard. For me, it's hearsay once removed, since Belle told me."

"I can't do that to my grandchildren." Tears spilled from Belle's eyes. "They've already lost their father. They can't lose their mother, too. Lorrie Ann is pushy and greedy, but I don't believe she could've killed that man."

"Then why tell me?"

"Please help us," Belle pleaded. "Figure out what really happened and bring this to an end."

We had the same goal, but I wasn't sure I could. The only thing I could think to do was persuade Lorrie Ann to tell the authorities what she knew. But I wasn't sure Belle would be happy with the outcome if I was successful.

Had Lorrie Ann been unable to pick Belle and Bard up at PT on Monday morning because she was aboard the *El Ay*? Had she and Peter killed David Thwing and had Peter somehow ended up in the ocean? As I walked rapidly toward the

Murray house, I pictured Lorrie Ann desperately trying to save her husband as he sunk into the watery depths.

But how had she, and the filled prescription bottles, ended up on land before I spotted the *El Ay* that afternoon? Could she have maneuvered the lobster boat close enough to shore to get off and then set it adrift in the narrows between Morrow Island and Westclaw Point? It was technically possible. But then how had she gotten back to town? It was a heck of a walk. Miles and miles. Unless Sonny had brought her back with the drugs. But I could still hear her voice shouting, "You were supposed to be there!" Why would she have said that, if he had, in fact, been there?

By the time I'd been through this set of questions without answers I was at Lorrie Ann's front door. I was relieved Livvie's minivan was the only car parked out front. The support group-slash-wake had moved on. I pressed the bell. The TV was on inside, though not at the decibel level it had been when the Murray children had the run of the household while their mother fell apart. I wondered about Lorrie Ann's descent from optimistic or in-denial spouse to total mess between my first and second visits. Had her downward spiral been driven by guilt?

Livvie answered the door. "I'm here to see Lorrie Ann," I whispered. "Can you take the kids out? I need to talk to her alone."

Livvie nodded. "Do them good to get out of the house."

"Thanks." I caught my sister's hand and pulled her toward me for a hug.

"Are you okay?" I whispered.

She broke the hug and faced me. "It'll take a while for things at our house to settle down. I just wish Sonny would tell the truth."

"To you or the cops?"

"Both."

I didn't know if it was a good idea for Sonny to tell the truth to the cops. I still wasn't sure how he'd been involved.

I helped my sister round up the three kids, get them into their jackets and shoes, and finally strap baby Toddy into his stroller. Livvie explained to Lorrie Ann that they were going out. She responded with a vague nod. The sky was covered with dark clouds and the wind had come up a bit by the time Livvie set off with the children.

"Are you sure you'll be okay?" I asked.

She gave the heavens an expert's glance, the kind that developed when your family's and your husband's family's livelihoods depended on the weather. "We've got plenty of time," she answered.

When I went back inside, the usually noisy house was so quiet, it felt deserted. Lorrie Ann was still seated at the old Formica table in the kitchen.

I sat down opposite. There was no easy way to have this conversation, but I hoped Lorrie Ann's rapid deterioration over the last four days meant she felt remorse about whatever part she'd played. Maybe she was ready to confess. "It wasn't Sonny who was on the *El Ay* with Peter when David Thwing died, was it?" I said. "It was you."

She sat, stone-faced, but didn't deny it. I continued. "You and Peter met a ship and picked up the oxycodone with Thwing. But something went wrong after that. Thwing's body ended up tied up in the trapline and Peter in the water. Sonny and the *Abby* never showed. That's why you shouted at him on the dock that he should have been there. You meant there with the *Abby* at the rendezvous point, not there on the *El Ay*."

I reached across the table and put my hand on her forearm. It was intended as a gesture of comfort, but I also didn't want her to bolt. Her muscles were tense, though she sat unmoving.

"Lorrie Ann, you have got to go to the police and tell them what really happened. I'll call an attorney for you. I know it feels like you'll be in terrible trouble, but David Thwing was a notorious drug dealer. You're a recent widow. This is your first offense. Maybe an accommodation can be made. A lesser charge."

"I didn't kill Thwing and I didn't kill my husband."

"I'm not saying you did. But you were on the *El Ay*. You were the one who delivered the drug prescriptions to your buyers afterward. You're the only person alive who knows what happened."

She jumped up from her chair and came toward me. "Get out of here," she hissed.

"Lorrie Ann, you can kick me out, but if I figured this out, the police will, too. You need to go to them, before they come to you."

Her face, already red, deepened to almost purple and contorted in rage. "Get out! Get out! Get out!"

I moved to the front door as quickly as I could. This conversation was going nowhere. But I couldn't help trying one more time as I left. "Get in front of this, Lorrie Ann. Come clean. Do it soon."

Chapter 32

I hurried to the marina. It was almost three, and Sonny and Kyle might return on the *Abby* at any moment.

As I came up over the crest at the edge of the parking lot, The *Dark Lady* was suspended in midair on the boatyard lift, halfway between the sea and Chris's trailer. The *Flittermouse* was docked at the marina, too. Quentin and Chris stood off to the side, heads bent deep in conversation. What could that be about? They didn't have a relationship as far as I knew. The only thing they had in common was me.

Chris spotted me and waved just as the *Abby* chugged into the marina. I waved back and mouthed, *See you in a minute*, pointing at the Ramsey boat.

Sonny and Kyle were tying up by the time I arrived at their slip.

"I need to talk to you," I called.

"In a minute, Julia," Sonny answered. "We're busy here."

"Not you," I responded. "Kyle."

"Me?" Kyle pointed at his chest with his thumb.

"Yes, you. Though you might as well hear this, Sonny."

They both moved closer on the *Abby*'s deck. I stood above them on the dock. "Kyle, I think you're the one who called Sonny from the PT waiting room. When you dropped your dad and Belle off, you waited until everyone went in for their appointments and then you called from the extension. You disguised your voice. You knew about Livvie's previous miscarriage. You gambled your brother wouldn't hear anything clearly after you told him Livvie was in danger."

"What?" Sonny roared. "Why would you do that to me?"

Kyle didn't deny it. Sonny stood beside him, clenching and unclenching his fists. I was afraid he might hit him.

"I'm sorry," Kyle finally said. "I heard Dad and Belle talking about the drugs, serious drugs. I wanted to keep you out of it. It's bad enough for our family that I'm . . ." His voice faltered.

"I can take care of myself," Sonny rumbled. "Haven't I always taken care of myself? And you. I've taken care of you."

Kyle looked down at the deck. "I didn't know what else to do."

"Really? Because I can think of a lot of what elses." Sonny sounded gruff, but the danger he'd react physically seemed to have passed.

"I'm sorry," Kyle said again.

"S'okay," Sonny said without looking at him.

"He's alive! He's alive! He's alive," a woman shouted. Lorrie Ann Murray ran into the marina, yelling as loud as she could.

She sped toward where Chris and Quentin stood by the *Dark Lady*. Sonny, Kyle, and I reached them right after Lorrie Ann did.

"A fisherman called me," Lorrie Ann panted. "Right after you left." She looked at me. "He said he saw a campfire on one of the islands outside the harbor. It's Peter. I'm sure it's Peter. We have to pick him up. Now."

We pelted her with questions.

"Which island?" Quentin asked.

"Why didn't the fisherman pick him up?" Chris wanted to know.

"A campfire? How do you know it's Peter?" I said.

"No time!" Lorrie Ann looked up at the cloud-laden sky. "We have to go now."

"We've got to call the Coast Guard," I said.

"No," Lorrie Ann wailed. "Please, please, please help me save him."

All eyes were on Sonny. Despite being the slowest boat we had among us, it made the most sense to take the *Abby*. A lobster boat would be the best craft for getting tight into shore. Sonny, an experienced pilot, could negotiate the inevitable rocks.

"I need fuel to go back out," he said. "I'll go—"

"No," Lorrie Ann repeated. "We have to go *now*." As if to emphasize her urgency, the wind came up in a mighty gust. There was a steady chop on the water, even in the protected marina.

That left the *Flittermouse*. As Lorrie Ann ran toward it, Chris pulled me aside. "What do you think?" he asked.

"This is crazy. Why won't she tell us where he's supposed to be?"

"Maybe she's afraid if she does, we won't bring her."

"She's grasping at straws. A campfire?" I said. "It could be anything, or anyone."

"Are you prepared to take that chance?" Chris searched my face for the answer. Was I? No. If it was Peter, he'd been out there for five days. With a storm coming, he had to be rescued. If Peter was alive, he had the answers to so many questions. We had to give it a shot.

I started toward the *Flittermouse*. Chris caught my arm. "Call the Coast Guard," he whispered. "I'll hold the boat until you're done."

I stepped behind his pickup and called the local Coast Guard station. "I'm in the Busman's Harbor marina with Peter Murray's wife. She says a passing fisherman reported a campfire and she'll take us to it. She's convinced her husband's alive."

"DO NOT GO ANYWHERE," the officer on the other end said. "Keep her there."

"She won't cooperate. She insists we go now."

"Hold on." There was a murmur of voices in the background on his end. I peered out from behind the pickup. The others had boarded Quentin's boat. Chris looked anxiously over the bow toward me. The Coast Guard officer came back on the line. "Give us your vessel name. Turn your transponder on. We'll track you."

"The *Flittermouse*. It's a forty-foot, single-mast racing sailboat. Please hurry."

"A sailboat?" the guy said as I ended the call.

I clambered aboard. Quentin started the engine. "We'll motor out of the harbor, then put up the sails," he yelled. "That will be fastest." He turned to Lorrie Ann. "Where are we going?"

Lorrie Ann shook her head. "I'll tell you when we get out of the harbor."

Chris, Sonny, and I gathered around Quentin at the helm, and I explained what the Coast Guard officer had said. I also told them I suspected Lorrie Ann had been aboard the *El Ay* with Peter and Thwing.

"You think this passing fisherman is made up?" Quentin asked.

"She knows a lot more than she's telling," I answered.

At the mouth of the harbor, the swells grew in size. Quentin directed Chris and Sonny, the most experienced sailors, to put up the sails, and the *Flittermouse*, built for speed, took off across the waves like lightning.

"Now," Quentin demanded of Lorrie Ann. "You have to tell us where we're going."

"Teapot Island."

That stunned us into silence. Teapot was a tiny, uninhabited desert island not far beyond the harbor mouth. Closer even than Morrow Island.

It was named Teapot because it looked like one from the air, with a rocky outcropping forming its spout. It was covered in dense pine, without a natural landing place even for boats smaller than the *Flittermouse,* which made it unattractive for day-tripping picnickers.

I moved next to Quentin, so Lorrie Ann couldn't overhear. "The Coast Guard must have looked there dozens of times," I said. "Helicopters and boats."

"At first, they were looking for someone alive who *wanted* to be found. They wouldn't have found Peter if he was hiding," Quentin pointed out. "And later, they were looking for a body washed up on the shoreline, not someone deep in the woods."

"Why would he hide?" I asked.

"If he killed David Thwing, he might," Quentin said.

The clouds darkened and the high wind turned from gusting to steady. Everyone aboard was an experienced sailor, but we all looked for something to hold on to. "Put on life jackets," Quentin directed. "Lorrie Ann, Julia, Kyle, go below until we get to the island." The three of us shrugged into life vests and I took one to Quentin. But we weren't going below. I could see Teapot Island in the distance.

The *Flittermouse* was fast, but it felt like it took forever to reach the island.

"There's a deepwater cove formed by the 'spout' on the other side," Quentin shouted. "That's where I can get the closest. Take the sails down," Quentin directed Chris and Sonny. "I can maneuver her better under power."

He expertly moved us into the cove. There was no doubt a storm was coming. Waves rolled the boat from side to side. The sky was so gray, it was nearly impossible to see, but based on the movement of the air, it did look like there might be smoke coming from the high ground at the center of the island.

"Peter, Peter!" Lorrie Ann shouted.

"He'll never hear you," Quentin warned her.

"He'll see us if he doesn't hear us," Sonny said. The boat's great mast was hard to miss.

"If he's looking for us. And if he knows we're friendly." I pictured Peter, alone and afraid, burrowing deeper into the island woods. But if, after five days, he was thirsty and starving, surely he'd come out.

"Sonny and I could get in the dinghy and go ashore," Chris said to Quentin.

"The dinghy's an inflatable with a little electric motor. Not enough power to fight these swells. In addition to the rocks, the currents are terrible here. I'd be afraid we'd lose you both." Quentin considered a moment. "I've got flares. In the Man Overboard kit in the stern. If Peter sees them, he might come to investigate."

Chris retrieved the flares and he and Sonny set two off. They made quite a flash against the darkening sky. We waited, jouncing up and down on the water, all six of us staring at the island's shoreline and into the woods beyond.

There was a movement in the pines. Lorrie Ann began to yell, and then Sonny did, adding his booming voice to her soprano. "Peter! We're here!"

A pine bow trembled and then Peter Murray stumbled out of the woods. He looked weak and confused, but alive and moving.

Except for Lorrie Ann, we were all shocked. Until that moment, I don't think any of us had believed Peter was alive.

Quentin took charge. "Sonny and Chris, there's a harness and jackline in the MOB kit. Toss it to Peter."

Peter seemed to understand what we were trying to do. Quentin expertly repositioned the boat, getting as close to shore as he dared. Chris threw out the harness. It didn't come close.

He pulled it back in, and he and Sonny heaved it together, with as much force as they could. We all watched, rolling from side to side with the surf, as the harness traveled through the air in what felt like slow motion. This time it landed close enough to shore. Peter waded toward it.

He secured the harness around his upper body and gave a tug on the line. Chris and Sonny pulled him in. The surf was rough and he disappeared under the waves several times. I held my breath along with him, but each time he resurfaced with the line, though he was clearly exhausted.

When Peter was alongside the *Flittermouse,* Chris and Sonny leaned over and brought him aboard in one fluid motion. They laid him on the deck, where he sputtered and choked. He was pale, unshaven, and shivering so hard it looked as if he was having convulsions.

Quentin began to maneuver us out of the cove. Sonny and Chris moved over to the rail on the island side of the boat, shouting to Quentin about obstacles to watch out for. We passed out of the protected cove, into the open ocean.

"What's going on?" Peter rasped.

Lorrie Ann didn't go to him. It was Kyle who rushed to Peter's side with a blanket.

"It's okay, man," Kyle reassured him. He pulled Peter gently to his feet and put an arm under his shoulder, preparing to lead him below deck. "It's over now. Time to tell the truth. The whole truth."

Kyle looked at the spot where Lorrie Ann stood. "Look at him!" he shouted. "He could have died. This isn't a game." Kyle's voice broke. "Thwing's dead. That's enough, man. I'm done with lying."

"Aieee!" Lorrie Ann jumped, folding herself over the boom, and propelled it across the deck. I shouted a warning and ducked out of the way. Quentin did, too.

Kyle saw the boom coming, Lorrie Ann hanging over it, screaming like a crazed chimpanzee. His mouth formed a perfect O as he dove for the deck, pulling Peter down with him.

Lorrie Ann dropped off, but as waves dipped the *Flittermouse* to its side, the heavy boom kept traveling. With a crash, it hit both Chris and Sonny and swept them into the sea.

Chapter 33

I struggled to my feet and ran to the side. Sonny and Chris's heads popped up in the waves. They were twenty feet apart, and the current was carrying them away from us and rapidly increasing the distance between them.

Quentin pushed Lorrie Ann roughly to the cabin door and sent her sprawling below decks. Then he locked the door behind her. Peter sat up groggily on deck. Quentin once again took control of the boat.

In the water, Chris and Sonny drifted beyond the rock outcropping that formed Teapot Island's spout. Sonny screamed in pain. He brought his right arm out of the water, where it dangled uselessly at an odd angle. Like Chris, he'd been hit high on the back and arms. Sonny's seemed to be broken. Neither of them had put on life vests when Quentin told us to. Those stupid, fatalistic macho men of the sea.

I grabbed the radio and shouted on the emergency channel, "May Day, May Day, May Day. Sailing vessel *Flittermouse*. Two men overboard. Teapot Island." I read off our location.

"Vessel *Flittermouse*, this is Coast Guard. Do you have them in your sight?"

"Five o'clock off my bow. One is forty feet away, the other sixty, both drifting, moving away from Teapot Island toward the open ocean."

"We were able to track you. We're nearby, heading to your position. Can you get one or both on board?"

I looked at Quentin. "The harness?"

He shook is head. "They're too far."

"I'm getting in the dinghy." The same one Quentin had told Chris was too dangerous. He didn't protest, which only underlined for me how dire the situation was.

"Maybe. One at a time," I told the Coast Guardsman.

I lowered the inflatable dinghy, climbed in, and started the engine. The little electric motor fought the increasing swells. It was two steps forward, one back as I battled the waves. I was soaked to the skin and shivering in seconds, not quite in as much danger of hypothermia as the men, but if I didn't act fast, I'd be the third casualty.

Sonny was closer and he was injured. My sister's husband, the father of my beloved niece and a longed-for baby. But if I got to him first and took him back to the *Flittermouse*, Chris might die. Chris, my love.

I lost sight of them both at intervals as the waves tossed me up and down. I didn't think Chris and Sonny could see each other, but Chris rose up on a wave and spotted Sonny, his right arm flapping as he tried to keep himself afloat. Chris motioned with both hands, urging me toward Sonny, mouthing, *Get him! Get him!* Chris, who'd shed his boots and jacket, kicked off toward the island. I saw one bare foot skim the waves. It would be minutes before hypothermia stopped him from moving, and he drowned.

I steered the little raft toward Sonny. His movements slowed as exhaustion set in and his body temperature dropped. I came alongside him.

"You have to help me get you into the boat."

Sonny nodded his understanding. I grabbed his shoulders and heaved. He howled in pain. I thought he might pass out and leave me with his dead weight hanging from the raft.

"Think of the new baby!" I screamed at him. "Page! Livvie!"

He gave one tremendous kick and I pulled him up over the side. Crying with relief, I turned the boat to the *Flittermouse*. If I tried to pick up both men in the little rubber raft, we'd all die.

It seemed to take forever as I fought the current to get back to the sailboat. "I have to get Chris!" I yelled to Quentin and Kyle as they pulled Sonny on board.

"You'll never make it," Quentin warned.

"I have to try." But just as I turned the dinghy around, a Coast Guard ship came into view. Quentin reached over and pulled me forcibly onto the sailboat's deck.

He ran back to the radio. "Vessel *Flittermouse*. We

have one man on board, one still in the water," he shouted.

"Do you have a visual?"

"One hundred feet off our bow."

I looked over. Chris was gone. "We've lost visual," I screamed.

"We've got this. Back away," the Coast Guardsman commanded.

I looked at Quentin, who revved the engine. No part of me wanted to leave, but having two boats in the small area would be infinitely more dangerous for Chris. The Coast Guard vessel had EMTs aboard. He was better off with them.

Two divers jumped off the Coast Guard ship and moved swiftly to the area where I'd last seen Chris. I couldn't see him anymore.

"Vessel *Flittermouse* return to port," the Coast Guardsman ordered.

"We need two ambulances to meet us," Quentin said. "And the police."

"They'll be there."

I grabbed a set of binoculars tethered to Quentin's console. I watched as the divers brought something to the surface. Chris's head! The three moved rapidly toward the Coast Guard boat. Hands reached out and hauled them aboard.

Chris's body, that body I knew so well, was inert. He neither helped nor fought his rescuers. He made no movement on his own.

I stood frozen on the deck, trying to breathe.

Chapter 34

We reached the marina before the Coast Guard ship. There were three ambulances waiting in the parking area. One for Sonny, one for Peter, and—my heart leapt with hope—one for Chris.

The parking lot was filled with cops, some wearing uniforms, others wearing windbreakers with their agency names emblazoned on them. I looked for Binder and spotted him in the lead as a group of lawmen made their way down the dock.

I scrambled off the *Flittermouse* and ran to him. "Peter Murray's alive," I said, panting. "And Lorrie Ann Murray tried to kill Kyle Ramsey, but Sonny and Chris ended up in the water."

"*Kyle* Ramsey? Are you sure?"

"Yes. Kyle said it was time to tell the truth. The whole truth. Then Lorrie Ann went after him with the boom." As I spoke, I scanned the marina behind Binder's back, searching for the Coast Guard ship.

"You're soaked and shivering." Binder seemed

to notice for the first time. "I'm putting you in an ambulance."

"No! Please. I have to know if Chris is alive."

Binder's eyebrows rose, comprehending. "I'll find a Coast Guard officer. Don't move."

Binder barked something at the men behind him, but I barely heard. The Coast Guard rescue ship entered the marina. I ran to meet it. "Chris! Chris!" I screamed.

I jostled my way to the front, where the EMTs waited with a single stretcher, craning my neck for the first sign of him.

Then I heard his unmistakable baritone, so dear to me. "I'm fine. I don't need all this fuss."

"You've been unconscious, had water in your lungs, and your body temperature is low. You're headed to the hospital," a woman's voice said firmly.

They brought him off the boat on a stretcher covered in a silver blanket. I wept as they transferred him to the EMTs' gurney and was still crying when I reached his side.

"I thought I'd lost you," I cried. "I couldn't picture my life without . . ." I broke down.

Chris snaked a pale, cold hand from under the blanket. "I know," he said. "Me, too."

The EMTs whisked him off the dock. The other ambulances were loaded. The police allowed Lorrie Ann to ride in the back with Peter, but Sergeant

Flynn also rode with them. Kyle was handcuffed and loaded into the back of a police car.

They wouldn't let me ride in the ambulance with Chris. I was neither a spouse nor a relative. Binder put me in his official car and turned on his siren. I was halfway to the hospital before I thought to call my sister.

The waiting area for the emergency room was strangely empty when we got there. Brittany, my phone-extension-finding pal, brought me a warm blanket and a pair of scrubs. I could hear the bustle in the back, as the ambulances were unloaded. Over the noise, I heard Chris insist, "I'm fine. I'm fine."

I'd changed into the dry scrubs by the time they finally let me see him. We were enjoying a deeply satisfying "You're not dead" kiss when Livvie arrived, auburn hair flying, eyes wild with worry. Sonny's arm was badly fractured and he was in shock. They were stabilizing him before they operated.

Two hours later, Chris was unhooked from the saline they'd used to bring up his body temperature and discharged. He, too, wore scrubs the hospital had given him. We waited with Livvie while Sonny was in surgery.

I realized I'd left the marina without thanking Quentin, either for finding Peter Murray or for his mad boating skills rescuing Sonny.

I called him on my cell. "Thank you, Batman," I said.

He chuckled appreciatively. *Of course he cultivates*

it. I handed the phone to Livvie, who cried so hard she couldn't speak. Finally, I took the phone from her gently and spoke into it. "Got that?" I asked.

"I did," Quentin answered. He sounded a little choked up, too.

Chapter 35

Binder showed up sometime after 8:00 PM. He greeted Chris and Livvie politely, then motioned for me to follow. We walked the hospital corridors as we talked.

"We have both Lorrie Ann and Kyle in custody," he said. "Each one blames the other for killing Thwing. I've just come from interviewing Peter Murray at his bedside. They're all lying, but I think he's telling the story closest to the truth."

"What happened on board the *El Ay*?" I asked.

"Your brother-in-law was supposed to show up with the *Abby* to pick up the prescription drugs." Binder glanced at me, trudging along at his side. I didn't protest Sonny's role. "As far as he knew, it was a normal run. Peter and Lorrie Ann believed once Sonny was there, and they were in possession of the oxycodone, he'd have to go along with smuggling it. They must have been awfully good friends."

Or, Peter knew about Bard selling his lobsters in

Coldport and threatened to reveal it if Sonny didn't cooperate. I kept that thought to myself.

Binder continued. "Kyle Ramsey overheard his father and Belle talking about Peter and Lorrie Ann's plan. He decided he wanted in on the deal. He was desperate for drugs, and for money to support his habit. He made the call to Sonny about your sister. Then Kyle took the *Abby* out to meet the *El Ay*."

So Kyle had called Sonny, but not to prevent his brother from involvement with oxycodone smuggling. To get him out of the way. I'd believed what Kyle had said about making the call to keep Sonny safe. I should have known better than to be taken in by the chronic lying and manipulative ways of the addict. Nonetheless, at the end, Kyle had wanted to tell the truth about what happened about the *El Ay*. Lorrie Ann had been determined to stop him.

If Kyle took the *Abby* out on the first trip that day, it also explained why Sonny hadn't gone out on the boat straightaway when he got back to the marina. It wasn't there. He must have realized his brother had taken it. That was why he'd continued to lie, insisting he'd gone to Bard's house and seen Bard and Kyle. He'd been covering for Kyle.

"What happened next is what the participants dispute," Binder said. "When the *Abby* drew up alongside the *El Ay*, Thwing recognized Kyle. He'd worked for a time at Le Shack."

I remembered Genevieve's abortive wave to Sonny from the Snuggles' front porch. From that distance, the Ramsey brothers looked so

much alike, she must have thought he was Kyle.
The healthier, heavier version of Kyle she'd known
when he'd worked at her restaurant.

Binder resumed the tale. "When Kyle worked at
Le Shack, ironically, he was fired due to his drug
problem. When Thwing saw him approach on the
Abby, he assumed they were being robbed, and that
Peter had orchestrated the robbery, telling Kyle
where they'd be. Thwing pulled a gun and threatened to kill Peter and Kyle. Lorrie Ann snuck up
behind Thwing with the gaff, swung it over her
head, crashing it into his skull. At least that's what
we think. She hasn't admitted it, but it fits the physical evidence.

"Once Thwing was dead, they compounded the
bad decisions each one had made up to that point
by making more terrible decisions. Thwing had
paid the supplier for the oxycodone when they
took possession of it. Peter and Lorrie Ann were
determined to sell it and pocket all the money. But
they were afraid he might have partners who would
come after them for the profits once the drugs
were sold, so they decided to stage a tragedy at sea.
They tied Thwing up in the line and left Peter on
Teapot Island. The *El Ay* would turn up empty."

Binder paused. "Sorting through all the versions
of the story, I think Kyle was a reluctant participant
from the beginning. He says he argued they should
go to the authorities and claim Thwing's death was
self-defense, but Lorrie Ann and Peter had a boat-
load of drugs they didn't want to throw overboard.
All three of them had reasons for wanting to stay
away from law enforcement.

"Kyle brought Lorrie Ann back to town on the *Abby,* along with the prescription drugs and a small amount of oxycodone for Kyle's personal use and so he could begin to find customers. Lorrie Ann took charge of the rest of it. She used the promise of more to keep Kyle in line, but he was unraveling." Binder paused. "She's admitted delivering the prescription bottles to Mrs. Gus and the others and given us the addresses. We're collecting them now so no one else gets hurt."

"It's a miracle no one did."

"It seems since the supply was so uncertain, most people ordered their prescriptions well in advance, so they'd have them for the future. But yes, it is very lucky."

Binder stood for a moment, as if considering this bit of good luck, and then continued walking. "Lorrie Ann 'borrowed' a boat from the marina in the middle of the night on Monday and took food, water, and a sleeping bag to Peter. But for some reason, after that first night, she couldn't return."

"She and her mother had a huge fight on Tuesday afternoon," I told him. "Her mother left the house. Lorrie Ann couldn't go to Peter that night because she was alone with her kids."

Binder nodded.

"The next day, my sister organized the lobstermen's wives so they spent twenty-four hours a day with Lorrie Ann," I said. "And your guys were dropping in to question her at least once a day, sometimes twice. She must have felt like a trapped rat."

"There's no natural fresh water on Teapot Island." Binder picked up the story. "Lorrie Ann was frantic. She was looking for any excuse to bring Peter home. I don't know what you told her when you visited her house today, but whatever it was made her decide to move up the date for Peter's 'miraculous rescue.'"

"I said I knew she was aboard the *El Ay* that day. I accused her and Peter of murdering Thwing, with Peter accidentally dying in the process."

"You were close," Binder agreed. "But not on the money. She may have hoped to disprove your story by showing Peter was alive. That way, she refutes your version and gets him off the island before it's too late. Then they could concoct another lie to explain Thwing's death."

"But before they could, Kyle spouted off about telling the whole truth."

Binder stopped walking. We'd wandered into a deserted hospital corridor without me even noticing.

"What happens now?" I asked.

"Lorrie Ann, Peter, and Kyle will all be charged with something. The prosecutors are sorting it out."

"And Sonny?"

"He wasn't there the day Thwing was killed. There's no evidence of his prior involvement with the prescription smuggling except the say-so of three people about to be charged as felons. I assume he isn't holding any drugs and there'd be no sign of extra money if we chose to look. So I doubt anything will happen to Sonny."

Almost the exact reasons Chris had given me for why he wasn't in danger.

"But," Binder continued, "Sonny would do well to stay on the straight and narrow from now on. In fact, I'd say that was good advice for all the men in your life."

"You don't have to worry. They will," I said. "I'm sure of it."

After Binder left me, I pulled my phone out of my pocket. There was a text from Livvie saying Sonny was in Recovery, and there were four calls from Owen Quimby, the last one with a voice mail. I deleted it without listening. Some options were no longer possible. Leaving Chris was one of them.

While I had time, I snuck upstairs to visit Mrs. Gus. Fee and Vee were in their accustomed places beside her bed. Mrs. Gus was, if anything, more restless, but her eyes were still closed.

"If they move her to a rehab facility," Fee said to Vee, "Gus will go back to work. But who will make the pies, I wonder?" She shook her head sadly. "I can't imagine Gus's without the pies."

"Her secret recipes are in a card box in her kitchen," Vee answered. "I can make the pies for Gus."

Mrs. Gus's eyes popped open. "Not with my recipes, you won't!" She tried to sit up in bed. "Where's my pocketbook? Where're my shoes? Time to go home!"

Her friends ran to her and hugged her, while I shouted for the nurse.

* * *

When they finally let Livvie in to see Sonny, I took Chris back to the cabin. He fell into bed, still in the borrowed scrubs, and was instantly asleep. I took a hot shower in the bathroom-without-walls and crawled in beside him.

In the morning, oddly, or perhaps not, we were tentative with one another. Something had shifted between us. Our relationship was in a new phase. It would take some getting used to.

Chris used his cab to drop me back at Mom's house. Livvie had kept her up-to-date with things last night while she stayed home with Page. Coming so close to losing Chris made me want to check in with everyone I loved.

Mom was in the kitchen when I came in, and she was in full makeup, fussing with her cappuccino machine.

"Julia, would you like an espresso?"

I sat heavily at the kitchen table. "Mom, when are you going to cut the crap and tell me what's going on with you?"

She turned around, mouth gaping. I'd never talked to her that way before. "Whatever are you talking about?"

"I'm talking about the cappuccino machine. And the fact that you're never home. And you're always tired. And for whatever reason, you won't tell me or Livvie where you've been or what's going on."

She pulled out a chair and sat at the table beside me, spreading her delicate fingers on its white enamel top. I sat up straight and squared my shoulders. I was ready for whatever she hit me with. At least I knew if she had a boyfriend, it wasn't Bard Ramsey. He was spoken for.

"I've taken a little job," Mom said.

"What?"

"I'm working at Linens and Pantries, the big chain store in Topsham." And then she burst into tears.

I almost did, too. Tears of relief.

"Everyone is so busy," she said. "Everyone's lives have gone on. Even Page has swim team. So I thought I should do something and I applied and they accepted me. Oh, Julia. It's awful. My schedule keeps changing. It's days. It's evenings. I have no routine. And I can't do anything or figure anything out. The store is as big as a football field, the cash register system doesn't make any sense, and in the evenings my supervisor is . . . a high school student." She put her head on her folded arms and sobbed. "I hate it."

I scooted over next to her and patted her shoulder. "Oh, Mom. Quit. Quit if you hate it."

"But—but—but then, I wouldn't only be an incompetent retail clerk, I'd—I'd be a quitter." More sobbing. "I never thought it would be this hard. I'm only fifty-three. I have to figure out something to do with my life."

I laughed. Hadn't I said those exact words recently?

"It's not funny," Mom scolded, though she did manage a little smile. "I bought the stupid machine with my employee discount. I wanted to spoil myself, to own something glamorous." She was crying again. "But, oh, Julia, I hate it so much. I just hate that thing."

"Come back to the clambake, Mom," I said. "Come back for next summer. Run the gift shop like you used to. It would be so good for Page and the new baby to have you on Morrow Island again. And for Livvie and me. The clambake needs you. Come out tomorrow for the last 'bake of the year."

She hugged me back. "I don't know. Maybe. It would be good to feel a part of something. I don't feel a part of Linens and Pantries." She dried her eyes with a napkin she'd plucked from the holder on the table.

Le Roi, sensing a human in need of comforting, jumped into her lap. His purr machine started before he even landed. Mom petted him, sweeping the length of his long, furry body. "And what about you, Julia?" she asked. "What will you do when the clambake is over for the season? Where will you and Le Roi live?"

"We'll figure it out," I answered.

Chapter 36

The storm cleared out and left a glorious day for the last Snowden Family Clambake of the season. The air was crisp as fall should be, but the sun shone brightly and the clouds were high.

The *Jacquie II* wasn't crowded. With only fifty or so people aboard, I was fine with that. We were running with a skeleton crew. Our summer employees had returned to school or headed to other seasonal jobs down south. Only a few stalwart schoolteachers and local high school students who could give us their weekends were on hand.

To fill things out, and because I longed to celebrate, I invited friends and family along. Chris and Quentin were there. Fee and Vee brought Genevieve Pelletier, who still hadn't returned to Portland for some reason. Lieutenant Binder and Sergeant Flynn, still in town completing paperwork, came, too. I'd even brought Le Roi in his carrying case for one last hurrah on the island before the long winter ahead.

Jamie was on the boat, too. Like Binder and Flynn, he was off-duty and dressed in civilian clothes. He brought a lovely, tall brunette with him whom he introduced as his girlfriend. I gave them each a hug. The tension between Jamie and me was gone at last.

Bard Ramsey was there, too, trying his best to act hale and hearty, when I knew his heart must instead be breaking. Kyle was out on bail until his hearing, but the road ahead would be a difficult one. I'd invited Belle and her grandchildren, but she'd declined. Peter was out on bail, but Lorrie Ann was still being held in custody. A broken family.

And my mother. For the first time in five years, my mother was on the *Jacquie II,* the boat my father had named for her.

The harbor was quiet as we cruised toward Morrow Island. The seals were in the water, just their heads visible, not hauled out on the rocks, sunning themselves as they did in summer. Many had already begun their migration south. As we passed Chipmunk Island, the last of the summer residents loaded suitcases and boxes onto boats at the dock. Busman's Harbor would shut off the water to the island the next day. The empty windows of the charming Victorian cottages stared blankly as the *Jacquie II* passed by.

When we landed on Morrow Island, I helped the passengers off the boat. Mom was the last to disembark. She gasped when she saw the burned-out Windsholme. She'd seen photos since the fire, of course, and had been involved in the decisions we'd made about the house so far, but seeing it in real life was a shock. I put my arm around her to steady her.

"Grandma, Grandma!" Page yelled, running to us across the lawn. She threw her arms around my mother. "I'm so glad you're here!"

Since it was a cool fall day, many of our guests gravitated to the clambake fire, Bard along with them. He and Sonny stood together, in family solidarity, and matching blue slings.

I checked on Livvie and her crew in the kitchen. They were in good shape. The staff was small, but experienced. I pulled her aside. "Are you going to be okay?"

"Sure." My busy sister looked over my shoulder to see what one of the cooks was doing. She had a meal to put on.

"No. I mean you and Sonny. Are you two going to be okay?"

Tears sprung to her eyes. "Oh, Julia," she said. "I almost *lost* him."

I took that as a yes.

I saw Lieutenant Binder across the dining pavilion and went to talk to him. Flynn was off circling Genevieve like a moon in her gravitational pull. "If I'd known they were an item, I wouldn't have tried to persuade you she was a suspect," I said.

Binder responded in a low voice. "She wasn't a suspect. She's a federal informant. She's the one who gave up David Thwing to the feds. She discovered he was using the business to launder money, and the business locations to smuggle in drugs."

"You're kidding." There were more layers to Genevieve than I'd suspected. "What will happen to her now?"

"She only gave up Thwing. She didn't know any of his suppliers, so she's safe to live her life. But Thwing built their restaurants and kept them running with drug money. She'll probably lose them all."

It was a courageous decision for an ambitious woman like Genevieve to risk her business by informing on her partner. "So that's why Flynn kept tabs on every move she made. I thought he had a crush on her."

Binder looked over at his partner and Genevieve. "Oh," he laughed, "I don't think you're wrong about that."

The ship's bell rang, signaling the start of the meal. Ordinarily, I worked as host and traffic cop, but with so little staff, I grabbed a tray full of cups of Livvie's delicious clam chowder and passed them out.

When the chowder cups were cleared, the main meal arrived. Steamed clams called steamers, twin lobsters, corn on the cob, a potato, an onion and an egg.

Fee and Vee sat with my mother, and when everyone was served, I visited with them briefly. The sisters reported that though Mrs. Gus would have to go to rehab, her doctors were optimistic about a full recovery. She and Gus had finally agreed to tell their children what had happened.

"What is her real name?" I asked. I remembered

the time I'd spent at her bedside, convinced the poor woman should have an identity of her own.

Fee answered, "It's Gus."

"No," I insisted. "What is *her* name?"

Fee gritted her teeth. "I'm telling you. Her name is Gus. Augustine. Gussie when she was little, but just Gus from junior high on. When she married Gus Farnham, it caused no end of confusion. That's when she decided she wanted us to call her Mrs. Gus."

"She picked the name?"

"Who else?" Fee dug into her lobster and I went back to checking on guests.

At a table near the kitchen, a crowd had gathered. A man named Bruce who said he lived in Paris—France that was, not Paris, Maine—claimed to be the best lobster-eater on the planet. Quite a claim in coastal Maine. As I watched, he threw away everything we'd served him except the steamers and the lobsters. "Distractions," he said with disdain. I had to admit, this late in the year, the corn was terrible. Traditional, but terrible.

By the time I got back to Bruce's table, the steamers were gone and the first lobster demolished. I watched in admiration, as he tucked into the second. He twisted off the claws, used a nutcracker to crack them, and pulled out the meat. He separated the tail from the body, then put his thumb to the end of it and slid the meat out whole. He dredged it in butter and bit in, closing his eyes and sighing in satisfaction. He made short work of the body, using his fingers and all the implements we supplied until every nook and cranny was picked clean. Then he sucked the meat from every one of the legs. It was a sight to behold. When he finished, the crowd cheered. I cleared his plate. There was nothing but shell. I pronounced him the Snowden Family Clambake's new champion. Our reigning champs, Bard and Sonny Ramsey, looked ready to dispute it, but since each of them had an arm in a sling, there was nothing they could do.

We brought out dessert, blueberry grunt with vanilla ice cream. Afterward, the guests lingered while the staff cleaned up. There were so few of us, we planned to go back on the same boat with the customers. The sun set over the point, and many of the guests wandered out to view it.

Chris and Quentin, who'd spent a lot of time together, walked around the outside of Windsholme and then slipped through the fence and disappeared inside. The captain blew the *Jacquie II*'s horn, our fifteen-minute warning, and the guests and staff prepared to board. I stretched and closed my eyes. The last clambake of the year. My last evening on Morrow Island. There'd be one more trip to shut down the clambake, button up for the winter, and get the clothes and books I'd brought out with me. But this was the end. We had survived.

I snuck down to the little house by the dock to say good-bye. I carried Le Roi in my arms. I didn't want him to wander off and hide before we got on the boat. As soon as I closed the cottage door and put him down, he meowed, loudly and insistently. I shushed him, which only incensed him. Finally he looked me straight in the eye, jumped on the kitchen counter, and hit the latch on the door. He kept at it until it turned, and then he batted the doorknob until it, too, turned. He reached a claw into the crack of the door and pulled it open.

"So that's how you got out," I called as I ran after him.

My mother and I were the only people left on the dock when Chris and Quentin walked down from Windsholme. They looked at us and we looked at them.

Quentin nudged Chris and said, "You tell them."

"Quentin and I have been studying the mansion. The kitchen wing and rooms above are sound. We can save it and preserve some of the building cost-effectively, though it will be smaller." He let that sink in. "After all," he added, speaking to me, "you may want to live on the island someday with your family, and Livvie and Sonny are already in the dock house."

"The wing over the ladies' withdrawing room isn't in bad shape, either," Quentin added. "In case you need three places. If Mrs. Snowden wants to live here summers, too."

Chris beamed at me. "What do you think?"

What did I think? I pictured his torn-apart second floor and wondered what we might be letting ourselves in for.

My mother had no such qualms. She threw her arms around his neck and hugged him. "Thank you, thank you, thank you."

My mother, initially a Chris-detractor, then a Chris-tolerator, was finally won over.

Chapter 37

On Tuesday morning Chris and I opened Gus's. The easy way we'd had of working together the first time we'd run the restaurant returned. I took orders, served, and handled the money, and Chris cooked like a maniac.

The place was full, and the main topic of conversation was still the arrests of Kyle, Peter, and Lorrie Ann. The war with Coldport was back on the conversational agenda as well. The police had charged Hughie B. Hubler with burning his own boat for the insurance money. Neither Thwing's murder nor the burned boat had anything to do with a lobster war. I hoped the long winter would cool everyone down.

At almost ten, when business slowed, Gus wandered in through the back door. "How's it going?" he asked Chris.

"Fine. No worries. How's Mrs. Gus?"

Gus's great white eyebrows swooped low over his piercing blue eyes. "So much better. They're moving her to rehab later today. The docs are optimistic she'll come the whole way back."

"I'm so glad." It was hard to imagine Gus without Mrs. Gus. She'd been the one behind the scenes. She kept the books, ordered the food, and most important of all, made the pies. They had been married more than fifty years, had raised two children, and were cherished by six grandchildren. And the whole town.

"Let me fix you breakfast," Chris said.

Both Gus and I snapped our heads around to stare. It was such a startling idea. Someone else serving food to Gus at his restaurant. I expected him to resist, but perhaps in a concession to his emotions of the past week, he agreed.

"Over easy," he said. "You crack the egg on the grill, then when the clear part starts to turn white, you spoon hot oil over the yolk."

Chris had already started back toward the grill. "I know how to make eggs, old man," he called over his shoulder.

Gus sat down at one of his tables and patted the chair next to him, gesturing for me to sit as well. "You come, too, Chris, when you're finished with my eggs. There's something I want to talk to you both about."

Chris brought Gus's plate over, the eggs, two pieces of toast, and the last of the morning's home fries, and put it in front of him. Chris stood, shifting nervously from foot to foot while Gus picked up his fork. The thin crust on top of the egg broke beautifully and the bright yellow yolk oozed out.

Gus mopped it up with his toast, loaded on a bit of egg white, and popped it in his mouth.

I held my breath.

"Delicious," Gus pronounced. "Perfectly cooked."

Chris sighed from relief and sat in the chair between us. It was funny to me how much Chris, who was always so sure of himself, cared what Gus thought. I was giddily relieved myself.

"Been busy in here?" Gus asked.

"So busy," I answered.

Gus nodded. "That's what I wanted to talk to you about. The restaurant is important to people—"

"Of course it is," I said. "And they care about you, too, Gus. Every single person who's been in here has asked about Mrs. Gus."

"Let me finish, Julia." Gus took another bite of egg and chewed slowly. "I was going to say, the restaurant is important at times like this, when everyone in town is confused and hurting. They need a place to talk out their worries. And with Crowley's closed after New Year's, my restaurant is pretty near the only place where everyone can gather."

He was right. The winter would be long and the weather bad. People might run into each other at the post office, but that was it. In the winter, Gus's would be a warm refuge with wet overcoats draped over every chair and steam fogging the windows. But what was he saying? Was Gus going to give up the restaurant?

"I think you two should run it," Gus finished quietly.

"Never!" Chris and I reacted immediately, with the same word.

"Gus's isn't Gus's without you," Chris added.

For a moment I thought Gus was going to walk away from his restaurant. I couldn't bear the idea of living in Busman's Harbor without Gus's.

Gus held up a hand. "Hear me out. I think you two should run the restaurant for supper. I'll keep doing what I'm doing, maybe close earlier in the afternoons. I'm an old man, you know." For a moment, the twinkle was back in his eyes.

"Chris here is a great cook," Gus said, "and Julia, you know all about the ordering and such. The town really needs a restaurant in the winter and you're the perfect pair to take it on. You can close up in the summer when you both have better things to do and the other places are open."

The thought was dizzying. I looked into Chris's green eyes. He held out a hand, palm down. I took the gesture to mean, *Don't react now. We'll talk later.*

Then Gus threw in the kicker. "Julia, there's an apartment upstairs you could live in. Do you want to see it?"

Gus ate his last bite of egg and led the way upstairs to the "apartment." The restaurant was in an old harborside warehouse, albeit a small one. I guessed by the look of it, the upstairs had been converted to living space sometime during World

War II, when shipbuilding in Bath had created a dire need for housing up and down the coast.

"Mrs. Gus and I lived here when we started out," Gus said. "But then the kids came along and we moved to our house. Never had much need for it after that."

The apartment was a large studio with an enormous, multi-paned window capturing a breathtaking view of the harbor. The place was piled with cardboard boxes holding napkins, plastic forks and the red-checkered boats Gus served most of his food in.

"I don't know what to say." I looked at Chris, who looked back at me. So much to discuss, so many decisions to make. But I could tell from his look, he knew, just as I did, we'd accept Gus's offer and run the restaurant as a team.

As Quentin had promised, when the right thing came along, I knew it instantly.

Recipes

Chris's Shrimp & Lobster Polenta

In the fall when Chris moves off his sailboat, the Dark
Lady, *to his cabin, Julia's surprised to discover he's a great
cook. He tells her put this delicious shrimp and lobster
polenta dish together in 20 minutes.*

Polenta

½ cup quick-cooking polenta
1 teaspoon salt
2½ cups water
2 Tablespoons olive oil

Sauce

3 Tablespoons olive oil
2 scallions sliced thinly
pinch of crushed red pepper
2 Tablespoons tomato paste
¼ cup white wine
¼ cup seafood stock or bottled clam juice
¼ pound medium shrimp (21-25 per pound)
    cut into 3-4 pieces
¼ pound cooked lobster meat
½ Tablespoon lemon juice
½ Tablespoon lemon zest
1 Tablespoon chopped parsley

To make the polenta

Boil water together with salt. Add polenta in a thin
stream and stir for about five minutes until thickened.
Turn off the heat. Stir in two tablespoons of olive
oil. Lay a piece of wax paper on top and keep warm.

To make the sauce

Heat olive oil. Add scallions and pinch of crushed red pepper. Cook for a couple of minutes and stir in tomato paste. Cook for three minutes and stir in wine and stock. Let bubble for a minute or two and stir in shrimp. Cook for two minutes and stir in lobster. Let warm through. Remove from heat and stir in lemon juice, zest, and parsley. Reheat and stir polenta, put in a bowls, and spoon sauce over top. (Serves two.)

Slow-Cooker Curried Fish & Butternut Squash Stew

This slow-cooker stew is delightful, mixing so many great fall flavors. The base can cook all day with the fish and kale added an hour before serving.

> 2 Tablespoons olive oil
> 3 ounces pancetta, diced
> ½ pound kielbasa, cut into half-inch rounds
> 2 medium onions, sliced
> 1-2 red peppers, quartered and cut into thick slices
> 3-4 fat cloves garlic, chopped
> 2 Tablespoons curry powder
> ½ teaspoon cayenne
> 1 Tablespoon lemon juice
> 1 Tablespoon kosher salt
> 1 Tablespoon brown sugar
> 1½ Tablespoon fresh ginger, grated

2 cups dried chickpeas, soaked overnight
1 pound butternut squash, cut into large
　　pieces
1 small to medium head cauliflower, cut
　　into florets
3-4 cups diced tomatoes or 1 28 oz. can
　　with juices
4 cups vegetable broth
1½ pound fish such as pollock or cod, cut
　　into thick pieces
8-10 ounces chopped kale
1 13.5-ounce can coconut milk

Heat oil in pan on medium heat. Add pancetta and lightly brown, about four to five minutes. Add kielbasa rounds and lightly brown, about three minutes.

Add onion, peppers, and garlic and soften, about three minutes. Stir in curry powder, cayenne, lemon juice, salt, brown sugar, and ginger. Deglaze pan with a ½ cup of broth, if necessary, and scrape everything into slow cooker.

Add soaked chickpeas, squash, cauliflower, tomatoes, and vegetable broth.

Cook on low for seven hours. Add fish and kale and cook another forty-five minutes. Add coconut milk, adjust seasonings and cook fifteen minutes to meld flavors. Serve with crusty bread.

Grandma Snowden's Pumpkin Whoopie Pies

We haven't learned much about Julia's father's side of the family so far in the series, but Livvie has continued one of their traditions by baking Grandma Snowden's pumpkin whoopie pies. Whoopie pies are the official, and well-loved, state snack of Maine.

Pumpkin Cookies

1½ cups all-purpose flour
½ teaspoon baking soda
½ teaspoon baking powder
½ teaspoon salt
1 teaspoon cinnamon
½ teaspoon ground ginger
¼ teaspoon nutmeg
¼ teaspoon ground cloves
1 cup packed light brown sugar
½ cup vegetable oil
1 15-ounce can of pure pumpkin (not pie filling)
1 egg
1 teaspoon vanilla extract

Cream Cheese Filling

½ cup (one stick) salted butter, softened
8 ounces cream cheese
3 cups confectioners' sugar
3 tablespoons maple syrup
1 teaspoon vanilla abstract

To make the filling

Beat the butter on medium speed until smooth (no visible lumps). Add the cream cheese and beat on medium speed until smooth, and combined. Add the powdered sugar gradually, beating as you do until it is mixed. Add the maple syrup and the vanilla and beat until smooth. Place the filling in the refrigerator while you make the cookies. This will make it easier to work with when you are filling the pies. Filling can be made a day ahead.

To make the cookies

Preheat the oven to 350 degrees. Line two baking sheets with parchment paper.

Whisk flour, baking soda, baking powder, salt, and spices together in a bowl. Whisk together sugar, oil, pumpkin, egg, and vanilla in a separate large bowl until combined thoroughly. Add in flour mixture.

Using a one-ounce ice cream scoop, drop a scant scoop of batter onto the parchment paper. Scoops should be two inches apart. (You will have batter left over.)

Bake twelve to eighteen minutes, until springy to the touch. These will be cakelike cookies. Place cookies on rack to cool.

Repeat until all the batter is used. (You will have thirty-two to thirty-six cookies.)

To assemble

Spread a heaping Tablespoon of filling on the flat side of a chilled cookie. Top with another cookie.

Hot Lobster Dip

Invited for dinner at the Snugg sisters' B & B, Julia's niece, Page, attacks this delicious hot lobster dip because she's famished after a long, dramatic family day. But you don't have to be starving to appreciate the flavor combinations of this reliable crowd-pleaser.

> 1 clove garlic
> ¼ cup snipped chives
> 8 ounces cream cheese
> 3 teaspoons Worcestershire sauce
> 2 teaspoons lemon juice
> ⅛ teaspoon cayenne pepper
> ½ teaspoon salt
> ⅛ teaspoon black pepper
> ½ pound cooked lobster meat, roughly
>   chopped
> 2 Tablespoons thinly sliced scallions

With food processor running, drop garlic clove through feed tube and finely chop. Add chives and pulse about six times to finely chop. Add cream cheese, Worcestershire sauce, lemon juice, cayenne, salt, and black pepper. Process until fully combined. Scrape down sides of bowl and fold in the lobster meat. Process about thirty seconds to combine. Spoon into baking dish or pie plate and refrigerate for at least two hours. Heat oven to 375 degrees. Bake dip for twenty to twenty-five minutes until bubbling. Garnish with scallions. Serve with crackers, chips, or slices of baguette.

Genevieve's Signature Mussels

Genevieve Pelletier has built the reputation of her restaurants on her mussels, and if you make this dish you'll see she certainly deserves the praise she gets for them. Genevieve serves this hearty dish as an appetizer, but it's more than capable of carrying a meal as the entree.

1 Tablespoon olive oil
6 ounces chorizo, divided. Half diced, half sliced into thin rounds
2-3 cloves garlic, chopped
¾ cup onion
¼ cup celery, diced
¼ cup red pepper, diced
salt and pepper
½ Tablespoon smoked paprika
1 cup diced tomatoes
½ Tablespoon chopped fresh thyme
½ cup white wine
½ Tablespoon Dijon mustard
½ cup heavy cream
1-1½ pounds mussels, scrubbed and debearded
1 Tablespoon chopped parsley for garnish

Heat the olive oil on medium heat in a wide saucepan with a tight-fitting lid. Cook the chorizo rounds until lightly browned. Remove with a slotted spoon and set aside. Add the diced chorizo. Cook until lightly browned.

Stir in garlic, onion, celery, and red pepper. Add salt and pepper to taste. Stir in smoked paprika. Sauté for three to four minutes.

Stir in tomatoes and thyme, cover pot, and simmer together for three to five minutes.

Add wine and let bubble on high heat for about a minute.

Stir in mustard and heavy cream and cook another minute. Taste and add additional salt or pepper, if necessary.

Add mussels and reserved chorizo rounds, stir, cover pot, and cook for five minutes, stirring once halfway through.

Spoon mussels into bowl, pour sauce over, and garnish with parsley.

Autumn Salad

With its pears, apples, and dried cranberries, this salad combines some of the best flavors of fall fruit. Genevieve

Pelletier serves it as a salad course, though it can also be a side salad or a full meal on its own. Though the dressing contains honey, it is not overly sweet.

Salad

6 ounces pancetta, diced
8 cups mixed salad greens
1 pear, cored and diced
1 apple, cored and diced
½ cup dried cranberries
½ cup pine nuts, lightly toasted
½ cup crumbled Gorgonzola cheese

Dressing

¼ cup vinegar
2 Tablespoons lemon juice
1 Tablespoon honey
1 Tablespoon finely chopped thyme
2 teaspoons finely chopped rosemary
salt and pepper
½ cup olive oil

Cook pancetta over medium heat until browned and just crispy. Remove from pan with slotted spoon and allow to cool on paper towels. Put greens, apple, pear, and cranberries in bowl. Prepare dressing by whisking together vinegar, lemon juice, honey, thyme, rosemary, and salt and pepper. Drizzle oil and whisk until dressing emulsifies. Add pine nuts, pancetta and Gorgonzola and dressing. Toss to combine.

Lobster, Shrimp & Fennel Scampi

This is the pièce de résistance of Genevieve's thank-you meal for the Snugg sisters. The lobster adds richness to the flavor that shrimp alone can't provide. The fennel gives the dish a satisfying crunch.

1 Tablespoon oil
3 Tablespoons butter
1 head fennel, cored, quartered, and sliced thinly, fronds reserved
4 shallots, chopped
4 cloves garlic, minced
salt and pepper to taste
½ cup white wine
2 Tablespoons lemon juice
¼ teaspoon lemon zest
1 cup seafood stock
¾ pound cooked lobster meat, chopped
¾ pound shrimp (preferably Maine rock shrimp)
1 pound linguini, cooked al dente in a pot of salted water
½ cup reserved pasta cooking water
½ cup chopped parsley

Heat the oil and one Tablespoon of butter over medium heat. Add the fennel and shallots and cook for four minutes.

Add the garlic and cook for two minutes. Add salt and pepper. Add the wine, lemon juice, and zest.

Turn the heat up to high and let bubble for one to two minutes.

Add stock and cook together for three minutes. Stir in shrimp and cook for two minutes. Stir in lobster and heat through a minute or two. Add pasta, the reserved pasta water, and remaining butter and toss together.

Garnish with chopped fennel fronds and parsley.

Vee's Apple Pie

Viola Snugg is a wonderful baker, as exemplified by the scones and muffins she serves to guests at the Snuggles Inn. Her pie is irresistible, as Julia discovers when she tries to take a sleepy Page home before the dessert course.

Pie Crust
3½ cups flour
2 teaspoons kosher salt
1½ cups shortening, lard, or unsalted butter
1 egg, beaten lightly with a fork
1 Tablespoon apple cider vinegar
¼-½ cups ice water, as needed
1 Tablespoon milk (to brush over finished
    pie before baking)

In food processor, using the metal blade, pulse flour and salt to combine. Add shortening and pulse until reaching the consistency of corn meal.

Add egg, vinegar, and ¼ cup of ice water. Pulse, adding additional ice water, if necessary, until ingredients barely come together in a dough ball. Turn out onto cutting board and pat together evenly into a large oblong. Divide into four pieces. You will need two for the pie. (You can freeze the other two for a later pie.) Refrigerate. Remove from fridge ten minutes before using.

Filling

1 teaspoon ground cinnamon
8 medium apples
¾ cup sugar
1 Tablespoon lemon juice
2 Tablespoons salted butter

Roll out bottom crust of pie and put in pie plate. Add apples. Over the top sprinkle lemon juice, sugar, cinnamon, and the butter in pats.

Roll out top crust and cover. Slit top. Brush with milk.

Bake at 425 degrees for ten minutes. Then lower oven temperature to 350 and bake twenty-five to thirty-five minutes more, until top is brown and fruit is bubbling.

Acknowledgments

There are so many people to thank for their support for *Musseled Out*, and indeed for the whole Maine Clambake Mystery series to date.

Captain Clive Farrin took me out on his lobster boat, where he and his sternman Cage Zipperer patiently answered my many questions. If you are ever in Boothbay Harbor, Maine, you should definitely take the tour, which is beautiful and informative. http://www.lobsterfrommaine.com/golobstering.aspx

And, if you want to experience an authentic Maine clambake on a private island, be sure to visit the Cabbage Island Clambake. The real family and island differ entirely from the Snowdens and Morrow Island, but you will get the same delicious meal. http://www.cabbageislandclambakes.com

I got the idea that Julia and her mother should drive winter beaters from a column by Maine humorist Tim Sample in the *Boothbay Register*. Since I know nothing about cars, Tim also supplied the makes and models. You can read the whole column at http://www.boothbayregister.com/article/winter-beaters/24807

Thank you to Richard Hayes for talking me through the rescue at sea and improving its authenticity. Toby Peltz and Kathy Fast also supplied feedback. Any mistakes, inadvertent or deliberate, are mine.

If you can't make it to Maine, but want to learn more about lobstering, I recommend these books, all of which figured in the research I did over a long, snowy New England winter. *The Secret Life of Lobsters: How Fishermen and Scientists Are Unraveling the Mysteries of Our Favorite Crustacean*, by Trevor Corson (Harper, 2004), was particularly helpful, not to mention a piece of well-written and compelling nonfiction. *The Lobster Chronicles: Life on a Very Small Island*, by Linda Greenlaw, (Hyperion, 2003), was the first book I read about the lobstering life, long before I started work on *Musseled Out*. I have no doubt of its influence. In the same time period, I read Eva Murray's *Well Out to Sea* (Tilbury House, 2010), which also had a tremendous impact. James M. Acheson's seminal work of anthropology, *The Lobster Gangs of Maine* (University Press of New England, 1988), supplied great context. If you want to read an account of the real rescue of a lobsterman at sea, I recommend Paul Tough's *New York Times Magazine* article, "A Speck in the Sea" (January 2, 2014). Finally, I was helped immensely by Barbara Delinsky's *Does a Lobsterman Wear Pants?* (Down East Books, 2005). This little book is the result of Delinsky's research for her own work of fiction, *The Summer I Dared* (Scribner, 2004). I love the idea of a fiction writer collecting her research for the benefit of another fiction writer.

Lobstering and lobsters are a complicated business, and all mistakes and exaggerations, inadvertent and deliberate, are mine.

As always, I would like to thank my agent, John Talbot; my editor, John Scognamiglio; and the entire team at Kensington Publishing, especially Adeola Saul and Robin Cook. Also, artist Ben Perini for all the terrific Maine Clambake Mystery covers to date.

A book can't be successful without finding readers, and I'd like to thank the Malice Domestic conference Agatha voters, *RT Book Reviews*, and the Maine Writers and Publishers Alliance for their award nominations for the first book in this series, *Clammed Up*.

Book bloggers have been especially critical to the success of the series, and happily there are too many to mention. However, I must give a shout out to Dru Ann Love, who put her hand up during a round of "author speed dating" at Malice Domestic, when I, dazed and confused, asked if anyone would take one of my Advanced Reader copies. I often feel like she started it all.

I'd like to thank my writing community for all the help and critical support: Sisters in Crime New England, The New England Crime Bake, Grub Street, and most especially my blogmates at Wicked Cozy Authors—Jessie Crockett, Sherry Harris, Julie Hennrikus, Edith Maxwell, and Liz Mugavero—and at

Maine Crime Writers, including Vicki Doudera, Kaitlyn Dunnett, Kate Flora, Sarah Graves, and Lea Wait.

Thanks to my most critical readers, my fabulous writers' group, Mark Ammons, Kathy Fast, Cheryl Marceau, and Leslie Wheeler. And for *Musseled Out* especially, Sherry Harris and Bill Carito, who both went above and beyond. What is the saying about my procrastination creating your emergency?

Finally, in author talks and blog postings, I've been open that I don't cook and do not develop the recipes that appear in the Maine Clambake series. Fortunately, I'm married to a superb chef who has the patience to work with me as I figure out what foods will tempt my characters in each book. All of the recipes in *Musseled Out* are Bill Carito's, except the apple pie, which is one of my specialties, and the pumpkin whoopie pies, which I supplied, because Bill "doesn't bake." I'm working on that.